Safeword: Oasis

MINA'S HEART

Michele Zurlo

www.michelezurloauthor.com

Mina's Heart (Safeword: Oasis 2)
Copyright © March 2013/May 2018 by Michele Zurlo
Print ISBN: 978-1-942414-61-2

Editor: Nicoline Tiernan
Cover Artist: Pyroclastic and Nic T.

Published by Lost Goddess Publishing LLC
www.michelezurloauthor.com

This book is a work of fiction. While reference might be made to actual historical events or existing locations, the names, characters, places and incidents are either the product of the author's imagination or are used fictitiously, and any resemblance to actual persons, living or dead, business establishments, events, or locales is entirely coincidental.

Warning: This book contains sexually explicit scenes and adult language and may be considered offensive to some readers. It is not meant for underage readers.

DISCLAIMER: Education and training are necessary in order to learn safe BDSM practices. Lost Goddess Publishing LLC is not responsible for any loss, harm, injury or death resulting from use of the information contained in any of its titles. This is a work of fiction, and license has been taken with regard to BDSM practices.

Chapter One

The door slid shut behind her, its hiss warning her of the precariousness of the situation. Mina took two steps into the large room. It was dark. Strange shadows populated the landscape, but the path to the center was clear, as was the single pot light casting a small circle on the floor.

"Stand in the spotlight."

His voice played over her nerves, simultaneously soothing and alarming. It took her back to simpler times, when she hadn't minded compromising her goals in order to be loved by a man.

Without speaking, she moved to the center of the room. Her legs felt leaden, as if she were trying to run in a dream, but she forced them to obey. Everything was on the line tonight.

Using the edges of the darkness as a guide, she centered herself in the narrow band of light. It was just wide enough to fit her petite form. Time ticked by as she stood there. With the light cascading directly down her body, the shadows became even darker, less distinct. He was somewhere in the room, and not necessarily where he'd been when he'd spoken last.

She felt his hand on her waist and the pull of his body behind her, and she struggled not to give in to the desire to lean back, to throw her arms around his neck and ask if they could turn back time.

He walked around her, dragging his fingertips over her lower back until the feeling dropped away. She wanted to turn her head, to meet his sea-green eyes, to seek his silent reassurance. But he'd warned her against doing anything he didn't specifically command, and besides, she wasn't sure he had any comfort to give her. She'd asked for this.

"Remove your shoes and stockings."

Mina crouched to unbuckle the straps of her high heels, mentally berating herself for not wearing slip-on shoes. She'd wanted to impress him, and these heels made her legs look long and sexy. She set the shoes next to her, just out of the spotlight, her stockings folded neatly on top of the shoes.

A scraping sound drew her attention. Thank goodness it was directly in front of her. Everett positioned a conversation chair a few feet away and sank down in it, his lanky frame dwarfing the small piece.

1

He sat back and folded his hands over his stomach, completely at ease in these surroundings that were so alien to her.

"Now the dress."

Her entire outfit had been designed to impress him. Six years earlier, when she'd known him as her kind and tender boyfriend, she never would have entertained the thought of wearing tight clothes or a short dress. This one was both. It was the little black dress every woman was supposed to have, only she'd purchased her first one two days ago.

It hugged her form, accenting her slight curves in a way that made them seem more substantial. She hated to take it off just yet, but she couldn't refuse to follow an order. Even hesitating was grounds for punishment. And she'd voluntarily agreed to those terms. No impact play. Spanking—the duration and severity to be determined by her Master—was to be the primary means of punishment.

She reached behind her, groping for the hidden zipper.

"You're forgetting something. Slaves with bad manners will be punished."

She lifted her gaze, searching the darkness, trying to read his expression, but she couldn't see him well enough. He hadn't sounded angry. Perhaps he was being tolerant because he knew it was her first time. He'd been so understanding all those years ago when he'd taken her virginity. "I don't know what I've forgotten."

"When you're given an order, you must acknowledge it."

Then she remembered. Isla had coached her, bullying her half the time and scowling the other half. Mina despaired of getting anything right. Worry had kept her up most of the night before, and now the prophecy was fulfilling itself. "I'm sorry, Ever."

"Master. You must remember to use my title, little slave. When I tell you to do something, you say, 'Yes, Master,' and then you do it."

She nodded. "Yes, Master. I'm sorry."

"I accept your apology. Please continue."

She shrugged out of her dress, catching it as it fell down her body. She folded it carefully and added it to the steadily growing pile next to her.

Only her black lacy bra and matching panties were left. This set of lingerie was the raciest she owned, though she fully admitted it wasn't that racy when compared with other things out there. The bra cupped her breasts, but the lace barely covered her nipples, and it left nothing to the imagination. The bikini-cut panties were made from the same material. She liked this shade of black. It made her skin look lighter, nearly obscuring the yellowish tones that came out when she wore orange or red. Except now that she was standing here, she remembered how much Everett loved to see her in red.

He liked her skin tone. He thought it was sexy.

She stood still, aware that he was watching her. He would look at her for as long as he wanted, and she could do nothing but stand here and take it. She wished he would talk. When he used to make love to her, he always spoke to her, his voice rough with passion. He would murmur the sweetest things, telling her how beautiful she was, how soft, how perfect. How much he loved her.

"Take off your bra. Slowly. Entice me."

Except for those five blissful months with Ever, she had never thought of herself as a sexual being. With any other man, it had been a chore. With Ever, it had been addictive, something she wanted every time she saw him. Well, that wasn't exactly true. She'd wanted more than sex.

But now wasn't the time to think about what she'd wanted. She'd thrown it away, and if she didn't get this right, she'd be fucking up a second chance with him.

"Yes, Master."

She cupped her breasts through her bra, lifting and kneading them as he would do. Then she pinched her nipples lightly, rolling them between her thumbs and forefingers until they were hard little peaks.

She searched the darkness for signs of his reaction. The light only gave her pieces—one bent knee, the shape of his shoulders, a glint from his cornea. She wished she could see his expression, but that was another privilege she would have to earn.

Crossing one arm over her breasts, she reached behind her and unhooked her bra. The straps slid down her arms, and she adjusted so that she once again cupped her breasts. Now she was the only thing holding the scrap of fabric up.

"Drop it." He growled the order. She wasn't sure whether that was a good sign, but his tone sent a shiver of anticipation through her. He'd always been commanding, and she'd mistaken his dominant tendencies for Neanderthal characteristics. It had taken her many years to appreciate the important differences.

"Yes, Master." She let the bra drop, guiding it to the stack of her clothes on the floor to her right. Then she stood still, letting him drink in the sight of her.

"Remove your underwear, put them in your mouth, crawl over here, and offer them to me."

This was the first time he'd expressed an interest in her panties, but she knew his order wasn't at all about that tiny bit of lace. He wanted her complete submission, and she wanted to prove she could give it.

"Yes, Master."

She hooked her thumbs under the bands holding her panties up and let them whisper down her legs. Then she knelt on the floor, noting how cold and hard it was. He'd thrown a rug over the cement instead of putting in wood or carpet.

Gripping her panties with her teeth, she crossed the impossibly wide gulf between them in the space of several seconds. She wasn't sure how close she was allowed to get, but now that she was out of the spotlight, she could make out his figure better.

His feet were bare. They stuck out of his jeans and were planted firmly on the floor. His legs, long and lithe like the rest of his body, were parted. She crawled between them and dropped her panties on his crotch. The way he was sitting and the lack of light went a long way toward hiding any evidence that her presentation made him hard.

She eyed his hands, still folded over his stomach, and waited for him to accept her offering.

Moving slowly, he wrapped his fingers around the soft lace, which was moist with her juices. He lifted it to his face, buried his nose, and inhaled deeply. The move rocked her to the core with its intimacy and promise. She remembered how much he'd loved to bind her wrists and lick her pussy.

"Stand up, slave." His eyes glittered hard, but she couldn't find evidence of any emotion.

"Yes, Master." She rose to her feet as gracefully as she could, mindful that she was still on display.

"Lift your leg. Put your foot here." He patted his thigh.

The position he indicated would open her farther, though she wasn't sure how much detail he would see. Her heart seized a little because she recognized his thoughtfulness. The first time he'd gone down on her, he'd blindfolded her to save her from being overwhelmed by embarrassment. Except that she was older and wiser, this was no different. She still had only a theoretical idea of what to expect from this encounter.

"Yes, Master." Her voice shook. Since she'd left him, sex had become a quick act committed in the secrecy of her dark bedroom.

She lifted her leg and set it on his thigh. The act of exposing herself like this made her feel vulnerable, but it also sent a rush of desire to her core. She imagined all the ways he would touch her, the gentle glide of his fingertips across her skin as he explored her calves and inner thighs. Given his reach, he could spend time getting reacquainted with her pussy and her breasts.

Open and ready, she awaited her Master's touch. One click, and he trained the beam of a small, powerful flashlight between her legs. She struggled not to squirm out of that warm spotlight.

"Touch your pussy, slave. Show me how you pleasure yourself."

She didn't pleasure herself. She'd tried before, but it just didn't work for her. But she couldn't tell him that. Failure tonight was not an option. The repercussions might just destroy her.

"Yes, Master."

She thought back to the ways he'd touched her, the pressure and patterns he'd used to bring her to orgasm, and she put those lessons into play. Grazing her finger lightly over her clit, she coaxed it to a throbbing peak. Then she drew her finger through her juices.

Some of the light reflected back onto his face, showing her nothing but a mask. His gaze focused on her pussy, but his expression, so often open and flirty, was shuttered. She wanted to know she affected him, but even a glance down failed to reveal the state of his arousal.

His lack of reaction killed her passion. She'd swallowed her pride a long time ago. "Master, please help me."

He lifted his gaze and his eyebrow. She couldn't tell whether he was amused at her request or angry that she'd spoken without permission.

"This doesn't turn you on?"

He'd cautioned her to be honest. She shook her head. "No, Master. I need your touch." His embrace, his kisses, his words of praise and love whispered in her ear. Suddenly she felt every moment of the past six lonely years without him. It had been her choice, and she bitterly regretted it.

He looked away, his mind clearly elsewhere.

Before it could flee completely, she slid onto his lap, straddling him, and cupped his cheek with her palm. "Please don't be angry with me. I've never been good at this. You know that."

He closed his eyes, but he snuggled into her palm. "I don't know how you've changed."

"I haven't." Her confession was inadequate at best, but completely true. Nothing had changed for her. She thought about him all the time. In the dark, when John, her former boyfriend with whom she'd spent three years, fumbled for her, she imagined Everett's hands on her, his lips claiming hers, and his cock filling her.

She thought Everett might take her in his arms and kiss her, but instead his face hardened. "I didn't give you permission to move."

But he hadn't stopped her. A cold feeling stole strength from her limbs as she realized he would never stop her from disobeying. He would merely mete out punishment afterward. In committing the act, she accepted the consequences.

She dropped her gaze automatically. "I'm sorry, Master."

"You must learn patience. I wasn't rejecting you, Mina. I didn't agree to be here because I wanted retribution. I'm here because I want to see if you can be the submissive I need." He spoke gently, with no undertones of anger or hurt. Amazingly, she heard hope.

"I can, Ever. I can be anything you want me to be."

He sighed. "I don't want you to be anything you're not."

Behind his statement was a censure she understood with absolute certainty. He would have accepted her in a vanilla relationship all those years ago, but now he wasn't willing to settle. "I'm sorry. Please tell me how to make it up to you."

"Get on your knees."

She slid to the floor, assuming the correct position. She'd practiced this with Isla, a Domme friend and coworker of Everett's.

He adjusted his position, shifting to sit up straight, and she realized he intended to punish her for her transgression. She focused on breathing through the panic preceding this first spanking. Isla had refused to discuss this with her, dismissing Mina's fears by saying the administration of a punishment was a positive sign. Doms who didn't care didn't bother to punish their slaves.

"Stand here." He pointed to a place to his right. Then he guided her down until she was bent over his knees with her hands on the floor for balance. He had her widen her stance and turn her toes inward a little. "Tell me why you're being spanked."

"Because I moved and spoke without permission."

"You did not speak without permission, slave. I asked you a question, and you answered it."

"Yes, Master. I moved without permission." The denim of his jeans was scratchy under her ribs and stomach, and the concrete floor was cold against her palms.

"You'll count these three out and thank me for each one."

He touched her ass with his palm, but his gentle caress failed to soothe her tight nerves. Years of watching her father hit her mother had her questioning again why she'd accepted this form of punishment. Her research had turned up a variety of punishments acceptable in the BDSM community. But in the negotiation phase, this was the only thing Everett had proposed. She hadn't wanted to take the chance she'd lose this opportunity to show him he'd misjudged her all those years ago.

The first spank landed with a loud smack, and a hot pain bloomed across her skin. Her breath caught even as a great shiver rocked her body. She barely remembered her line.

"One. Thank you, Master."

The second and third ones came quickly. She wanted to get up afterward, to retreat and hide, but he pressed his hand on her lower back and ordered her to stay put.

"Tell me what you feel right now."

Her feelings were easy to identify, not complicated at all, and she knew better than to hide them. "Humiliation, shame, fear."

"Why fear?" Everett expected her to feel humiliated—she was a proud woman—and ashamed—she hated to make mistakes. But he hadn't expected her to be afraid. Sure, he hadn't tempered himself when he'd spanked her, but he hadn't struck her hard either. She needed to know what would happen when she misbehaved.

When she didn't answer, he flipped her up so that she sat on his lap. The room was warm, and the aftercare blanket was in the cabinet behind him, so he cradled her in his arms. She held herself stiffly against him.

"You knew the consequences for misbehaving. You agreed to them before you set foot in my house."

"Yes, Master." She avoided his gaze, which irritated him greatly.

"Mina, explain why you're afraid of me."

She shook her head. "I'm not afraid of you. I'm afraid of the punishment."

But it was over. He'd expected to help her process her feelings of humiliation and shame, not fear. It troubled him that she was afraid. A spanking like this wasn't pleasant, but it wasn't horrible. Her ass might burn for a little while, but that was all. It was a reminder, not meant to cause lasting discomfort. He remembered before, how the mere mention of a spanking had bothered her. He needed to know why she was so afraid, why she'd fled from him years ago, and why she'd agreed to spanking if she hadn't overcome her fears.

"Mina, look at me."

She did, and what he saw cut him to the core. Her brown eyes were dark and wide, bright with unshed tears. She was terrified after the fact. If anything, the first spanking should have set her mind at ease. It should have proved to her that she could take it.

"Are you hurt?"

She shook her head. He watched her try to form words and fail.

"Tell me why you're afraid."

This time she closed her eyes, and a single tear escaped. "That is a discussion for a later time. I want to continue the scene."

He recognized the return of her stubborn streak, and her demand made him smile. All was not lost, and she wasn't afraid of him. Still, he couldn't let her think she'd won. "We can't, Mina. Not until this is straightened out. I don't wish for you to be afraid." He did, however, bank on apprehension and taut nerves.

"I'm not afraid of you, and I won't misbehave again. If I promise to talk about this with you later, will you at least kiss me?"

He wanted to kiss her. He wanted to take her upstairs and fuck her until she couldn't walk away from him ever again, but that wasn't an option. Not yet. First he had to know if she was serious about wanting to be his submissive.

"You need me to touch you, don't you?"

"Yes, Master." He'd once convinced himself that he didn't need to hear her use that title, but now he knew he never would have been happy that way.

He closed his hand on the inside of her knee and brought it up a little higher on his chest, and then he shoved her other knee until her legs were parted. Taking her right hand in his, he guided it between her legs. "We'll do this together, slave. But next time I give this order—and rest assured I will give it again—you will do this alone, for my pleasure, and I will watch."

Her entire body relaxed, conforming more to his. Six years ago, he would have wondered if this was the first time she'd masturbated, but he dismissed that idea now. When she'd left him, she'd been well aware of the pleasures of the flesh. Even if she'd never touched herself in front of him, he'd coaxed her to orgasm with his mouth, his hands, and his cock. She wouldn't be able to resist touching herself.

He cupped her hand and pressed her fingers to her clit. He was there for guidance and backup, nothing more. She was very wet, evidence she'd found the striptease arousing. He wasn't under the impression she'd enjoyed the spanking. She'd made it clear from the very beginning that she didn't want any kind of impact play. That was strictly a punishment.

Sliding their fingers through her slick folds, he concentrated on the places he knew drove her insane, but he also paid attention to the places in between. A small sigh escaped her lips. She rested her head against his shoulder, her lashes fluttering softly against his skin and her shoulder-length dark hair falling like silk over his arm. She pressed kisses along his collarbone and gripped his knee with her free hand.

"Play with your breasts, honey."

If she was surprised by his term of endearment, she didn't show it. Ever mentally berated himself for using it, though. He hadn't moved past what she'd done to him, and he didn't want her to think sex would salve that wound. It was only a small part of the problem.

She released the hold she had on his knee and cupped one breast. He watched, careful to keep a steady stroke going between her legs. She lifted her hips, urging him to her opening, but he ignored her offering. If she'd done what he'd originally asked, she would have been able to have control over those details. But she'd given it up the moment she asked for his help.

She dragged her fingers lightly along the underside of that perfect-sized round globe, and he filed away her preference for that kind of touch. He'd experiment with it later. Then she circled her nipple. He eased two of her fingers and one of his inside her pussy. She was tighter than he'd expected. Her muscles jumped and twitched, squeezing his finger against hers.

"God, Ever, yes!" She arched, thrusting her hips against their hands, and pinched her nipple.

He hated to interrupt her in the midst of a good time, but he had to correct her. "'Master,' slave. You must remember to use my title."

She tilted her head back and looked at him. Her almond-shaped eyes were wide with the weight of her mistake. "I'm sorry, Master. You make me feel so good that I forget myself."

He twisted his lips in a wry smile at the way she'd blamed him with a compliment. He liked her stubborn and willful side, but he needed to help her understand that certain things would earn a punishment. Not accepting responsibility for her mistakes was one of them, but he decided to defer telling her until after she'd had an orgasm. He needed her to see that their sexual relationship had always been D/s. They just hadn't used those terms or protocols.

With the arm supporting her shoulders, he lifted her closer and claimed her with a kiss. He thrust his tongue into her mouth and tangled it with hers. She kissed him back, a little bit thankful and very sassy, and she pumped her hips in time to their duel.

He felt her caress the side of his neck, and then she continued around to the back, seeking the place just below his hairline that made him go crazy. When she found it, he lost some of his iron control, kissing her harder and pumping his finger into her faster.

His cock, already chomping at the bit to get inside her, pressed painfully against his jeans and her ass, which also rubbed against him as she fucked their fingers. She'd always had this much of an impact on him, from the first time he'd kissed her even after she'd told him she didn't kiss on the first date. She'd made the mistake of presenting it as a challenge instead of a limit. One he would respect, but the other he could only shatter.

She played him until he growled a warning, and then she fanned her fingers through his hair and tugged lightly. Perhaps she meant to guide him down her neck, where he could kiss and lick at her many erogenous zones, but he had a different plan in mind.

Breaking away suddenly, he tried to don his darkest expression. From the way her brown eyes lit and her eyelids fell to half-mast, he knew she'd failed to understand his warning. She moaned again. Clinging to him with that one hand on the back of his neck, she ground against their hands.

"Master, yes. Harder! Oh God, I love the way you kiss."

It was an honest compliment, but it was also an attempt at manipulation. Partly as punishment—and he figured he'd helped her over her initial problem—he withdrew his finger and eased it into her mouth. She lay across his lap, masturbating, and he fucked her mouth with his finger, a preview of what was to come. Mina wouldn't be worried, though. He remembered how much she'd loved to suck his cock.

Her hips lifted so high she almost did a backbend, and her body stiffened as she came. A deep blush bloomed on her chest, climbing to include her neck and cheeks. She moaned, the vibrations echoing around the finger he still thrust into her mouth.

She lowered her hips slowly until she rested on his lap, and she extracted her fingers from her pussy. He gave her mouth a temporary reprieve as he grabbed for her wrist. Then he guided her fingers where his had just been. Not only was it incredibly hot to watch her feasting on her own juices; it was another way he exercised his control over her.

"Suck on them as if they were my cock."

He watched the languor of her orgasm fade. They were just getting started. He'd always been like this, and she'd voiced amazement several times at the amount of foreplay—for him, this counted as foreplay—he required. She'd never complained, which was a good thing. From the beginning, he'd loved her sexual stamina.

She closed her eyes and moaned. Her tongue danced over those digits, dipping down to lick her other fingers and the palm of her hand. Those luscious lips, not yet swollen with evidence of his domination, savored every drop of her essence. It served to remind him that she'd never neglected his balls. Sometimes she'd paid more attention to them than his cock. Because he was her first sexual experience that way as well, he once asked her where she learned to give such a mind-blowing blowjob. She'd smiled and blushed, and then she'd mumbled something about the Internet.

The visual she presented made his cock ache and demand similar treatment, so he put a halt to her activities.

"Go and stand underneath the spotlight. Lace your fingers behind your neck." He knew Isla had taken some time to show her basic poses and to walk her through the meaning of the negotiated terms. Everett had complained—loudly—when they were discussing her wish, that she had no fucking clue what she was asking for. Knowing his history with Mina, Isla had just patted him on the cheek, blown him a kiss, and told him not to worry about it.

He figured if Mina could research giving head, then she could research BDSM. That, and he trusted Isla implicitly. His friend and fellow Domme wanted him to either move forward with Mina or put her firmly behind him.

She stood under the spotlight with perfect posture, her gaze lowered and her body relaxed. She was the portrait of perfect submission, and his heart ached, mourning what they'd lost and not quite believing this wasn't a dream.

Getting to his feet with far less grace than she had, he ambled toward her. As proof she was hyperaware of him, her breathing sped up as he came closer. He'd spent some time in that spotlight because he wanted to know what a submissive would see, so he knew the quality of her perception. Right now, she could see him, but she couldn't make out the details. Soon it wouldn't matter.

He took a blindfold from his pocket and held it where she could see. "Remember this, Mina? It's the same one."

All those years ago, he'd used this to mask her vision. He'd wanted to lick her pussy, her first brush with sex, and she hadn't been able to relax enough to enjoy it. Once he'd bound her wrists and blindfolded her, she had been fine. He hoped to achieve the same result today.

She lifted her gaze, surprise ruining her submissive position. "You kept it?"

He heard her hope and her unasked question. He harbored the same hope, but he didn't know the answer to her question: Was it too late for them? So he answered the question she'd voiced. "Yes. I hoped to one day have you in this position." He'd built this playroom with her in mind, but he couldn't tell her that, not yet.

Whether she suddenly remembered her status or she was simply overcome, she dropped her gaze once again. "Thank you for giving me this chance, Master. I won't let you down."

She trembled with the force of her convictions, or maybe it was just nerves. He slipped the blindfold over her eyes and adjusted the strap to cinch under her hair. That way it wouldn't slip off with her movements. By the time he finished with her, she wouldn't be able to move much, but she would have some maneuverability.

"What's your safeword, slave?"

"Oasis." She responded without hesitation, just as she always had.

"Hold your arms out in front of you."

"Yes, Master." She held her arms out as he directed, but with her palms up.

While that pose would be easier to hold for a longer period of time, he wanted her palms down, so he turned her wrists to correct her position. Then he wrapped neoprene cuffs around each one. They were lined with a soft material, and they fastened with Velcro. Easy on, easy off, nearly impossible to escape. The D ring wasn't as strong, but it would get the job done.

An access panel near the door hid the buttons that would unwind and drop the chains connected to winches built into the structure of the house. He pressed one, but he watched her. She stiffened when she heard the clinking sound, but then her shoulders relaxed. He knew holding her position for a long time wouldn't be fun, and he had no plans to keep her that way.

Wordlessly, he lifted her arm above her head and attached the snap to the hook. Then he repeated the action with her free arm. Now she was bound at the wrists, chained to the ceiling. He returned to the panel and made an adjustment to the chain. He wanted her flat on her feet for now.

"Go ahead. Test them."

She yanked against the bindings, but she wasn't able to accomplish anything. This would do very nicely.

Mina's heart beat a little faster. It always had when he'd bound her wrists. Fear didn't play into it. She'd always trusted him. He'd established his trustworthiness from the beginning, even as he barreled through her limit about not kissing on the first date. She hadn't known what he was doing back then because he'd never explicitly discussed his need to dominate her. She hadn't understood his honor code, but she did now. She understood so much more about him after researching and negotiating.

This was one of her favorite things, yet she wasn't sure how she felt about it tonight. From the clanking sounds it had made when she'd tugged against it, that was definitely a chain holding her in place. Before, she'd always been tied to his bed, or he'd simply held her wrists down. This was different, a little impersonal.

He slid his hands around her ankles, wrapping cuffs that felt similar to the ones he'd put around her wrists. Then he spread her legs wider, forcing her to shift her weight to the balls of her feet. She heard the rattle of chains again, this time sliding against the floor. A click, and she felt the slight weight holding her ankles so she would not be able to alter her spread position.

As the realization of her helplessness crashed down on her head, hot cream rushed to her pussy. The scent of her arousal reached her nose, and she knew Ever could smell it from wherever he was standing.

Behind her, as it turned out. He rested his fingertips on her waist. "You like being bound like this, don't you, Mina?"

She didn't mind his gloating tone. He'd always been cocky and confident. What rocked her in that moment was his use of her name. He hadn't called her "slave," a term she felt kept the wall between them firmly in place. She liked the way he said her name, and she missed the way he used to call her "honey" and murmur sweet phrases in her ear.

She tried to speak, but her throat was a bit dry from all that heavy breathing. She swallowed to wet it. "Yes, Master. Putting myself at your mercy is definitely a lot more erotic than I thought it would be."

His fingers slid across her skin and dropped away. She listened intently to the sounds of him moving around the room. Seconds later, she felt something small and round against her bottom lip.

"Drink some water."

She accepted the fact that he was going to be pouring it into her mouth, and she parted her lips. He fed her in sips, his competent actions advertising that he'd done this before with other women. Probably recently. She ingested the bitter taste of her own folly with the soothing coolness of the water.

"Thank you, Master." She signaled a stop with her gratitude.

He licked a stray drop from her lip before she could get to it. She hoped the quick swipe of his tongue would lead to one of those drugging kisses of his, but it didn't. The next time he touched her—only moments had passed, but it seemed forever—he drew his fingertips over her hips.

She shivered at the lightness of the sensation, and she wondered what he planned to do with her in this position. The research she'd done indicated this was the time for impact play, but she's specified no flogging.

The caress moved up her ribs. He stroked the undersides of her breasts softly, coaxing her nipples to sharp points without once touching them. Then she felt the press of his lips at the place just below her ear that sent tremors racing down her body.

"So soft, so responsive, so mine." He repeated the caress on her other side. "I'm going to show you how a master uses his slave, Mina. You aren't allowed to climax until I tell you to. Do you understand?"

"Yes, Master." She knew she was supposed to ask first. Heat rose to her cheeks as she remembered Isla telling her that she had to ask. More heat scorched her chest as she remembered the last time they'd been together, her first punishment. She'd begged, but he hadn't let her come. She had forgotten when she'd masturbated on his lap, but he hadn't punished her or even mentioned it.

He was behind her now. He pulled her hips upward, rolling them forward, and she felt the tip of his cock nudge her entrance. No condom for this. She'd been explicit in her request once all the medical tests had come back clean. He was the only man she'd ever let take her without a condom. She wanted nothing separating them.

Reaching around to the front, he guided his cock into her wetness. His thrusts were shallow, short jabs that targeted her sweet spot with unerring accuracy. He grasped her hips hard and fucked her quickly.

She wanted to feel more of him against her body, not just those three points of contact. She wanted him to stimulate her clit, touch her breasts, caress her body, and kiss her. She wanted to be surrounded by him, engulfed by his body, but that wasn't the lesson he sought to teach. As he'd said, he was using her body.

And she loved it. Serving him this way reduced her from a cherished lover to a comfort object. She should have hated it, but because she knew him so well, because she trusted him, she could accept this temporary reassignment. She could revel in the decadence of submitting to him in a way that fulfilled his needs.

And damn if he didn't see to her pleasure when he could have just taken what he wanted without reciprocating. Tension built inside her abdomen, and he stopped his actions, pulling out and stepping away.

She whimpered a protest. If he heard it, he didn't respond.

Something soft whispered against the underside of her knee. It continued upward, stroking her thigh and her butt. Analyzing the sensation, she knew he wasn't using his hands. Pictures of various implements and toys filed through her mind, a pornographic slide show that wasn't providing answers. She'd concentrated on researching things that could cause pain, and this did not.

As he traced his way around her body, she thought the soft touch might relax her, but it had the opposite effect. Combined with the need pulsing between her spread legs, it made her skin hypersensitive. Each stroke awakened more nerve endings, setting them on high alert.

Then he tickled the undersides of her breasts, a place she hadn't realized was so responsive, and she moaned loudly. The sound echoed in the silence of the room, shattering some of the tension. His lips closed over hers, and he teased the seam of her mouth with the tip of his tongue. Helpless in the face of his masterful onslaught, she parted her lips, submitting in all the ways he demanded.

Abruptly, he pulled away. This time he approached her from the front. The tip of his cock slid into her wet and waiting pussy. His thighs pressed against hers, and he gripped her ass. Again he fucked her with short, hard strokes, and she could do nothing but stand there and take pleasure from him.

Her breaths grew ragged, and she let her head fall back. Heat spiked from her pussy to her navel, and she felt the first stirrings of her orgasm.

"Master, may I come?"

Immediately he halted his actions and pulled out. "No."

He refused her in the simplest terms, his tone completely lacking emotion, as it might if he were having coffee and the server asked if he wanted a refill. Well, maybe not exactly like that. He'd thank the server. Mina didn't expect to be thanked, but she also didn't expect to be refused. He used to love to watch her climax.

The next thing that pressed against her skin was a vibrator. She recognized the sound and the shape. Once she'd realized that John wasn't going to be able to satisfy her in bed the way Ever had, she had purchased a pink vibrator. John had been upset at the implication he wasn't good enough, so she'd pretended to throw it away. In reality, she'd just hidden it with her feminine hygiene products because she knew John would never look there.

Even then, in the back of her mind, she had known Ever would have welcomed the purchase. He would have used it on her. Those bitter thoughts had damaged her relationship with John, not that he would have been able to make her happy anyway. She'd never managed to move past her feelings for Everett Burke.

Ever ran the tip of it along her inner thighs, teasing with proximity. It pulsed in short bursts, so some areas received more stimulation that others. Then he played around with it, holding it against her nipples, skimming it along her sides and neck, and then pressing it to her lips.

She knew what he wanted, so she opened her mouth. He slipped the tip inside, just barely, forcing her to pursue it with her tongue. Part of her wondered why he didn't just put his cock in her mouth. She loved licking it and sucking on it, listening to the sounds he made when she drove him to a place of extreme pleasure.

He cupped the back of her neck, just as he did when she went down on him. "Yes, honey. Just like that."

She made a noise, a desperate sound, but she was beyond caring. He took the vibrator away, drawing it down her body. He parted the lips of her pussy with it, rubbing it back and forth. She wanted to thrust her hips, but he'd bound her too well. She whimpered, simultaneously begging for more and letting him know how much she loved what he was doing.

She felt his lips against her throat. "No coming, slave."

"No, Master." God, she wanted to come!

He moved his lips down her neck and swirled his tongue around one nipple. He coaxed it to a peak. She expected him to suck it into his mouth, but he bit it. Hard. She cried out at the sudden and unexpected pain that lent sparks of white to the darkness of the blindfold.

The list of her hard limits played through her head. She'd only outlawed impact play. This didn't fall under that umbrella. She understood that, but it wasn't being flogged she feared; it was the pain.

"Ever, don't do that."

He laved her other nipple, teasing it to a point. Heat radiated from the one he'd bitten. It felt like his teeth were still around it, but now that the initial sting was subsiding, it pulsed with a sensation bordering on pleasure.

Just as she was becoming used to the aftereffect, he did the same thing to her other nipple. She sucked in a breath, uncertain whether she wanted to be upset with him for doing something she'd just told him not to do or because it hurt.

"Damn it, Everett. I told you not to do that!"

He smacked a kiss on her cheek, a loud one. "That's twice, slave. You can scream and beg as much as you want. I love to hear it. However, slaves who forget their place and give orders are punished. Swearing at me isn't going to make me want to go easy on you either."

As he spoke, he slid the vibrator into her pussy. The sensation competed with the pain in her nipples, which was turning into something unexpectedly pleasurable.

"I'm sorry, Master. I'm just—I wasn't expecting for you to hurt me."

He brushed his palm across one nipple, knocking something metal against her breast. "Does it hurt more than it feels good, slave? Think for a moment before you answer. Concentrate on the feeling."

Mina tried to banish all thoughts and focus on the feeling, but that was quite a feat in the face of the fear clogging her mind. "It's about even, Master. It feels like you're still biting me."

"They're nipple clamps." He fiddled with one, and the pressure eased a little. Pleasure began to outweigh the pain.

"Now it feels good." Her brain raced. She didn't recall giving permission for the use of nipple clamps, but she didn't remember banning them either. "Were there questions about these on the survey?"

"Yes." He adjusted the other, and the pressure on that side morphed as well. "It was in the section on toys. I thought about bringing up the discrepancy when you outlawed impact play and pretty much everything else that can cause pain, but then I decided not to rock that boat. I want to see what you can take."

It wasn't an acceptable excuse. This was definitely something to discuss. "Ever—"

"If you object, call the safeword. Otherwise, shut up."

She shut up. The pain had diminished, and now she barely felt the clamps at all. And she was a big chicken. She was reluctant to remind him about how she'd walked out on him for the wrong reasons, especially not now that she was bound and at his mercy with a vibrator in her pussy—exactly where she wanted to be.

His body heat moved away from her, but he prodded her mons with his fingers, splitting her even wider, so she didn't worry. Then she felt his lips lock on to her clit. He wiggled the vibrator, teasing her sweet spot. She gasped. The coil of tension—sexual and emotional—contracted sharply and burst. She moaned, louder and louder until it turned into a keening cry. The orgasm washed over her, battering her with feelings she couldn't hope to contain.

Between her legs, Ever manipulated the vibrator and sucked her little nub, prolonging the flood of feeling. Then the vibrator was gone. He stood and devoured her mouth, giving her another taste of her juices on his breath.

"Naughty slaves steal orgasms. You need to be taught a lesson."

He removed her blindfold. Light flooded her field of vision, so bright after that prolonged period of darkness. She blinked at him until his face came into focus. Then she just gaped at him. He'd made her come. If he didn't want her to climax, why hadn't he stopped when her moans had turned urgent?

"Are you going to punish me?"

He sat down on his chair, propped his elbow on the arm, and rested his chin on his fist. "Master."

She'd forgotten to use his title, which probably only compounded the punishments. She was really racking them up. "I'm sorry. Are you going to punish me, Master?"

He appeared to consider this. "Punishment—yes. Spanking—no. I think we'll reserve that for willful disobedience."

Once more, her mind returned to the massive amount of paperwork. An edge of panic began to set in because she couldn't remember everything. She wanted another look at the agreement.

"Breathe, Mina. Tell me what has you so upset."

"I don't remember what other punishments I agreed to."

He didn't appear surprised by her answer. "You didn't agree to any punishments. You agreed to spanking, but spanking isn't always a punishment. Under the right circumstances, it can be quite pleasurable."

She couldn't see that happening, but she didn't dismiss it either. The nipple clamps weren't something she ever thought she'd like. "But you used it as punishment. Master." She added his title belatedly. She'd forgotten it a lot tonight.

The corner of his mouth twitched in a semblance of a smile. "I know. It's what you expected. It calmed you down and let you focus on what you needed in order to have an orgasm. As your Master, I'll always give you what you need, which may not necessarily be what you want."

As the weight of his words sank in, so did the guilt, settling on her shoulders more oppressively than any chains. "You've always done that."

He rose, and she realized that not only was he still naked; he hadn't climaxed yet tonight. He closed the distance between them and crooked his finger under her chin, forcing her to look at him. His green eyes glittered with harsh light. "Forty-eight hours. Two days, Mina. That's what you asked for. That's what I'm going to give you. If you seek to understand the nature of being a submissive, I'm willing to answer any questions you have. If you want to discuss the past, this is neither the place nor the time."

Since she feared that discussion, she swallowed and took a breath. The harshness left his eyes, but so did any trace of tenderness.

"Pain is not required for a punishment. I'm going to punish you right now, slave, and I guarantee it won't hurt."

He twisted a small screw on a nipple clamp with his thumb and caught it as it dropped away. She gasped as blood rushed to fill the void. It burned a little, but not enough to be a punishment. He removed the other one, and she breathed through it.

"But before it's over, you'll be sobbing and begging me to make it stop." His arrogant half smile made her heart stutter. "Or maybe you're too stubborn to beg. We'll see, won't we?"

He disappeared into the darkness, leaving her alone in the light. If it was possible, she was more afraid of this punishment than of one that involved pain. Her pulse pounded in her ears, interrupted only by the muted sounds of Ever moving around somewhere outside the pool of light.

When he returned, he attached some kind of stand to the floor between her legs. While he was down there, he stuck a finger under her bindings and poked at her feet. "Wiggle your toes. Does it hurt? Tingle?"

"No, Master. It's fine." She flexed her fingers as well. "My hands are okay too. Of course, you could untie me and let me see to that erection problem you have."

He chuckled as he stood up. "So kind of you to offer, but believe me when I say I'll take everything I want from you, and there's not a damn thing you can do about it."

The threat filled her with a comforting warmth.

But that thought didn't occupy her mind for long. He held up a long, thick dildo and drizzled lubricant over it. There was no way that thing was going to fit inside her. Ever's cock stretched her enough. This was larger.

Then he knelt and pressed it to her opening. "Relax. You should enjoy this part. Breathe out."

She wasn't sure about that, but she exhaled because he told her to. He slid it inside her. The fit was tight but not uncomfortable.

Between her legs, he fiddled with things she couldn't see. From the bits she could discern, she figured he was somehow attaching the dildo to the stand he'd secured to the floor.

Next, he freed her ankles, a move she found puzzling. Then he produced a roll of plastic wrap, which he wound from her waist to her knees. At last, he retreated to his chair, where he picked up a remote and pressed a button. Between her legs, the dildo stirred. Powerful vibrations pulsed at irregular intervals.

"You've heard the story about the kid who steals a cigarette from his father's pack and is forced to smoke the whole thing?" He stroked his cock, and she understood he was going to force her to orgasm until she begged him to stop.

The spirit of rebellion stirred to life in her chest. The vibrator inside her felt so damn good. There was no way she'd be able to resist. Still, she did have one hell of a stubborn streak. It had been her downfall more than once. "He became a nicotine addict?"

Everett laughed. "Smart chicks are so hot." Then he turned up the rate of vibration. Her entire body shuddered. An orgasm wasn't far off.

Mina's knees bent, and she dangled from the wrist cuffs. Ever sat up a little straighter, ready to dash the two steps it would take to grab her and hold her up if necessary. The wrist cuffs were meant as restraint. He'd never expect her to support the full weight of her body with those delicate, slim wrists.

But she recovered quickly. He pressed a button on the remote and turned the vibrations to a regular pulse. She looked at him, and he knew she had no problem seeing him. Her eyes had adjusted to the uneven light levels quickly.

She'd popped off three spectacular orgasms. Add that to the two she'd already had, and she had to be getting tired.

"Ready to beg, slave?"

She shook her head.

He couldn't help but smile at her stubborn streak. She was determined to outlast him. Between the way she was bound and the way his cock begged to get inside her, she just might win this one. Of course he couldn't let her know that.

20

She wiggled her hips, and he realized she was fucking the dildo. Wicked minx. He got to his feet and brought the rate of vibration back up. Sweat beaded her brow and trickled down the valley between her breasts. The scent of her sex filled the air in the room. Presented with this erotic sight and the smell of her juices, he couldn't resist.

He stood inches from her and took his cock in hand.

Her gaze flickered down. She licked her lips and focused on his cock. "Oh God, yes."

"I'm not going to fuck you, slave. I'm going to ejaculate on your stomach."

Her breasts seemed to swell before his eyes. "Yes please, Master. I've waited so long for this."

She never ceased to amaze him. He slid his hand up and down his cock, and the action only seemed to drive her insane. If he'd known this would get the results he'd wanted, he wouldn't have spent the last forty-five minutes forcing her up the face of that cliff. This was the free fall he needed to see.

"Yes, yes, yes!"

The faster he pumped his fist, the louder she became. Her breaths turned to ragged moans. She called his name and his title, and she came again the moment his hot semen hit her skin.

And then she was spent. She slumped forward as far as the chains would let her go. He caught her, supporting her weight with an arm around her waist as he released her from the cuffs. Unwrapping her from the plastic proved troublesome, because the languor of his orgasm hadn't faded.

Finally he had her free. He eased the dildo from her pussy and tossed it in the direction of the sink. Hopefully it landed where he meant it to go. He'd have to clean up in the morning. Right now he had to care for his stubborn submissive.

Mina woke to find herself in a soft bed. She had a vague recollection of Everett holding her in the shower as he washed the sweat, semen, and juices from her body. Then he'd toweled her dry, and she'd glimpsed the tender caregiver she'd come to know all those years ago. After that, her memory failed.

The room was large. Moonlight streamed through a curtainless window, rendering everything in shades of silver and black. She sat up.

As the covers fell away, she realized she was naked. Of course. He'd specified that she would be naked for the entire weekend, so why would he dress her simply to sleep?

Because he'd been in the process of building it when she'd left him, she'd never been inside his house, but she knew the land well. They'd spent many afternoons picnicking or hiking through the woods, and he'd discussed the plans for the house with her often. At the time, she'd known he was seeking her input on the design for the house because he pictured a future with her, and that had alarmed her as much as it had warmed her heart.

Despite all the things he'd done for her, there were some things she needed to do for herself. Ever had been a light sleeper, so she was careful to move slowly and watch where she was going. Still, he snaked out a hand. It landed on her leg before she could exit the bed. "Where are you going?"

He barely moved his lips, leaving her to mostly guess what he said. From what she could discern, he did the same with his eyes. He wasn't really awake yet.

"Bathroom," she whispered, not wanting to disturb him further.

He rolled over and groaned. Then he shifted his leg and tossed the covers aside. As he crossed the room, moonlight lit his body, revealing that he'd slept naked as well. He opened a door and flipped on a light switch. A yellow pool of light illuminated his messy hair and sleepy expression. He still hadn't opened his eyes.

She watched as he trudged back, his feet shuffling along the carpet, and then he fell back into bed, facedown. "I put your stuff in there."

"Thanks." Seeing as it was the middle of the night, she didn't add his title.

He didn't take his face out of his pillow to call her on it, which muffled his correction. "Master."

Her mistake. She'd agreed to be his for two days. "Thanks, Master."

When she returned to bed a few minutes later, he wrapped his arm around her waist and pulled her across the king-size mattress until she was nestled against him. He turned her so that she was on her back, and then he threw a leg over hers and pressed a kiss to her neck.

It didn't stop there, and she wasn't surprised. She knew he generally woke up horny, and as the submissive she couldn't deny him—not that she wanted to.

His firm lips fluttered softly against her neck and along her jaw. When he made it to her mouth, he licked the seam of her lips. "You brushed?"

And perhaps she hadn't rinsed as thoroughly as she should have. In her defense, her body still felt heavy with lethargy left over from the many orgasms he'd forced on her, which she would never complain about. They were addictive. She hoped for another soon.

"Yeah. You cleaned my body, but that still needed to be done."

He shifted, nudging her legs apart with his knee, and settled on top of her. The tip of his erection brushed her inner thigh. "Waking up your master in the middle of the night and criticizing him isn't a great battle strategy."

"I wasn't aware we were fighting."

He reached between them and positioned his cock at her opening. "You've always fought me."

She opened her legs farther and tilted her hips to give him a better angle. "I'm not fighting you now."

"Yes, you are." He slid home. "But I'm not going to let you win." With that, he pinned her wrists on either side of her head and captured her mouth with a kiss that both possessed and controlled.

A cloud passed over the moon, and he became a shadow hovering over her. He withdrew most of the way and thrust deep. Whether in deference to the lack of foreplay or due to his semisleepy state, he fucked her slowly, claiming her with every stroke.

"You're so beautiful, honey. So tight. You feel so good around me." He increased his pace, rocking his body into hers harder and deeper. She met his every thrust.

It felt good to finally have him take her like this. She'd missed being close to him. She wanted him to release her wrists so she could touch him. "You can't even see me."

"Don't need to see you. I dream about you here with me, like this."

Probably to shut up anything she might say to ruin the moment, he plunged his tongue into her mouth, tangling it with hers in a duel she couldn't hope to win. She didn't even try, choosing surrender instead.

Then she got her wish. He released her wrists. He ended the kiss, but his lips hovered so close to hers that she felt like they were still touching. Tunneling one arm under her shoulders, he lifted her closer, sealing her chest to his. He pumped into her, faster and faster.

"Come with me." It was an order, but it was a plea as well. This was something he'd always said to her, often coupling it with an affirmation of love.

23

Mina sensed the sentiment was still there, buried under the weight of the heart she'd broken. The unspoken declaration wrapped around her core, liquid heat combining with the fire he stoked between her legs. His breathing grew ragged, and she knew he was close. So was she.

She hung on to his shoulder with one hand and the back of his neck with her other, tangling her fingers in the soft hair at his nape. Taking the chance—because it was incredibly selfish to expect him to put himself out there first—she whispered the words. "I love you, Ever."

He cried out as she spoke, so she wasn't sure he heard. They came together. He thrust one last time, and then he rolled to the side so he wouldn't crush her.

She looked over at him. The clouds moved away from the moon for a moment, and she saw that he'd fallen back asleep.

She berated herself for thinking it would be that easy, and she didn't stop the silent tears that leaked from her eyes.

Chapter Two

Most of her friends had found jobs or internships right away. Mina delayed the job-application process to return home. Her mother, Jin Ae, had been alone for four years. In the divorce, she'd been awarded the small bungalow-style home in which Mina had been raised. It was her duty to see to her mother's health and well-being, and she couldn't do that from California, Texas, or Virginia, the places where she'd been scoping out jobs developing new tech.

Vermont didn't offer much in her field, so she aimed to persuade her mother to sell the house and move with her. It would take some time to do, but Mina was convinced it wasn't an insurmountable task.

Her plan was to begin slowly. She'd integrate herself back into her mother's routine and then show her mother there was nothing in Vermont worth staying for. Because her father had been strict and controlling, neither Mina nor her mother had been allowed to truly become part of the small-town community. They'd been welcome. The people had always been friendly, but the Sungs had held all nonfamily members at arm's length.

Mina wanted a new start in a new town where she and her mother could participate in community life. She was tired of watching from the periphery. Being away at college had taught her that there was more to life than staying at home and suffering in silence as her father beat his wife and bullied his daughter.

Leaving that house was a necessary part of the healing process. The first weekend, Mina ran to town to do some shopping. She liked running these kinds of errands because it got her out of the house, and she really needed to get out. It was June, and her mother hated to venture farther than her immaculate garden.

The stores in town hadn't changed a bit. In the past, Mina and Jin Ae had rushed through their errands because the tyrant waiting in the car timed everything. If they took longer than he thought was necessary, then he became angry. When he became angry, things never turned out well.

One of the first things her mother had done after separating from her father was to get a driver's license. Now that she could run errands on her own, she avoided it at all costs.

Breen's small grocery store had fresh produce and hanging baskets overflowing with pretty flowers. In the past, Mina would have hurried by, trying to avoid looking at what would be considered a frivolous purchase. But now she was finding she couldn't help but stop to look.

A particularly pretty basket of red-and-white pansies caught her attention. She drew her finger over one soft petal and smiled.

"Beautiful, aren't they?"

The strong male voice startled her at first. She hadn't been aware of anyone nearby. She glanced up to find a massive chest occupying all the available space next to her. His short-sleeved cotton shirt was blue, and it clung to his muscular torso and emphasized his impressive arms. Following a path up his shirt, she found herself drowning in a set of foamy green eyes.

The corners of his lips were lifted in a smile that dripped sensuality. Immediately she imagined what they'd feel like against her own, and then she recognized him. The high school she'd attended hadn't been very large. Though Everett Burke had been three years ahead of her, they had been in a couple of classes together. And she had been friendly with his younger sister. She couldn't say they'd been friends because her father hadn't allowed her to have friends. School and family came first. His parents had raised him that way, and now it was her turn. Mina vowed that when she had kids, they would be allowed to have friends, attend parties and sleepovers, play sports. Anything they wanted.

She hadn't known Everett well. Their conversations had been few and far between, and they'd always been academic. While he'd frequently acknowledged her with a smile and a nod outside the classroom, they'd only ever spoken when a teacher had put them together for group work. Even then, she'd refrained from saying much. She'd found him both attractive and intimidating. He was far larger than her father, which meant he could cause far more damage, and he had been a senior when she was a freshman.

His size hadn't changed with time, though he had filled out a little more.

She lowered her gaze. "Yes. I was thinking they would look nice on the back patio, but I'm afraid of getting dirt all over my car."

"I have some newspaper in my truck. I meant to get to the recycle center yesterday, but I didn't get out of work in time." He flashed that sinful smile. "I guess the universe had a reason."

He lifted two hanging baskets, both full of the red-and-white flowers she had admired.

"Wait." She put her hand on his arm, the first time she'd voluntarily touched a man, much less one she found attractive. His warm skin heated her palm, and his muscles felt firm under her hand. What would it feel like to have his skin brush against hers? She froze, staring at the place where she touched him, and hoped he wouldn't get angry.

"You don't like these? Tell me which ones you like best."

This would be her first frivolous purchase. She didn't want to go overboard. "I was just going to get one."

Everett considered each basket, and then he shook his head. "You need at least two, possibly three or four, in order for them to look good. One isn't enough."

Mina shook her head. "I didn't bring that much money."

He just grinned. "That's okay. They're on me." Lifting his gaze and his volume, he shouted over her head. "Wild, add two of these."

Mina knew Wilder Burke as well. These handsome twins greatly resembled each other, but they weren't identical. Though they were the same height and they shared a build, Everett was just a little broader in the shoulders, and he had green eyes to Wilder's blue ones. Plus he was better looking.

Too late, she realized he meant to pay for them. "I can't let you do that."

"You don't have a choice. Where is your car? I'll load them up for you."

His high-handed manner gave her pause. He'd always been confident and commanding. Every girl in school had a crush on him or Wilder or their best friend Micah. Micah's younger brother, Jude, was good-looking as well, but he was younger, and that automatically counted him out until the older boys had graduated. Then every girl spent the next two years trying to make Jude O'Connor notice them. She didn't know which heartthrob had come next, but she was sure there was somebody now over whom the girls drooled.

Her arms were full with two bags of groceries, so she couldn't take the baskets from him. His affable, firm expression let her know there was no point in arguing. She inclined her head toward the sedan she'd rented. She didn't want to buy a car until she convinced her mother to move.

He followed her over, grabbed some newspapers from the bed of the truck parked in the next spot, and lined her trunk. "When did you get back in town?"

Mina set her bags down on the ground and helped him spread the paper. "Wednesday. I'm staying with my mom for a little while."

He nodded as if she'd confirmed something he already knew. "A bunch of us are going to Elmhurst tonight. Can I pick you up at six? We could get dinner first."

Elmhurst was a popular hangout, mostly because it was the only hangout. By day, it was a bar and restaurant. After eight on the weekends, it turned into a low-key karaoke and dance club. It took Mina several moments to process Everett's question. She'd been asked out before, but not like this. She wasn't sure if he was asking her if she'd go out with him or if he was assuming she'd go and he was just confirming the time.

"Are you asking me on a date?"

Ever ran his hand through his hair, a nervous gesture he wished he hadn't made because he hadn't checked his hand for dirt yet. A smooth move to compound his mistake. He heard the incredulity in her question, and he didn't blame her one bit.

He'd meant to ask. He'd rehearsed this scenario and ones like it in his head since the summer after his junior year in college. Four years ago he'd come home to watch his sister Danica graduate from high school, and all he'd been able to do was stare at Mina Sung, the most beautiful girl in the world.

Danica had brought Mina home from school twice in twelve years, and Danica had never once been invited to Mina's, so the girls weren't very close. Mina's parents were strict and old-fashioned, and Mina hadn't been allowed to go anywhere or do anything. Ever had toyed with the idea of asking her out, but he knew her parents wouldn't permit her to date.

Now that she was older and they had both returned from college, he figured this was the perfect opportunity to get that date he'd only dreamed about. But he'd fantasized about this moment so often he'd skipped huge parts of the conversation. Those parts included flirting and actually asking if she was interested.

Since he'd already stuck his foot in his mouth, he decided to brazen it out. He tried for his most charming smile. "Yes."

Her brows drew together sharply. "That wasn't a question. You just assumed I would go." She closed her trunk.

He couldn't let this chance pass. Luckily he had several tricks up his sleeve. He leaned against her car casually, as if she hadn't made a move to end the conversation. "Are you busy?"

"I think you meant to ask if I was even interested." She planted her fists on her hips, but she didn't look angry, just a little nervous. He could deal with that.

Leaning down, he closed some of the distance her shortness put between them. "I know you're interested. No woman who touches a man the way you did is uninterested."

"The way I—" She put her hand to her chest and sputtered. Small spots of color darkened her cheeks. "I didn't touch you."

Now he was gaining control of the conversation. His goal wasn't to humiliate or embarrass her, but he didn't want her to think it was okay to hide her thoughts and reactions. He schooled his features into a neutral expression. "You grabbed my arm when you were trying to stop me from buying flowers for you. It's okay. I felt it too."

She dropped her gaze, and his jeans grew tighter at her unconscious display of submissiveness. "I didn't mean to do that. I insist on paying you back for the flowers."

Everett shook his head. "Not going to happen. I've been waiting to ask you out for four years."

Now she looked directly at him, studying him with undisguised curiosity. "Why now?"

He took her hands in his. The fact she didn't resist spoke volumes. "Why not now? The timing finally seems perfect. You're twenty-two, an adult who can make her own decisions about where she goes and who she keeps company with."

She thought about that for a minute, as if it was the first time she'd thought about her situation from that perspective. "All right, I will have dinner with you. I will meet you at Elmhurst at six-thirty."

It wasn't the gallant setup he'd wanted, but it would do. He leaned down the rest of the way and kissed her cheek. "I'll see you at six-thirty, Mina Sung. Wear a pretty dress."

Mina stared in shock at Everett's retreating figure, and not because his ass looked so sexy in those jeans, though that view did take some of the edge off her chagrin. No man had ever kissed her before the first date. Sure, they tried afterward, and she usually refused. Everett hadn't asked. He'd just taken what he wanted.

She couldn't say why, but his action made her knees weak. She gathered her wits together and got into her car. Learning to drive had been a rebellious act she'd perpetrated her first year in college. Her roommate at the time had insisted that everybody should know how to drive, even if they never got a car. Once Mina had a taste of this life, she embraced it.

At six-thirty exactly, she walked down the sidewalk on Main Street, heading toward Elmhurst. The building wasn't large, and it was very, very old. Over the years, they'd remodeled to keep up with changing times. A timeline on the wall kept track of when they got indoor plumbing, electricity, an HVAC system, and wireless Internet. Lloyd, the owner with the ageless face, was very proud of his contributions.

She had chosen a colorful skirt that went down just past her knees. It said she was interested and happy to be there, but she wasn't easy. The matching blouse had short sleeves in deference to the weather. As he'd directed, the outfit was pretty. It wasn't sexy or revealing. She wasn't comfortable wearing things like that.

Ever broke away from a group of people and came toward her, his hand extended. It looked like he wanted to shake her hand, which was fine with her. She met him halfway. But he had other ideas. He raised her hand to his lips and kissed the backs of her fingers. Nobody had ever done something like that before. It seemed like a line from a movie, a gimmick designed to get her into bed. And he was charming and sincere enough to pull it off.

"I won't sleep with you."

His brows lifted in surprise, but he seemed otherwise unaffected. "Noted. You look lovely tonight. I like what you've done with your hair."

She lifted her free hand and nervously patted the back of her head to make sure the sleek knot hadn't fallen down. It hadn't occurred to her that he would like her hair up. She'd thought it was another warning that she wasn't going to be an easy conquest. *Hair up equals uptight.*

This wasn't going the way she thought it would, beginning with her opening statement. "Thank you."

Releasing her hand, he reached for the door and opened it.

She peered over his shoulder at the group of men and women who were pretending not to watch them. "Aren't your friends coming?"

Ever shook his head. "They'll join us later if we want them to."

Mina didn't know what she wanted. Now that she was here, she was losing her nerve. Dating a hometown boy had never been on the

30

list of things she wanted to do with her life. If everything went as planned, she would be moving across the country in the next few months. Her heart was set on California.

Since it was too late to back out, she let him steer her into the restaurant. It was dinner, not an engagement. His hand lingered on the small of her back. The gesture was perhaps meant to be unobtrusive, but she was hyperaware of the small pressure of his fingertips and the way his heat caused her stomach to flutter. Though she couldn't rationalize it, she felt cherished and possessed. It both pleased and terrified her.

A hostess sat them immediately. Everett pulled out her chair, a courteous move she hadn't expected. Their server, a man whose face looked very familiar but who Mina couldn't quite place, arrived before the hostess left.

She turned to smile over her shoulder at Everett. "Thank you."

Mina ordered water with a twist of lemon, and Everett ordered a soft drink. When the server left, she anticipated an awkward silence. After all, what did she know about Everett Burke except that he was handsome and a few years older? What could they possibly have in common?

He folded his hands on the table and regarded her with a twinkle in his eyes. "What was the first thing you decided to do in college that you weren't allowed to do at home?"

The question startled her. Why would he think she had a rebellious streak? She'd spent more Saturday nights studying than partying. Was his purpose to find out the lengths to which she would go to have fun? Mina shook her head. "I don't know what you mean."

"I had dessert for dinner and stayed out all night. My mother would have killed me if I'd sat down to dinner with a huge piece of cake, and my parents were both firm on the midnight curfew. They still use it if I stay with them. It's just one of the many reasons I got an apartment as soon as I could." He flashed that charming grin again.

The server brought their drinks and took their order. Mina hadn't looked at a menu, but Elmhurst wasn't a fancy place. Once in a while they served a fish dish, but mostly they served burgers and fries. That was what she ordered.

Everett followed suit and thanked the server. Then he turned his attention back to her, not that it had ever fully left. "Your turn."

She didn't pretend to have lost track of the conversation. "I'd have thought you would've done things wilder than that. I can picture you at a frat party every weekend."

31

He shook his head, but he allowed her evasion. "I wasn't interested in being part of a fraternity. I lived in the dorms my freshman year and got a tiny student apartment with three other people after that. New York isn't a cheap place to live."

She hadn't known he'd gone to college in New York. She'd thought both he and Wilder had stayed home to attend the University of Vermont. She wanted to ask about that, but when he lifted his drink and sipped slowly, she realized he wasn't going to say more until she answered his original question. "I learned to drive."

"Ahh." His head bobbed as if some great understanding had come to him. "Freedom and independence. Smart move, though you probably didn't need to drive much at Harvard. The public transportation system is pretty good."

"That, and I didn't have a car. When my parents divorced, my father agreed to pay tuition, room, and board. Nothing more. My mom didn't have money for frivolous things. I had a job in the library to cover expenses." This was the first time she'd ever mentioned to anybody that her parents were divorced. In this small town, she couldn't pretend nobody knew or cared. It was likely they all knew.

But Everett didn't seem to fixate on her disclosure. "That's funny. I worked in the library, too. I worked on their computer systems and spent a lot of time lost in the stacks, reading. What was your major?"

She couldn't picture Everett Burke, handsome charmer, sitting on the floor of a dusty aisle with his face buried in a book. In a woman, maybe. She wasn't sure she believed him. "Computer engineering. I can write programs, but I love developing hardware more. You went to NYU? What was your major?"

He nodded to confirm which school he'd attended. "Anthropology and statistics. You wouldn't think they go together, but they do. Studying culture is all about analyzing statistics."

"What can you do with that degree around here?" The judgment inherent in the question didn't occur to her until it was out there, hanging in the air and dripping with her incredulity.

He only chuckled. "You'd be surprised. I'm working for my parents' company. Wilder and I have expanded the company's reach to service the entire country, not just the New England area. We've doubled in size, and the growth means we get to travel all over the place."

In this economy, the fact any company could grow amazed Mina. She had no idea what his parents' company did, and she didn't want to draw attention to her ignorance by asking. So she just smiled encouragingly. "Congratulations. It must feel good to know you've made such a difference. I bet your parents are proud of you."

"They are." Everett smiled. "I'm lucky to have such a close-knit, supportive family. They didn't expect us to stay around, but they welcomed us if that's what we chose. Wilder and I decided to stay. Marielle, my older sister, moved to Hawaii to study marine life. Danica is on her third university. She keeps changing her mind about what she wants to do."

Mina could see that. Danica had been a very vivacious, impulsive person in high school. It made her interesting to observe from a distance, but Mina had never wanted to get caught up in the whirlwind that was Everett's little sister. They might be the same age, but they had little in common. The few times she'd been assigned to work on projects with Danica had been enough excitement to last her for years.

"That must drive your parents crazy."

Everett shrugged. "We all would've been surprised if she suddenly slowed down and focused on one thing. I'm sure she'll never settle on one career. We love her for who she is, and we just want her to be happy."

That was the sweetest sentiment Mina had ever heard a person express. She'd listened to other people utter the words, but this was the first time she'd heard the genuine love and affection suffusing Everett's simple statement.

The server arrived with the food. Mina had been too nervous after their morning encounter to eat much at lunch, so she dug into the juicy burger, relaxed, and enjoyed the rest of her conversation with Everett.

Ever watched as the tension eased from Mina's shoulders. She'd been so wound up when she'd arrived, he wondered if she'd changed her mind about wanting to spend time with him. Just to be safe, he kept the flirting to a minimum. It brought to his attention exactly how much he flirted with just about every woman he knew.

Some of the witty innuendos he'd squelched were good ones, too. When he eventually asked what job she had done at the library, he didn't make a joke about more interesting ways to dust those aisles of books and collections that nobody visited unless they were looking for some on-campus privacy.

He'd figured out the moment she blurted her first sentence that she wasn't comfortable with heavy flirting. Dialing it back tested his patience a bit. The only people he didn't flirt with were family members. Even Micah and Jude weren't safe from his penchant for jokes of a sexual and insinuating nature. They'd just learned to go with it.

That night, he completely abandoned his friends. They understood the importance of a proper first date, and he knew they wouldn't expect him to spend time socializing with them.

After dinner, he could tell Mina wasn't going to be comfortable with karaoke. She was too introverted to dive into something so public. No matter. They could work their way up to that, just as he could ease her into his large and boisterous group of friends. He'd introduce her to them a few at a time, keep the atmosphere relaxed.

She reached for the check as Benjy left the table, even though their server had clearly set it next to him. Ever had never in his life let a woman pay for dinner. He hadn't been raised that way. He set his hand over the slip of paper and regarded her with an expression that forbade any argument.

She retreated, but it was a slow process, and he watched her wage an internal struggle the entire time.

He leaned forward, because his words were for her ears only. "Mina, I don't like that you didn't let me pick you up, but I let you have your way because I really want to spend time with you. Please don't make the mistake of thinking there will ever be an occasion where I will let you pay the check."

"That's so sexist." Her brows dipped with amusement. "I know I'm the one benefitting from it, but I can't say I'm in favor of it. I'll pay next time."

That would never, ever happen. "It's good to know there will be a next time. I'd like to see you tomorrow." He removed his hand from the check and reached across the table. It wasn't a way to tempt her resolve, because he might just turn her over his knee if she touched that slip of paper. He closed his hand around hers, knowing full well she wasn't completely comfortable with his public display.

The analytical part of him watched her to make sure she was okay with his show of dominance. She seemed to be intrigued by it, no doubt about that.

She nodded at him. "I'm free tomorrow."

"Great. Now that we've established that, let me make clear my stance on feminist issues. I believe a woman can do anything a man can do, and she can probably do most of those things better. Women tend to be more intelligent, thoughtful, and levelheaded. However, I firmly believe it's my place to always show you respect. I will open doors, wait to sit down until you're seated, and pay for dates."

He let her absorb that for a few moments. Watching her think was a mesmerizing activity. From what he could tell, the conclusion she seemed to arrive at was the adoption of a wait-and-see attitude. He continued before she could vocalize her reaction.

"I'm not all that sensitive or enlightened. You won't see me watching movies about relationships or reading self-help books. I tend to tell rather than ask, which you've already experienced, and I expect to get what I want, when I want it. I have a quick temper, but it's gone as fast as it appears. I'm not perfect, and I don't strive to be what I'm not."

She patted the top of his hand with her free hand and flashed a grin. "At least you're in touch with your inner caveman. It's not all tragic news."

He chuckled at her dismissive summation.

"Since we're airing faults, I should tell you that I'm very stubborn. When I decide on something, it doesn't matter how much evidence stares me in the face proving I'm wrong. I will ignore it. I never back down from an argument. I also don't watch movies about relationships, but I will read self-help books, especially if they're about time management. I'll actually read anything—billboards, back of the shampoo bottle, the tiny print at the bottom of a contest entry form. It doesn't have to be interesting."

Everett liked stubborn women. They developed into strong submissives, and he liked his women strong. Opinionated. It kept him on his toes and made their surrender that much sweeter.

"I also like to pay for my half of the meal. I prefer to drive myself around and meet you places so I'm not stuck there if I want to leave. I believe in leaving my options open." She lifted her brows, challenging Everett directly, but he mostly noticed the way her brown eyes lit at their interaction.

He met that challenge the same way he approached negotiation. "Very well. I can bend on letting you drive. You can pick me up at my apartment tomorrow at eleven. I'm treating you to lunch."

With that, he released her hand, extracted a credit card from his wallet, and handed it to Benjy, whose timing was very fortunate for Mina.

Chapter Three

Normally Mina would bid her date good night at this point. He'd all but admitted he had a Neanderthal view of gender relations. But she found his old-fashioned values attractive. He had treated her as if she mattered every second they were together. He'd opened the door and paid for dinner, but those were surface features.

He'd also spent every moment with his attention completely focused on her. She had the sense he knew she'd encountered a bitter section of tomato on her burger and eaten it anyway. If she asked him, he could probably tell her the exact ratio of ketchup to mustard she liked for her fries. He listened when she talked, responding to what she meant as well as what she said.

If this was chivalry, why was it considered a bad thing?

He walked her toward the parking lot at a snail's pace, holding her hand firmly in his. "I know you don't want to stay for karaoke, but I don't want you to go home yet. My apartment isn't far from here. Want to come over and hang out?"

Mina recognized the subtext. She'd been here before. "I told you I'm not having sex with you. I don't even kiss on the first date."

Everett lifted her hand and brushed his lips across the back of it. "I didn't ask you to come over and have sex. I asked you to hang out. We'd be doing the same thing there that we did in Elmhurst, only without a crowd. You can take off your shoes and get comfortable. I'll even give you some cake. It's chocolate."

She laughed nervously, not all that certain he was telling the truth. Men always tried to get her in bed. "Did your mother make it?"

"Hell no. She's a great person, but she can't bake to save her life. I made it. From scratch."

From the amount of umbrage in his tone, she figured he had actually made the cake. She truly wanted to know how far he'd gone to set this up. "Did you bake it just for me?"

He shook his head a little regretfully. Then he lifted her hand, which he still held with his larger one, and kissed it again. "I made it yesterday, so it's mostly gone. There's just enough left for us to finish it off. However, I can promise something special for tomorrow, and that'll be just for you."

They'd arrived at her rental car. She dug for her keys in her purse, but he took them as soon as she found them and stuck them in his pocket. She looked up, ready to launch a protest, but he captured her face between his palms. The hold was both firm and affectionate. Then he slid his fingers into her hair, wrecking her carefully upswept arrangement.

"You said you don't kiss on the first date?" He peered deep into her eyes, asking silently for permission and relaying a lot about his intention.

She tried to shake her head, but he held her still, forcing her to speak. "Never."

"I'll respect that," he said. "Feel free to sit this one out."

With that, his mouth descended over hers. She could have panicked and pushed him away, and she knew he would have stopped. But she didn't want that. She wanted to know what it felt like to be kissed by a man who'd figured out how to sidestep the many restrictions she placed on him.

He brushed his lips lightly across a part of her that had suddenly become hypersensitive. He massaged and explored, leaving her mouth to skim across her cheeks, temples, and eyelids. By the time he made it back to her mouth, she'd parted her lips to suck in more air. He took it as an invitation to deepen his forays.

When his tongue slipped into her mouth, Mina wrestled with a split second of indecision. In her entire life, she'd allowed only three men this liberty. The first one had treated her mouth like a Popsicle, slurping and sucking the flavor away. The second had left her feeling like he'd simply licked her face inside and out. The third had been exceedingly gentle, to the point where she wasn't sure if he had any muscle tone in his lips.

Everett wasn't anything like that. His kiss was firm and commanding, a sensual feast she couldn't hope to resist. A powerful, hot liquidity washed through her system, sapping her muscles of necessary strength. He took what he wanted—her participation truly wasn't required—and left her weakened, clinging to him for support.

When he at last brought the kiss to its stunning conclusion, he wrapped his arms around her body and held her against him. She felt the rapid beat of his heart, and she knew he'd been affected just as deeply.

After several moments spent luxuriating in his embrace, she drew a shaky breath. "You are one devious man."

"Yes." He chuckled, rocking his chest against hers. "Wild got the scruples, and I got the cunning. Now that you know what you're in for, do you want some cake?"

Mina laughed at the proud way he embraced his fault. She wasn't as sold on the cake as she was on the prospect of receiving a few more kisses like that. For the first time ever, she honestly considered going to second base on the first date.

Things wouldn't go further than that. She was very experienced in putting a stop to wandering hands. When she initially got to college, she had avoided dating because she didn't know how to interact with men on anything but an academic level. The few who had managed to make her see them differently hadn't made it past her defenses.

From the time she was little, she'd listened to her mother lecture her not to have kids until she was forty. Jin Ae had been eighteen when she'd married her high school sweetheart and nineteen when Mina was born. From that moment forward, her mother had been locked into a role. While she'd never expressed regret that Mina was in her life, she often said she wished that she'd waited ten or twenty years so she would've been better prepared.

The unspoken part of her mother's warnings was clear: don't get trapped in an abusive relationship. Keep your legs closed and your options open.

And so she'd never let a man do more than touch her breasts, and two of the three had been restricted to touching over the clothes. Somehow she knew Ever would find a way around any restrictions she set. While that scared her a lot, she had a built-in escape plan because she didn't want to stay in Vermont for more than a few months.

Just from the way he kissed, she knew she wanted to experience some heavy petting from Ever. With that in mind, she smiled and nodded. "Cake sounds yummy."

"Great." He clicked the button to unlock her doors. "You can drive us this time."

Mina drew her brows together. "You're going to leave your truck here?"

"I didn't bring it. Wild drove." He opened the door and motioned for her to get inside.

She was a little affronted that he'd just assumed she'd go home with him. "So you planned to ask me to your place the whole time?"

He stared at her for a long moment, the reflected pinks of the sunset clashing hard with his unusual green eyes. She had the feeling of being dissected yet again. When he spoke, she knew that was exactly what he'd been doing. "Mina, if you don't want to come to my place, we can go anywhere you want. If you have an issue with using your car or with riding together, I can get Wilder's keys, and he can go home with Micah. You seem to want to ascribe a lot of motives to me that don't exist. I was pretty clear in stating what I want from you."

He'd only said he wanted to spend more time with her. That kiss had shaken her more than she'd realized. Recognizing that she hadn't been nice, she lowered her gaze in an act of contrition. "I'm sorry, Everett. You *were* clear. You said cake and conversation." She lifted her focus to find him staring at her with quiet expectation and no small amount of pride. It sent something strange and exciting aflutter in her midsection. "But then you kissed me after I said I didn't kiss on the first date."

She didn't know what kind of response she'd expected—a little bit of remorse, perhaps? He displayed nothing approaching repentance.

Instead he flashed a devilish grin. "There's a good chance I'll do it again. Don't worry; I won't expect you to kiss me back until the second date. I'm a patient man. I can wait until tomorrow."

Having taken men to task many times, Mina didn't know what to do with the fact that Ever didn't react the way he was supposed to. He didn't seem acquainted with shame or guilt. Shaking her head and wondering what trouble she was courting, she got into the car and put on her seat belt.

Ever held her hand as she drove. It turned out he lived in an apartment complex less than a mile from town, so the trip was short. She waited in the car until he came around and opened the door. It seemed like the right thing to do.

He grinned as he helped her out of the car. "You're learning. I like how quickly you pick up on the important things."

This old-fashioned show of manners wasn't important to her, but it was to him. In a departure from her normal attitude, her date's preferences made a difference to Mina. She felt connected to him, a perception that had been missing from her association with any previous man she'd dated.

But his compliment had been delivered with a flirtatious twist of his lips, and that deserved an equal response. She returned his grin. "Smart women are hot."

He laughed. "That's definitely part of what I like about you."

The lobby of the building was clean and modern, which made sense because it had been built the summer before. Mina couldn't remember what they'd torn down to make room. Signs in the lobby pointed the way to the swimming pool and workout facilities. Everett led her through the maze of empty chairs and sofas to a pair of elevators.

"How long have you lived here?"

"Since it opened. My grandparents left Wild and me some land. I'm saving up to build a house."

He didn't look all that much like he wanted to talk about it, so Mina dropped the topic. If she had been in his shoes, she would have lived with her mother to save up the money. As it was, she scrounged for freelance work. She was saving her earnings to put down on a nice little bungalow just outside Santa Monica. Once she convinced her mother to move, she could reapply for the job she wanted and head west.

"What about you?" he asked, returning her attention to the moment. "What are your post-college plans?"

Telling her date she had zero intention of staying in the state where he owned land and was planning to build a house would probably put a damper on things. Mina shrugged. "I have several offers, but I'm going to stay around here for a little while. My mom needs me."

He nodded at that. "Family is important. Just don't let it hold you back."

The elevator doors slid open, and he ushered her inside. She laughed nervously at his warning. "Are you saying I should accept a job on the other side of the country?"

He ran his thumb along his jaw as he considered her question. Since he lived on the third floor, the trip didn't take long. They were at the door to his apartment before he answered. "If that's what you want, then nobody who cares about you would begrudge you the opportunity."

She had a similar opinion, but her mother wasn't the problem. Jin Ae had urged Mina to accept any job Mina wanted. Her mother had told Mina that she shouldn't be a factor in her career decision. But she was. Mina, as she had her whole life, felt responsible for her mother. Growing up, she'd maintained perfect behavior and grades because she knew her mother would be punished for her transgressions. Her father had stated on many occasions that her behavior reflected her mother's parenting ability.

Ever paused with his hand on the knob. "I didn't plan on having company tonight, so please excuse the mess."

He pushed open the door and reached inside to flip on the switch. True to form, he expected her to enter first.

The interior wasn't what she had anticipated, especially after his warning. It opened to a narrow foyer with a dining room on the right. The light from the foyer fell across a tall, square table stained dark. A laptop and several stacks of papers occupied space there, which wasn't something she would consider messy. It was obvious he did some work from home. Frames of various sizes hung on the walls. There wasn't enough light for her to make out anything.

A door opened to the left. Through it, she could make out an unmade bed. Beyond that door, a narrow metal-and-glass table held three small baskets. Ever threw his keys in the first one. The second was full of potpourri, and the third was brimming with odds and ends. She made out some coils of rope, a Swiss army knife, and some clips like the kind she used to hook her water bottle to her backpack when she went hiking.

Everett closed the door to the bedroom and tossed one of those charming grins in her direction. "I've never voluntarily made a bed in my life."

She laughed at his unapologetic explanation. "That's okay. I stopped making my bed the day I left for college." It was a small act of rebellion, but she derived immense pleasure from it.

He kissed her cheek and guided her forward with the gentle pressure of his hand on her lower back. That expression she liked was back on his face, the one full of pride and anticipation. "I knew it. You totally cut loose once you got to Harvard. Unless you're expecting serious company, what's the point? You're just going to mess it up again."

The apartment opened up past the foyer, revealing a spacious kitchen behind the bedroom and a living area behind the dining room. A rectangular island divided the long room, and the far wall was full of windows. The living room had sliding glass doors that opened to a balcony. The lack of light meant Mina couldn't get a true sense of the balcony's size.

It wasn't neat, exactly. Lived-in would be a more apt description. A glass and a mug were on the counter next to the sink. Two cereal boxes shared space on the island with a stack of paperback novels and some folded laundry. In the living area, throw pillows were stacked on one end of the sofa, and a pile of blankets was wadded at the other end. The wood floor looked like it had been swept but not mopped recently.

"I have a cat," he said. "I hope you're not allergic."

On cue, a tiny feline climbed from beneath the blankets. It was a bundle of tan fur with black-and-white patches. It yawned and stretched before meandering toward Everett. "A kitten?"

"Yeah. The vet says she's about eight months old. I've had her for about six weeks. She's very affectionate." The kitten brushed up against Everett's ankles, arching and purring loudly. He scooped her up and set her on his shoulders. She settled down as he stroked her with one hand. "Her name is Jolinar. I call her Jolo."

Mina scratched the kitten behind her ears. The little creature rubbed her head against Mina's hand, adjusting to make sure the scratches happened exactly where she wanted them. She'd always wanted a kitten, but her father frowned on having pets. She'd been allowed a goldfish for a few months when she was in grade school, but it had died rather quickly, and that had been the end of that.

After a few minutes of bonding, Ever crossed to a post where a bit of wall separated the glass doors in the living area from the windows in the kitchen. Small platforms extended from the sides at random locations. Jolinar hopped to one a little higher than Everett's head and began furiously licking all the places she'd been petted.

Ever pursed his lips in a wry frown. "I found her wandering around, starving, her fur a mess, on the land I'm clearing for the house. You'd think she'd be grateful."

He headed to the kitchen and opened the refrigerator. Mina watched as he took clean plates from the dishwasher and cut pieces of cake for each of them. As cakes went, the appearance was unremarkable.

"If she was grateful, then she'd be a dog." Mina reached for the knob on a likely cupboard in search of glasses. She'd spied some milk, which seemed like the perfect accompaniment for chocolate cake.

Ever pointed her in the right direction, flashing one of those smiles that made his eyes sparkle mischievously. "True. I don't think I'm quite ready for a dog yet. No yard." He cleared a place at the island and put down the plates. "What about you? Any pets or aspirations for one?"

Mina shrugged. "I'm not ruling it out, but I'm not settled enough to be responsible for a pet. My mother has feeders all over the yard. She seems to have developed a special relationship with birds and rodents. I think I can safely rule them out as pet options."

She thought it was sad that her mother spent time feeding wild animals. It seemed those little things were her only companions. Her mother needed to get out more. The move would be good for her.

Ever regarded her soberly. "I like to watch wildlife. It's very peaceful and sometimes wonderful. I can see why your mom would set out feeders. How did she like the flower baskets?"

Mina handed him a glass of milk and climbed onto a high stool next to him. Ever's feet touched the floor, but she had to perch hers on a rung. At the mention of the baskets, she blushed a little, but not because it had been the first time a man had bought her flowers. "She loved them. We didn't have any hooks to hang them, so we took the hangers off and put them on the back patio."

Half of his mouth lifted in a teasing grin. "You didn't tell her they were from me."

No, she hadn't mentioned running into Everett or that she'd be having dinner with him tonight. Her mother thought she was meeting friends in town. Throughout high school, Mina had assured her mother she had friends. The one time her mother had advocated for Mina to be allowed to go to a friend's house on the basis that if she didn't socialize, she couldn't keep friends, her father hadn't reacted well. Mina didn't want her mother to have to suffer from guilt on top of everything else.

"She was so delighted by them that I couldn't tell her they were mine. I hope you don't mind." To cover her embarrassment, she shoveled a bite of cake into her mouth. She didn't expect much, and she found herself pleasantly surprised. It was moist and flavorful. The cream cheese frosting was just sweet enough. "Mmmm. This is really good cake."

"Thanks." He finished chewing his mouthful. "I don't mind about the flowers. They brought joy to you both, so they've served their purpose."

He had a crumb of chocolate at the corner of his mouth. She reached out, intending to brush it away with her thumb. He seemed to guess her intention, because he held still. Something came over her, and at the last second, she leaned forward and licked it away with the tip of her tongue. He tasted every bit as delicious as his kiss.

Never in her life had she been so bold. The moment she pulled away, she froze, not certain to which degree her behavior had mortified her.

Ever's eyelids fell to half-mast, and he regarded her with a sultry expression. "Moves like that will get you thoroughly kissed."

She took stock of her emotions. "I'm okay with that."

Almost before she finished speaking, his lips closed over hers. At the same time, he snaked his arm around her and cradled the base of her skull with his hand. He tangled his fingers in her hair, knocking her hairpins loose. He plunged his tongue into her mouth, not bothering with the soft sensuality of his earlier foray, and stole her breath with his mastery.

She was conscious of the feel of his hands moving through her hair, freeing the long strands from their confinement. Her breasts seemed to swell, and she found herself leaning against his body. Somehow he had moved without her knowing, and now he stood in

43

front of her, his thigh wedged between hers. She scooted forward and pressed her mons against his leg.

A delicious sense of anticipation built in her core. It was hot and wet, burning with a sense of something more. She wanted to rub against him, but she didn't have the courage. He skimmed one hand down her spine and slid it under her ass, lifting her closer. It solved part of her problem, but it also created a powerful need.

All this time, he ravaged her with his lips. He abandoned her mouth to nibble along her jaw and nip at her earlobes. When he pressed his hot kisses on her neck just below her ears, she moaned loudly.

The noise seemed to fuel him even more. He must have taken it as permission, because he pushed up her skirt with his free hand and caressed her bare leg. Up and down, he seared the tender skin with his hot hands until at last he lifted her leg and secured it around his waist. These high stools put her in the perfect position.

Until now, she'd kept her hands on his shoulders, too timid to explore him the way she wanted. His behavior made her bold. She teased her fingertips down his chest. When she arrived at the waist of his jeans, she tugged at his shirt, wanting it out of the way so she could touch his skin the same way he touched hers.

Her move seemed to jolt him away from the place passion had taken him. He wrapped his hands around her wrists, halting her tentative exploration.

"Please don't stop." She didn't know where that heartfelt plea had come from, and the fact that it tumbled from her mouth shocked her into silence.

Everett put her hands back on his shoulders. "Honey, if we don't stop now, we're going to go farther than you want. I love that you're so affected by me, but I can't let you do something I know you don't want to do."

She didn't want to stop. Primal needs rushed to the fore, taking over her brain. "I've changed my mind."

He pressed his forehead to hers and inhaled. "For now, you have. But tomorrow you'll regret it. In times like this, it's my job to take care of you. That includes making sure that you never regret what happens between us."

Mina felt herself fall a little further for Everett Burke. This was definitely a benefit of his protective and slightly alpha nature. It just made her want him even more. She did something the thought she'd never do: she begged. "Ever, please."

"The first thing you did when we met tonight was lay down a hard limit. You decided on it when you were sane and rational. I want you to understand that in the heat of passion, I will never lose control. I will always take care of you, and I will never, under any circumstances, do something you truly don't want me to do."

His sincere declaration took her aback. In a million years, she'd never thought a man would turn her down, especially not after she'd begged. Yet she didn't feel he'd rejected her. Evidence of his desire branded itself into the thigh he'd trapped between his legs, and still he held fast to his principles.

She nodded her acceptance of his ruling. "I just don't want you to stop kissing me."

He chuckled and played with a handful of her hair. "I don't want to stop kissing you either. You taste like heaven with a dash of chocolate thrown in."

To her disappointment, he made no move to kiss her again. She wasn't skilled in the art of seduction—she wasn't even particularly skilled at kissing—so she had no idea what her next move should be. He continued to play with her hair and study her face.

"Right now your lips are a little swollen, and you look so ripe and ready. I think I could kiss you all night. I'd strip away your clothes and kiss every inch of your body until you're writhing under me, screaming as you come in my mouth." He brushed a strand of hair away from her face. "Would you like that? While it is sex, it wouldn't technically violate your rule of no intercourse."

Nobody had ever talked to her like that before. She had the sense that Everett could—and would—get quite graphic. She felt her eyes widening with shock, which she was sure only made her appear more wanton than he'd already described.

"You'd keep your clothes on?" She didn't ask to make sure. What he offered was very one-sided. She knew tat he wouldn't let her reciprocate even if she begged, which wouldn't happen because she wouldn't know what to do anyway. She'd never in her life seen a naked man.

"I would probably take my shirt off."

That was a sight she'd very much like to see. Before her brain could think on his offer too much, she found herself nodding eagerly. He lifted her against him, banding one arm around her waist and cupping her ass with the other. She wrapped her legs around him and held on as he carried her into his bedroom.

The change of location made her a little leery until he turned on the overhead light. He knelt on the bed with one knee and set her down. She unlocked her legs and slid to the mattress, careful to keep her low-heeled shoes off the bed. In another move she hadn't expected, he stood up instead of scooting her to the center of the bed. Suddenly self-conscious, she straightened her skirt, which had ridden up high enough to expose her panties.

"If you want me to stop, say 'Oasis.' That's an important point to remember, Mina. Simply telling me to stop won't have an impact. You must use the safeword."

Though she had never heard of a safeword, it didn't take a genius to figure out what he meant. It seemed Everett Burke was into playing sex games, the kind where a woman might utter fake protests. Mina couldn't see herself doing that. She simply nodded at his directive.

He stared at her. "Say the safeword."

"Oasis?" It came out like a question, not because she wondered about his command, but because she didn't understand why he'd want her to repeat it.

"Yes. Now say it like you mean it."

Now she understood. He was testing to make sure she would use the right word in the right way. "Oasis."

He melted her leg muscles with that special smile. "Very good. We'll start slowly. I'm going to kiss you and touch you."

He toed out of his shoes. Then he bent down and removed her shoes, sliding his hand up to caress each bare calf. He spent some time there, seeming to measure the places where he could wrap his entire hand around her flesh and simultaneously enjoying the texture of her skin. Good thing she'd shaved. His thorough exploration both calmed her and made her feel anxious. She wasn't used to being with anyone who was so blatantly enamored with her body.

Then he bent his head and kissed the inside of each ankle, his actions slow and almost reverent. "Move back and lie down with your head on a pillow. Get comfortable."

She did as he directed, and that sense of uneasiness returned. He watched from his crouched position next to the bed, his observant eyes no doubt capturing every detail. He seemed almost predatory, yet that sober air of protectiveness hadn't faded. Her perception of him altered subtly as she realized he was deadly serious about the things he'd said to her tonight. He truly saw it as his duty to care for her, and he enjoyed assuming that role. It was part of his core identity.

When she calmed down, he stood and swiftly pulled off his shirt. She wanted time to look at him, but he didn't seem interested in posing for her. He tossed the wadded piece of fabric onto the floor and shoved the messy covers to the foot of the bed. He had a determined air about him that made her expect he would lie between her legs and get to work right away.

She'd never let a man touch her where he was about to touch her. She didn't mourn the loss of her innocence, but while she embraced the pleasures this new experience would bring, she was still very apprehensive about having a man's face between her legs.

He settled over her body with his pelvis pressing her thighs open and his stomach against hers. She hadn't been aware of her shirt riding up, and the feel of his flesh was surprisingly intimate. He stared down at her, his eyes so light they seemed to glow. From the hungry way he regarded her, she wondered if he might skip the preliminaries and just devour her from head to toe. She wouldn't have a problem with that.

"You haven't done this before, have you?"

His unexpected question had her squirming. Was it that obvious? What was she doing wrong? Though most of his weight rested on his elbows, he had positioned himself in such a way that she couldn't move very much. Instead of feeling trapped, she felt protected, sheltered from the place her fears might trap her.

She wasn't sure exactly what his question implied, but she kept their purpose for being in that room in mind and gave her head a quick, small shake. He kissed her, claiming and massaging her lips with bold strokes, and she felt her honesty had been rewarded. He wasn't gloating as she thought the first man to claim her like this might. He seemed to have accepted the fact and moved forward from there.

When he at last broke away, he gripped the side of her head and lavished kisses on her cheeks and eyelids before moving to her throat. He slid her shirt up, lifting her shoulders to tug it over her head. Her heart beat faster as she watched him lean up even more and take in the sight of her lying there wearing only a white lacy bra.

Though his expression didn't change, his eyes smoldered. He resumed kissing her, but his attention had moved to her chest. He slid his strong hands up her rib cage and cupped her breasts. His heat seared through the thin layer of material, and her nipples pebbled in anticipation of direct contact.

He lulled her with the spell of his deft caresses so that she didn't know he was going to unhook her bra until she felt the sudden looseness around her ribs. Right away, she grabbed his wrists to stop him. That piece of clothing didn't need to come off for him to do what he was going to do.

Rather than heeding her unspoken protest, he rotated his wrists. Suddenly he was the one holding her captive. He gathered her wrists in one hand and pressed them to the pillow above her head. Then he lifted the cups away from her breasts. Having never been exposed this way, she wiggled, trying to escape and cover herself. She didn't know why; she certainly didn't want him to stop. Everything he did felt so good. Even the way he held her down appealed to a need she never knew she had.

Everett paused, regarding her with a furrowed brow. "Honey, if you want me to stop, you have to use the safeword. I have no problem holding you down or tying you up. If you misbehave much more, though, I have to warn you that I will turn you over and spank your ass."

Cold fear traveled the paths of her veins. Though nobody had ever laid a hand on her, she'd seen her father hit her mother. She lived in fear of that happening. Immediately she stilled.

Instead of looking pleased at the way she'd acquiesced, he appeared bothered by her compliance. He released her wrists and peered down at her with a frown. "Talk to me, Mina. Tell me what's wrong."

"I don't want you to hit me." The confession tumbled out, her deepest fear revealed.

His frown deepened. "I'd never hit you."

"You just threatened to spank me."

He appeared to consider something, but she wasn't sure it was related to their conversation. At last he nodded. "All right, no spanking. I'll bind you instead."

The wetness between her legs increased tenfold. She whimpered a little bit, a series of sounds that took her completely by surprise.

Everett chuckled, his frown melting away. "You like that idea."

She very much liked that idea. But she couldn't just let go of all her inhibitions at once. "Will you turn the lights off? I would be more comfortable in the dark."

He cocked his head to the side as if she'd just made an outrageous request. Surely he'd made out in the dark before. "I'll make it dark for you, but I want the light. Men are visual creatures. I want to see your gorgeous body bared for me. I need to see and hear your reactions so I can make sure I'm pleasuring you the way I want."

After pressing a kiss to her lips, he rolled away from her and off the bed. He crossed to his dresser and pulled out a drawer. She watched him rummage for something. "What are you looking for?"

"I'm going to bind your wrists and blindfold you." He returned with a bunch of black straps in his hands. "Take off your bra, honey. I'll handle the rest."

She looked at him, taking in his broad shoulders and the lean muscles of his chest. Evidence that he'd been outside shirtless showed in the darker hue of his tanned skin. A small sprinkling of hair began just below his belly button and disappeared into his jeans. His brown, sun-streaked hair was a little messy from their activities, and his eyes smoldered with glints of amber. He was the single sexiest man she'd ever seen.

"Trust me, Mina. I want you to enjoy this experience."

He was so sincere. All traces of his flirty charm had vanished, though he hadn't used that piece of ammunition very much at all tonight, almost as if he knew that too much would drive her away. She didn't want to be another of his conquests. Though he didn't have a reputation for dating a lot or sleeping around, there was no way a man as attractive and built as Everett Burke suffered from a lack of female attention.

She took a deep breath and held it as she peeled away the paltry barrier barring his gaze from her breasts. As soon as she had exposed herself, that prideful possessiveness came back into his eyes, only it was even more intense than before.

He just looked at her, taking in the sight of her lying half-naked on his bed. She wondered what he thought about her petite figure, and she was glad she could fill out a B-cup. Even as those thoughts winged through her mind, she could feel her skin heating up with the force of a self-conscious blush, and she fought the urge to cover herself. She knew he wouldn't like if she did that.

He came closer and climbed on the bed. She was grateful he didn't comment on anything. Given the expression on his face, words weren't necessary. He straddled her waist, the roughness of his jeans scratchy against her stomach. He towered over her in true alpha-male fashion, and she had the sense that he liked it as much as she did.

Then he lifted her head and slid the blindfold into place. She had forgotten the many black straps he held in his hands. It was a sleeping mask, the kind she used whenever she studied well into the night and needed to nap the next day to catch up on her sleep. He adjusted it until no light seeped in at the edges.

"How's that?"

"Dark."

He laughed quietly, and she hoped it was at her dry tone and not something else. Next he took her wrist in his hand and wrapped something soft around it. Then he did the same thing with her other wrist. She felt his weight shift on the bed as he leaned forward, and she heard the sounds of fabric—most likely those black straps—rasping against the headboard. He positioned her hands on either side of her head.

Snapping sounds, one near each wrist, startled her with their finality. He slid his finger under one of the bindings on her wrist, then repeated the action with the other. "How do they feel?"

They were surprisingly comfortable. "They're soft."

"Good. Pull on them. Let me know if it hurts anywhere when you do that."

She gave them an experimental yank. Other than the pressure she created around her wrists, it wasn't unpleasant. Being bound like this was different from when he held her down. Then it had seemed personal, a direct action on his part. The cuffs removed that personal attention. She liked it, but it didn't make her pussy tingle the way he had when his hands had been around her wrists.

"It doesn't hurt."

He slid down her body, resuming his earlier position between her legs. His bare chest brushed against her breasts. They swelled toward him, and her nipples hardened where his skin met hers. He moved back and forth, stimulating them even more. She arched, seeking firmer contact. He closed his palm over one globe and his lips over her mouth.

In seconds, he swept her away with the sweet bliss of his kisses. She felt secure in the darkness, with his hands and lips guiding her pleasure, and her wrists bound. It stripped away her ability to do anything about her shyness and naïveté, freeing her to enjoy the way he made her feel. She trusted him not to cross the boundary she'd set, though she half wished he would ignore it.

His lips moved to her neck, spreading fire that tingled in her bared breasts. Simply uncovering them had freed her to revel more in the pleasure he induced. He took the lobe of her ear between his teeth, and a shiver rocketed through her body.

"Beautiful. You are so indescribably lovely. Stop biting back your reactions. I want to hear you. Those sweet moans and gasps are music to my ears." He ground his pelvis against her pussy, and she felt hard evidence of his desire. The friction elicited one of those gasps from her. "Yes, like that. I want to hear everything. You're allowed— encouraged—to talk. I need you to tell me when to move to the right, harder, slower, faster, whatever helps you get there. You're allowed to make as much noise as you want, especially if you're calling my name or begging."

That last part caught her off guard. "Begging?"

"Yeah." He nipped at her other lobe. "You know. 'Oh, Ever, yes! Please don't stop.' Things like that. Whatever comes to mind." He raised the pitch of his voice to mimic her feminine tones, though the smug laughter lurking behind it almost ruined the attempt.

Now that she was tied to the bed, he brought out all the flirty charm he had kept on a leash throughout their date. She liked his confidence and his sense of humor. Though she couldn't see his face, she knew he wore a cocky grin. She felt her lips twist with a wry smile. He'd calmed her mild panic rather nicely. "'Yes, Ever. Please don't stop.' I'll keep that in mind."

She wasn't sure she could do the other things he'd directed her to do. Bossing around a man was nowhere near her comfort zone, and doing it in the bedroom—especially since he didn't expect any kind of reciprocation—just seemed tacky.

He kissed his way down her body, lingering over her breasts until she writhed under him and sounds of pleasure squeaked from her throat. She'd never heard those noises come out of her mouth before. They were wanton, nearly primal, and she questioned her decision to take such a hard line and deny herself these pleasures for so long. She wasn't just a twenty-two-year-old virgin; she had zero experience when it came to sensual pleasures. She'd never even masturbated.

She was intensely thankful for the restraints and the blindfold. With them, Everett had made it possible for her to forget her inexperience, inadequacies, and her limitations. Now she could concentrate on the riot of sensation coursing through her system.

He'd slipped his hand up her skirt when her attention had been focused on the magic of his lips skimming along the underside of her breast. She stiffened as one finger hooked beneath the edge of her panties. He traced her folds, spending more time exploring there than she ever had.

"You're so wet, so wonderfully wet and ready." He grazed the tip of her clit, and it felt different from those few times she'd tried to play with it.

A shock of pleasure ran up her belly. Her legs moved farther apart, and her hips lifted in offering. Mina didn't know where her body was getting its directions from, because she wasn't in control of anything. She gasped. "There. Yes. More. Harder."

He circled his finger a few more times, increasing the pressure with each pass. She pumped her hips to his rhythm, chasing more of this wondrous feeling.

He eased his hand away, and she whimpered at the loss. But she understood what he meant to do. She lifted her hips to help him

51

remove her skirt and panties. He pushed her legs wide open and settled between them. She felt so exposed. This way, she knew he could see every inch of her. For long moments, he did nothing, and she knew he was looking at her. He'd said he was visual, that he liked to see her.

Then he settled over her body and plundered her mouth with his tongue. This was different from before. He wasn't taking his time, easing her into passion. He was taking his due, demanding her unconditional and complete surrender, which she gladly gave.

Once he seemed satisfied with her submission, he moved back down her body, tracing every inch of her skin with his large hands. This time when he shouldered her legs wide apart, she didn't think to resist. She had no modesty where he was concerned. In that moment, she belonged to him.

His hot tongue stabbed at her clit, taking up where his deft finger had left off. She moaned and murmured his name, which just seemed to feed his fire. He closed his lips around her nub and sucked it into his mouth. The little bursts of pressure had an edge of pain, but it felt so unbelievably good. She wanted more.

"Oh God. Like that. Holy shit, that feels good."

She felt his smile against her pussy, and the vibrations of his chuckle triggered a tide so intense it threatened to swamp her. She cried out in ecstasy at the same moment he pushed a finger into her vagina.

Nothing had ever been in there before. She'd never even used a tampon, because her mother had told her it would hurt and she'd bleed for days. Ever's finger didn't hurt like she thought it might. There was a small tearing feeling, but the pain she'd expected didn't come.

The feel of his tongue and lips distracted her from even that little bit of nothing. She decided that if her mother was wrong about the pain, she was wrong about the bleeding. It wouldn't be the first time her mother had told her something outrageous, like when she'd convinced her that very small children operated stoplights because they were the only people who could fit inside. This had come after learning about children used as chimney sweeps, which had been true, so Mina hadn't questioned her mother's admonition.

She dismissed it and forgot about it completely, and Ever found a spot inside her that made her entire body feel like it was on fire. She wanted to tell him to stay there, but she lost the ability to form words. Set adrift in a dark sea, she felt it sweep over her, and she screamed as it took her under.

Ever loosened her cuffs before he headed to the bathroom to wash his hands. When she'd confessed to having no experience with oral sex, he thought she'd just never trusted a man enough to let him go down on her. As he washed the small bit of watery blood from his hand, he realized she'd never let a man touch her at all.

He vaguely remembered the last virgin he'd dated. He hadn't slept with her. Her lack of experience had nothing to do with his decision. He couldn't sleep with a woman unless he had strong feelings for her. Simple attraction wasn't enough.

Even the woman who'd claimed his virginity had been experienced. Now that he understood the stakes, he was determined to take this slowly. She had obviously decided to save herself, and he was determined that her first time would be special. It would be romantic, an experience she would treasure for the rest of her life. He would make sure of it.

He ran a clean cloth under cool water and returned to the bedroom. His bathroom wasn't connected to the bedroom, and he knew better than to leave his submissive tied up when he wasn't there with her. Though he'd loosened her cuffs, she hadn't moved.

He allowed himself a moment of pride and arrogance. He was relatively certain that he'd given her the first orgasm she'd ever had. She'd moaned and whimpered, her body writhing and bowing with abandon until she'd cried out her climax. The delicate flutters of her pussy had matched the shallow rise and fall of her chest as she struggled to catch her breath. Ever was completely entranced by the beautiful woman in his bed.

Taking things slowly was the only course of action, he decided. Not only where sex was concerned, but where submission was concerned. He'd topped her, and she'd responded well to his dominant personality. But she hadn't enjoyed everything. She didn't understand his need to take care of her, and she had panicked when he'd mentioned spanking her.

Domestic discipline appealed to him greatly. He'd always wanted to find a submissive who shared this value. Unlike many Doms, even his twin brother, Ever didn't feel a need to use floggers, whips, crops, or canes. He liked bondage and submission, and he needed a strong woman to dominate. She would challenge him, which would probably lead to a spanking for her, but it would also make him a better man.

Yes, easing her into his world was the correct course of action.

He settled on the bed next to her and pressed the cooled cloth between her legs. It would relieve any swelling or pain she could experience. He hadn't been very rough with her. Once she was in the throes of pleasure, she'd liked when he was more forceful. When she wasn't, she responded to gentleness.

She whimpered, wiggled her hands free, and tried to pluck at his wrist to get his hand away from her pussy. No doubt she would be shy now that they'd been intimate. He would have to make sure she didn't retreat emotionally from him because she felt exposed and vulnerable.

He halted her attempt and soothed her with a kiss to her brow. "Let me do this, honey. Let me take care of you."

She didn't say anything, but she stopped her struggle. He saw to her comfort, and then he climbed into bed next to her, pulling the sheet from the foot of the bed to tuck it around her cooling body, and he held her in his arms.

Normally he would remove her blindfold, but he left it, allowing her the moments she needed to pull herself together. There would come a time when he wouldn't allow her to hide behind a blindfold. It would become a device used to deny her the knowledge of what was to come.

After a few minutes, she turned toward him and snuggled her head against his shoulder. "That was amazing, Ever. Thank you."

He brushed his hand through her hair, a deft move that also dislodged her mask. She peered up at him with wide eyes and a shy smile that stole his breath. He kissed her, a tender show of affection that let her know exactly how much he cared about her.

Chapter Four

Mina woke up with a tingling between her thighs that was more insistent than anything she was used to. It was an itch demanding to be scratched. She checked the digital display on her cell phone and calculated three hours before she could head to Ever's place.

With a groan, she rolled from bed. After he'd rocked her world last night, he'd held her in his arms while they talked. Some of the questions he'd broached had been uncomfortable, and the way he'd sandwiched them between bouts of casual topics had been a little disconcerting.

For example, when Jolo scratched at the door, he'd asked if she minded if he let the cat into the bedroom. She hadn't. As he'd walked to the door to let her in, he'd asked whether she liked the fact he'd used two fingers, or would she prefer he use one or three?

She hadn't been lying in the dark estimating how many fingers he had inside her; she'd been too busy enjoying the orgasm.

Then, in a discussion about favorite songs, he'd asked how she liked being restrained and whether she thought she would be up for having her legs bound as well. He definitely knew how to throw her off balance.

She went for a short jog, and then she took a long shower. Her mother spent the morning in the garden. When Mina joined her, Jin Ae smiled from her position kneeling in front of a patch of freshly turned earth.

"How was your date?"

She hadn't told her mother she was going on a date. "How did you know?"

Jin Ae's smile turned into a short laugh. "You were excited and nervous." She glanced up at Mina. "You're allowed to go out."

Until that moment, she hadn't realized she'd been afraid her mother might prohibit her from seeing a man. "It was good. He's nice." Nice was the understatement of the century. "He insisted on opening doors and pulling out my chair. It was a little weird, but I had a nice time."

Jin Ae leaned back on her heels and regarded Mina with a frown. "You used 'nice' twice, and you hate that word. What's wrong?"

Mina hated the word because it meant nothing. She shook her head. "Nothing's wrong. I'm seeing him again today."

"Does it bother you that he has manners? I know you think it's a fault, but it's really not. You deserve to be with somebody who treats you well." Jin Ae stabbed her trowel into the dirt and turned it over. "The Burkes are a nice family. Macy Burke is one of the only people who remembers to invite me to town functions, and Russ Burke comes over after each snowstorm and does the driveway. Doesn't even ask or stop by to say hello. It's just clear when I wake up."

Mina stared at her mother with a little bit of wonder. She hadn't known her mother was at all acquainted with Ever's family. "Do you go?"

"I helped with the Memorial Day parade, and I'm signed up to run the snow cone maker at the Fourth of July celebration."

Her mother dropped that bomb as if her participation in town life was inconsequential, when in fact it put a huge crimp in Mina's plans. How could Mina convince her mother to move if she was finally making connections after all these years? And Mina knew she didn't have the right to sabotage her mother's happiness or urge her against forming friendships for which her mother had longed.

"That's wonderful."

"Perhaps not as wonderful as you dating Everett Burke. He's a good boy. You can invite him over for dinner."

Mina didn't know about that, or how her mom knew who she'd been with. Ever was a great guy, but he didn't figure into her life plan. "Mom, you know I don't plan to stay in Vermont."

Jin Ae nailed her with a shrewd look. "If you didn't plan to stay in Vermont, you wouldn't be going on your second date in two days with a man not known for playing the field."

Mina fidgeted. She hadn't thought about what Ever might want from her at all. In fact, she'd mostly thought about how much she wanted him to be her first lover. In her head, she hadn't considered him for the long term. During her entire jog and even in the shower—especially in the shower—she'd thought about what it would take to seduce him today.

She'd decided not to begin with a statement declaring she wouldn't sleep with him. That seemed to have been the only thing holding him back last night.

But now that she considered things from his point of view, she decided seducing him would most likely backfire. Besides, what the hell did she know about the art of seduction?

Her mother was studying her, probably looking for Mina to confirm her suspicions. Mina couldn't do that. She got to her feet. "It's just a date, Mom. It's nothing serious, certainly not enough to bring him here."

With the plates and cups clean and drying in the rack, Everett turned his attention to the spinach and red peppers on his cutting board. On the other side of the island, Wilder had spread out several different gauges of rope.

"Was it everything you thought it would be?"

Ever studied his brother, looking for the intended joke. "Are you asking about my date?"

Wilder chuckled. "Yeah. I know she enjoyed herself. Thin walls."

Once again, Ever was relieved Wilder had the apartment next door. He'd rather nobody overheard his bedroom activities, but if he had to live in a place with barely adequate soundproofing, then he was glad Wilder was the person he was bothering. If only he could convince Wilder to put himself out there again.

"She's coming over at noon. I'm going to take her out to the property for a picnic. I think it went well." Ever attacked the waiting ingredients with practiced skill. Cooking brought him a lot of pleasure.

Frowning, Wilder untwisted a length of rope. "I seriously didn't peg her for a submissive. My radar must be off."

Everett had no doubt about her submissiveness. "She's submissive, but she doesn't know it."

Wilder lifted his gaze. It was filled with alarm. "How can she have spent an evening with you and that topic not come up?"

The fact his brother had leaped to that conclusion didn't surprise Ever. Nobody knew him better than Wilder. "She's inexperienced. Very inexperienced. I'm treading lightly. I want her to be comfortable with it before we have the big conversation."

Though she hadn't minded the blindfold or the restraints, she'd nearly freaked out when he'd mentioned spanking her. He would have to test her to see what she was open to, and ease her into those things. If he had to, he could talk himself into living without seeing his handprints on her reddened ass. Though he preferred it, he didn't need her on her knees.

A bit of shock crept into Wild's expression, mingling with the alarm that hadn't diminished. "Ever, I think you're making a mistake.

Dad always says to be up-front about who you are and what you want."

He was well aware of his responsibility as her Dom. "Wild, she needs to be eased into this. She's fragile and delicate and incredibly naive. If I have a frank discussion with her before she's ready, she's going to flee. If I wait until she's ready, then she'll be mine forever."

Though they'd only had one date, he had already decided she was the one for him. His father had always told him he'd know his soul mate when he met her, and that assurance had definitely proved true.

Wilder snorted. "If she thinks you're playing vanilla games and finds out you're lying to her, you're going to lose her anyway."

"I'm not lying." The accusation stung, especially coming from his best friend. "I'm waiting for the right time. There is a difference."

He wasn't sure what the right time would look like, but he trusted he'd know when the time had come.

She arrived at Ever's apartment almost an hour early. It was easier than facing her mother's calculating, silently knowing looks. Wilder answered her knock. He and Everett truly resembled each other, but where Ever tended to be relaxed, Wilder radiated thoughtful intensity.

He smiled as he opened the door wider to admit her. "Good morning, Mina. Come on in. I'm not sure Ever was expecting you quite yet."

Perhaps she had miscalculated. The need to escape her mother's knowing gaze had made her forget what went on in the hour before a date. She spent a lot of time on her hair and makeup, though Ever had told her just to wear shorts and dress comfortably. The lack of pizzazz in her clothing had to be accounted for in the care she took with the rest of her appearance. And it had to look effortless. The makeup had to cover her flaws and also be invisible.

She took a half step back from the door. "I should come back later."

Wilder caught her by the wrist. "Nope. If I let you escape, then he'll get pissed at me, and his yelling might ruin his soufflé."

"I'm not making a soufflé, you idiot. It's quiche." Ever came down the hall to the foyer, the soft smile on his face completely at odds with the way he spoke to his brother. He took her arm from Wilder and pulled her inside, straight into his arms, where he planted a firm kiss on her lips. "You should stay."

The door closed behind them. Wilder headed back to the kitchen.

She rested her hands on Ever's chest, enjoying the way his heat permeated his shirt. "Are you sure? I didn't mean to be so early."

"I know." He grinned and winked. "You just couldn't stay away from my animal magnetism."

Truthfully, no, she couldn't. She'd definitely developed a weakness for him. She returned his grin. "Something like that."

"C'mon." He turned and herded her toward the kitchen. "You can watch Wild practice tying knots while I finish making lunch."

A large wicker picnic basket rested on the counter near the refrigerator. Plates, cups, and forks waited in the drying rack next to the sink. Wilder sat on a stool at the island, an array of colored ropes on the granite countertop in front of him.

Mina lifted her brow in amazement. "A picnic?"

"Yep. It's a nice day for it." He guided her to the stool next to Wilder. "Sit. Wilder needs a hand."

Wilder looked a little surprised at that pronouncement. "If you're okay with it."

She shrugged. "Sure. What are you doing?"

"Practicing my knots. It works better if I have someone to work with."

There was a lot of rope on the counter. Mina wasn't sure what she was getting herself into. It seemed a bit kinky. "You want to tie me up?"

He seemed disturbed by her question. His blue eyes clouded over. "No. If you'll hold out your arm, that's really all I need."

Ever stirred something on the stove. "Don't worry. I wouldn't allow him to do anything more than that."

She offered her arm to Wilder. He pushed the short sleeve of her shirt up and centered a green rope just below her shoulder. Then he wound it underneath. She felt the tickle of his fingertips brush against her skin as he manipulated the rope. He worked with a quiet intensity that was both calming and alarming. It was almost as if she didn't exist. The ropes were everything to him. The thought saddened her a bit.

Looking up, she saw Ever watching her. His attention was focused on her face, not on the knots his brother tied around her arm. She offered him a smile.

Abruptly, he turned back to the stove. "How was your night? Did you sleep well?"

"Yes." And she woke up hornier than she'd ever been. She couldn't imagine what it must have been like for Ever. He hadn't come at all. "You?"

59

He shook his head. "I would have slept better if I'd been able to drive you home. When do you think you're going to get over this need to drive yourself around everywhere?"

She didn't know whether to laugh or take him seriously. Wilder glanced up from his macramé and noted her confusion. "If he drives you home and sees you inside, then he knows you're safe for the night."

Ever transferred the picnic basket to the island counter and began packing plates and flatware, yet his attention was mostly on her.

"I don't need you to look out for me like that."

Ever scowled, his brows drawing together menacingly, but he didn't stop loading items into the basket.

Wilder bent her arm and worked on a fancy series of knots on the inside of her forearm. "It's not about you. It's about his peace of mind and his need to take care of you."

It was irritating that anyone felt the need to look out for her. She wasn't an obligation. And why wasn't Everett speaking for himself? She pursed her lips at Wilder. "Are you his paid spokesperson?"

"Nope." Wilder didn't seem fazed by her hostility. "I'm the twin, which means I have years more experience reading the fine print."

She blinked. "The fine print?"

Now Everett spoke up. "The fine print. All the rules and regulations that go along with dating somebody like me. Don't worry, my hot smart chick. You'll figure it all out eventually."

After that cryptic comment, she kind of wanted Wilder to translate. She looked to him, but he just sighed. "If he won't speak plainly to you, feel free to give him hell. It's the least of what he deserves."

She felt like they were having a different conversation from her. Ever grinned, and Wilder sighed as he unraveled the design he'd so painstakingly woven. "Are you coming on the picnic with us? Is it a double date?" she asked.

The shades of sadness flickered across his face and clouded his eyes. "No."

She'd stumbled onto a sore spot. Not sure what to do or say, she looked to Ever. The smile had vanished from his face, and he regarded his brother with fierce sympathy. He shook his head, a signal that she needed to let the subject alone.

As Wilder finished removing the rope, he coiled it up and gathered the rest of what he'd laid out on the counter. "Now that I've crashed your party, I'm off."

"Are you sure you don't want to join us?" Mina felt bad for him. What if he'd come to Ever's apartment because he needed to talk?

Wilder chuckled, sounding a lot like Everett. "Thanks. I'm sure. You two have fun." With that, he disappeared through the front door.

Mina looked around. A set of keys lay on the counter near where Wilder had been sitting. "Ever, I think Wilder left his keys here."

He nodded. "Looks like. Can you run them over?" He pointed to the wall behind him. "He lives there."

"You have apartments next to each other?" She found that a little unexpected.

"Yep. He's building his house next door to where I'm building mine. We shared a room for eighteen years, by choice. College was the only time we've spent apart."

As she took the keys next door, she reflected on the closeness between Everett and Wilder. They had an enviable connection. She'd always wanted a sister who could be a close friend and confidant, but her parents hadn't wanted more children. Mina wasn't certain her father had wanted children in the first place.

When she returned, Ever handed her an oven mitt. "I need to jump in the shower. Can you watch the quiche? It should be done in four or five minutes."

It was on the tip of her tongue to tell him that she'd prefer to get into the shower with him, but she lacked the courage to say it out loud. She took the mitt from him instead. "Sure."

Everett took a quick shower and tried not to think about the way Mina had looked the night before, bound and blindfolded, writhing and moaning as he licked and sucked her pussy. He wanted to see her like that again, only this time without the restrictions they'd both placed on the night.

After he dried off and fixed his hair, he realized he'd left his clean clothes in the bedroom. Rather than put back on the sweats he'd slept in that were now a soggy, crumpled heap on the floor, he deposited his dirty clothes in the laundry, wrapped a towel around his hips, and headed into the hall. With any luck, Mina would be busy with the food, and she wouldn't notice a towel-clad man hurrying from the bathroom to the bedroom.

No such providence. He emerged to find her standing at the opening to the kitchen. Her dark gaze traveled from his face, down his neck, and over his bare chest. It lingered in the area his towel covered, and he felt his body respond to her unspoken appreciation. At last she shifted her gaze down his legs and to his feet before she raked it back up.

"See something you like?" He didn't have the ability to stop flirting, especially when a beautiful woman he desired regarded him like dessert.

Half her mouth lifted in a sultry smile. "Lose the towel, and then I'll tell you."

He struggled to remember his resolve and her status as a virgin. He managed what he hoped was an amused grin, and he disappeared into the bedroom. If she came after him, his resolve wouldn't hold.

Mina debated following him, but he closed the door solidly behind him, a definite hint he didn't want her in there. It wasn't quite a rejection. His manner had seemed more like he wanted to wait, that he had planned a series of activities for them today and nothing she could say would derail his plans. She understood on an instinctual level he needed things to happen on his terms.

She wasn't sure she was willing to accept that. A bigger part of her wondered whether the debate mattered. She'd be gone as soon as her mother agreed to move.

She returned to the kitchen, where three quiches cooled on the stove. She didn't know if two were for Ever, or if Wilder had planned to accompany them until she'd brought up his lack of a date. Seriously, though, if Wilder wanted a date, she didn't see how he'd have trouble finding one. He was very attractive—not as handsome as Everett, but definitely a hottie.

Arms slid around her waist, pulling her backward. She turned her head to snuggle into the embrace, and Ever's shower-clean scent engulfed her senses. His body seemed to wrap around her as well, holding her tight and keeping her safe. The contradictory responses he aroused puzzled her to no end. One moment she was questioning his nearly pathological need for control, and the next she luxuriated in his affection.

Her lack of experience wasn't to blame either. She didn't need to have dated anybody else to know that Ever was a singular man. He would eventually make sense. In the meantime, he could be a fun enigma to figure out.

He turned her around and kissed her soundly, gripping her hip with one hand and the side of her head with the other. A light, tingly feeling zipped through her body, which seemed to swell into him, trying to burst out of her clothes.

When he broke the kiss, he rested his forehead against hers, and she knew he'd been affected just as much as she had. It made her feel special. Then he pressed another kiss to her lips and stepped back.

"Let me pack up the quiche, and we can get going." He put two of them into the basket and handed her the third. "We'll drop that by Wilder's place. He inherited his cooking ability from our mother, so he's in danger of starving to death."

They smelled good, and Mina's stomach gurgled with anticipation. Everett took her to the mountains above the town. She knew the area pretty well, having grown up here, but she didn't recognize the narrow road he turned down.

"I have to widen this a little more. Once the house is built, I'll have asphalt put down." He slowed his truck to a crawl as he guided it over the deep ruts.

"This is the land your grandparents left you and Wilder? Did they leave anything to Danica and Marielle?" The land was beautiful, lush with forest vegetation. But it seemed unfair that the male children would inherit everything.

"Yeah." He chuckled. "They wanted cash. Marielle has a kick-ass condo on the beach in Hawaii. Danica's money is stuck in a trust until she's twenty-five. My parents could give it to her now, but they know she'll just blow it."

Mina hadn't known Danica that well, but she didn't think Danica was as thoughtless and impulsive as Everett did. Danica might not invest the money the way her older sister had, but she would no doubt use it well.

Ever brought the truck to a halt. He gestured to the right, where a clearing revealed a sloped piece of land. "That's where I'm going to build."

She studied the incline thoughtfully, trying to picture a house there. "You're going to built it into the hillside?"

He nodded. "Four bedrooms, five bathrooms, three stories. Solar cells on the roof. It'll have glass lining most of the back where it overlooks the drop-off."

"It sounds wonderful." She couldn't see living in a house that large and ostentatious. Her next place would be a small, two-bedroom house or apartment in sunny California.

"It will be." He sighed. "It's going to take a few more years to save up before I can start construction. In the meantime, we can have a picnic and admire the view."

The afternoon flew. Mina ate more than she thought she would. It turned out Everett had some real talent in the kitchen. They rambled all around his property. He showed her where Wilder planned to build his house. It was close enough to walk over, but the thick stands of trees afforded plenty of privacy. He held her hand, and he kissed her a lot, the type of deep, toe-curling kisses that left her breathless and wanting more. Then he'd move on, his fingers intertwined with hers as he guided her through the woods.

Standing near a precipice overlooking a small stream, he took pity on her. He wrapped his arms around her from behind, cupping her breasts in his palms. He held her in place with her back pinned to his chest, and he nipped at her earlobe.

She melted into him, trusting him to support her weight. He hummed against her neck, making an approving sound. Wordlessly, he lifted her shirt and unclasped her bra, and then he returned to cupping her breasts, this time without a barrier. She gasped as he pinched and rolled her nipples.

"I'm going to make you come, Mina. Spread your legs a little farther apart, and keep facing forward."

He didn't ask, not that she expected that from him. If she objected, he had instructed her in how to stop him. Obediently, she widened her stance. The cotton shorts she'd chosen made her butt look cute, but they were stretchy as well. He'd told her to dress comfortably.

He kept one hand high on her body, holding her to his chest and stimulating her breasts at the same time. The other he slipped past the waistband of her shorts, directly into her wetness.

"Mmmm." He opened his mouth wide and bit her neck. A hundred bolts of lightning shot from that point to where he circled his finger around her clit. "You're so wet, so responsive. I could keep you like this for hours, play with you all day, taste you, touch you until you beg me to make you mine."

She was ready to beg right now. "Ever?"

"Shhh. Just enjoy what I'm doing to you."

"But I want—"

He pulled his hand from her shorts and shoved two wet fingers into her mouth. She wasn't sure whether she should suck on them. "Mina, when I tell you to stay quiet, I mean it. One more word, and you'll be choosing between a spanking and a gag."

There was that threat again. What was it with him and spanking? The spanking was obviously an empty threat, but she wasn't so sure about the gag. She opted to keep the question to herself. Closing her mouth around his fingers, she sucked them with gentle pulls. He exhaled hard against her neck and twisted her nipple. It didn't hurt like she thought it would. Little blasts of heat pulsed from the tip, spreading over her breast.

She whimpered with him in her mouth, and when he slid his fingers in and out, she sucked and licked, simulating a blowjob the best she could. If she wasn't allowed to tell him what she wanted, he couldn't object to her showing him that she was willing to go as far as he wanted to take her.

He ground his hard cock against her ass. "Little vixen."

She moaned at the accusation in his tone, giving her consent however she could, but he extracted his fingers and returned them to her pussy.

"Not a sound." He pushed those fingers inside her, plunging them deep. "You're going to come for me, but you're not allowed to shout or cry out. Hold it in."

She'd been loud the night before. No doubt her screams would echo all over the valley if she let loose. He massaged her intimate tissues until he found the spot that made her gasp. Then he spread her pussy lips with the palm of his hand. As he slid his fingers in and out, establishing a rhythm that she couldn't hope to resist, his palm rubbed and scraped her clit.

She moved her hips, fucking his hand as they stood on the edge of the mountain. The way he plucked at her nipples echoed in the throbbing of her pussy. It stung a little, but it felt so damn good at the same time. She wanted to make noise, to say his name, to release the wealth of moans trapped inside her. They only added to the tension, the coil of heat low in her abdomen.

Pressing her hand to her mouth, she did her best to stifle the sound of her climax. Ever held her body against his as the strength left her limbs. Vaguely, she was aware that he'd withdrawn his fingers and licked them clean, and then he'd fixed her shorts.

"Ever?" She figured it was safe to speak now.

"Yes, dear?"

"I want you to make love to me."

He buried his face in her neck, but she heard his muffled response anyway. "One day, I will. But not now."

Any lethargy fled. She turned in his arms and forced him to meet her eyes. "Why not?"

He pressed his lips together as he thought.

She didn't want him to take his time to formulate a response. She wanted the truth. "Everett Burke, don't you dare lie to me."

That got him. His eyes widened. "I would never lie to you. There's a time and a place for every discussion. That's not lying."

She tried to pull out of his arms, but he wouldn't let go. "The time and the place is now. I know you're attracted to me. Why don't you want to have sex with me? Why won't you let me make you feel the way you make me feel?"

He exhaled hard through his nose. "Because you're a virgin, Mina. It's not just sex, and you're not in love with me yet, so it's not making love either."

She yanked hard this time, and he released his hold on her. She wasn't under the delusion she was free because she'd pulled hard enough. He allowed her to take a step away from him. "How did you know I was a virgin? For Christ's sake, I'm not that bad at kissing."

His brows shot up, and she could tell he was suppressing the urge to laugh. "No, you're very good at kissing. It was a hunch, one you just confirmed."

She couldn't believe this. The one time she actually wanted to sleep with a man, and he turned her down because she hadn't said yes to someone else before she'd met him. What kind of hypocrisy was that? "This is bullshit."

Everett watched her stomp around. She was pissed. If he weren't afraid she'd launch herself at him, he'd spend some time admiring the way her eyes flashed and rosy spots of color bloomed on her cheeks. She set her lips into a thin line that made him want to kiss them until they were swollen again. She clenched her fists and muttered under her breath in Korean.

He knew she spoke the language because he'd overheard her speaking to her mother one time in a store years ago, but he didn't understand a word she said. He spread his hands wide, palms up. "Mina. Be reasonable."

She whirled to face him, and that glare only grew brighter. "Reasonable? You're prejudiced against me because I'm a virgin. That's not reasonable."

Where the hell had she come up with that? "I have no problem with you being a virgin."

"No?"

"No."

She parked her hands on her hips. "Then prove it. Have sex with me."

If he were to use tactics like this on a woman, the entire world would judge him harshly. Yet he couldn't muster up any ire at her. She was just too damn cute. He shook his head. "I'm not going to have sex with you just to prove a point."

She narrowed her eyes until they were barely slits. "You don't play fair."

"No, I don't." There was no use in denying it. She would figure it out sooner or later. Because she was so intelligent, he knew it would happen sooner. His admission seemed to take some of the wind out of her sails.

"Take me back. We're finished here."

She tried to storm past him, but he caught her easily. She struggled in his arms. While he found her stubborn display of anger endearing and cute, he also found it exasperating. "Stop fighting me, Mina." He had a strong urge to turn her over his knee, but he didn't say that aloud. Besides, that idea seemed to be temporarily off the table. That didn't mean his need to discipline her had vanished. The unspoken warning hung in the air with the reverberation of his command.

Immediately she stilled. Though her face was turned to the side, he could see the way her thoughts raced through her mind, because her face was too expressive to hide anything. When she lifted her gaze, she nailed him with daggers. "So, what now? You're bigger and stronger than me, so that gives you the right to bully me?"

He laughed. He couldn't help it. Her bullying tactics hadn't worked, so now she turned the situation around to make him the bad guy.

She renewed her struggle, but he merely tightened his grip. "Mina, honey, maybe you want to ask me why I won't have sex with you right now."

Her entire body went rigid. "You have an STD?"

He wanted to laugh again, but out of frustration, not amusement. She was a feisty one. While it was vexing, it just made him fall for her a little more. "No. I'm clean. My employer requires a complete health check twice a year. I just had mine. I can show you the report if you'd like."

She peered up at him again. "You work for your parents."

He shrugged and eased his hold. "I don't get special treatment." Though he didn't want to, he released her once again.

She ran a hand through her hair and pursed her lips. "Okay, tell me why you won't have sex with me *right now.*"

He'd asked for this, yet it wasn't as easy to put his reasoning into words as he'd hoped. But he knew if he took too long to start talking, she'd just get pissed again. "You're twenty-two, and you're a virgin. The fact that you've never let a man touch you tells me that sex means a lot to you, maybe more than it means to most people. You're saving yourself for someone special. I want you to be sure it's me, Mina, because I never want you to look back at anything we do together with regret."

Her shoulders slumped, her face crumpled, and she turned away. Crap, he'd failed. He should have taken more time to formulate his response.

He closed the distance between them and hugged her from behind. "Please don't cry. I'm not doing this to hurt you. I'm doing this to protect you."

"I'm not crying."

She might deny it, but he heard the tears in her voice. Still, he knew better than to call her on it. Her convoluted reasoning would somehow lead her to the conclusion she wasn't crying and he was calling her a liar.

"Of course you're not." He turned her in his arms and held her until she stopped sniffling.

"You're a very sweet man, Ever, but you're sorely misguided."

Had he heard her right? "Misguided?"

"Yes. Maybe I just never met a man I wanted to have sex with before you. Most girls dated in high school. I wasn't allowed friends, much less boyfriends. I didn't learn how to date until college. Perhaps it's not that I've saved myself; it's just that I started a few years later than everybody else."

Her argument took him by surprise. He supposed, looking at it that way, she was right. If most women had their first sexual experiences in their late teens, then she was only a couple of years behind.

"Nice," he said, not bothering to hide the depth of his appreciation for her argument. Of course he had to follow it up with a joke to defuse her anger. "Were you on the debate team at Harvard?"

She wiped her eyes with the back of her hand. "You're not buying that either, are you?"

"No, but if you want, I'll teach you how to give me a blowjob."

Her chin came up defiantly. "You're assuming I've never done that before, either?"

He responded with the barest lift of his eyebrow. He'd bet his land on it. Before yesterday, she'd claimed to have never kissed on a first date.

"Fine," she said, giving in without a hint of grace. "I'll let you teach me."

She extracted herself from his arms and headed away from him.

"Where are you going?"

"To the truck," she called over her shoulder. "How else are we going to get back to your apartment?"

"If you keep going that way, you'll end up at Wilder's place." He pointed in the opposite direction. "Truck's back that way."

He didn't bother to temper his laughter at the way she turned around and lifted her chin higher, as if she'd intended to go that way all along.

Mina bit her lip, something she almost never did, as she waited on Everett's sofa. The bright summer sun streamed through the windows, reminding her it wasn't even close to sunset. She couldn't remember the last time she was this nervous. Even last night, her first time naked with a man, she hadn't resorted to torturing her face.

Ever whistled as he came out of the bathroom. He'd let her use it first, which was good because she always had to go when she was anxious.

He sat on the couch next to her, his arm splayed along the spine and his leg bent between them. She stared at his shorts and wondered if she was going to have to undress him the way he'd undressed her.

"The first thing to keep in mind is that this should be fun for everyone involved."

He said it with a straight face, but he'd also asked her if she had been on the debate team at Harvard with a straight face, so she knew he had mastered ironic delivery. Mina glanced around the room to see who else might be involved. Not even the kitten was around. Then she looked back at him. His expression hadn't changed.

"You're kidding, right?"

That smile curled at the corners of his mouth, rendering him even more devastatingly handsome. "Nope."

She didn't believe him. Perhaps she hadn't done this before, but she'd listened to her girlfriends discuss it at length, and she'd spent some time researching it on certain websites, just in case. It was enjoyable for the man, which was why she wanted to do it. Except for the satisfaction of proving to him that she was up to this new challenge, she didn't expect to enjoy it herself.

"Are you going to sit there and tell me that you had fun when you went down on me?" It amazed her that she was able to be so blunt. With anybody else, she would have been tongue-tied. Well, she wouldn't have found herself in this situation at all because she wouldn't have been begging, bargaining, and bullying for sex.

That was also another anomaly for her. Men had begged and bargained for sex with her, but she hadn't caved. She was a little ashamed to have resorted to bullying, but not enough to apologize.

In the past when she'd argued with anyone using those tactics, she'd won. Ever hadn't caved, and he hadn't come close to looking like he was going to lose his temper. He'd seemed more upset when she had misbehaved while he'd been fingering her.

His grin only widened. "Oh yes. I could spend hours with you tied to my bed, licking and sucking on you, making you moan and beg and scream. That's definitely fun. For both of us."

"Fine." She conceded the point because it wasn't worth arguing about. "Are we doing this out here or in the bedroom?"

The smile vanished from his face. She wondered what she'd said to make it go away. She didn't have to wonder for long.

"Mina, you don't have to do this. You shouldn't do this unless it's what you want to do. I want it to be a positive experience, something that brings us closer together. Maybe it's not intercourse, but it's sex. I don't have sex with just anybody."

Despite what she'd heard, she had assumed he was like most men, not picky about his bed partners. Now she felt real shame. She should have known better. Even in high school he hadn't had a reputation for playing the field. "I'm sorry. I do want to do this. I want to give you back some of what you've given me. I don't expect to enjoy the act, just the feeling of having made you happy."

His breath caught, and a sudden hunger blazed like blue-green fire in his eyes. Then it was gone. "While it makes me happy that pleasing me is enough motivation for you to consider doing something, for this, I'm going to have to insist you do this because it's what you want. When I give you an orgasm, it's because I want you to have one. It's not to make you happy or to appease you. It's a selfish act on my part; one that benefits you. It's also a gift, and while reciprocation is a good intention, it's not enough."

She truly didn't understand why he insisted on dissecting her motivation like this. What did it matter why she wanted to suck his cock? It should be enough that she did.

She tried to reach for a middle ground. She couldn't promise to enjoy doing something she'd never done. "Okay, well, I don't have anything on which to base wanting to do this except for the fact that I want to give you an orgasm."

He nodded. "That'll do for now. Come sit on my lap."

She slid over, and he dropped his arm from the spine of the sofa to wrap it around her waist. He scooted her bottom until it was directly over his cock.

"Always start with a kiss." With that, he kissed her, stealing her breath and her will. As he broke away, he stood, lifting her in his arms. "Always remember that I'm in charge when it comes to sex. That'll never change."

He deftly maneuvered her down the short hall and kicked his door open. He deposited her on the bed, disturbing the sleeping cat, who stretched lazily.

"Come on, Jolo." He scooped her up and took her out of the room. When he returned, he closed the door. "Nothing kills the mood like looking up and seeing your cat watching."

Mina considered this. "You know she's judging your performance."

His smile said he wasn't concerned about not measuring up. Without another word, he shed his shirt and shorts. He stood before her wearing only light blue boxer briefs. She forgot how to breathe.

He'd removed his shirt the night before, but she'd been wearing a sleeping mask, so she hadn't been allowed the chance to study him the way she'd like. Even this morning when he'd emerged from the bathroom wearing only a towel, he hadn't lingered long enough for her to look her fill.

He had the look of an athlete, with lithe, defined muscles and broad shoulders. She let her gaze roam all over his chest and follow the band of his underwear from one hip bone to the other. It didn't flow smoothly, because his hard cock made it bow out.

71

He stood with his hands perched loosely on his hips, watching her look at him and openly enjoying her awestruck perusal. There was a definite difference in his bearing from earlier, when he'd caught her looking and asked her if she'd seen anything she liked.

She forced her gaze lower, taking in the powerful thighs that had been hidden by his long, baggy shorts. He was magnificent on so many levels. "Will you turn around?"

He granted her request without question or comment, and she realized he knew this was the first time she'd been this close to a soon-to-be-naked man. Since he was in the mood to humor her, she decided to go for broke.

"Will you take off your boxers?"

One shove, and they fluttered down to his ankles. He stepped out of them and kicked them toward his hamper. They landed in a pile of clothes that had been there yesterday as well.

She knew she was stalling. Tearing her gaze away from his dirty laundry, she feasted her eyes on his naked ass. It was sculpted perfection, tight and curved enough for her to grab a handful.

Then he turned back around, and she nearly died. The narrow trail of hair that ran down from his belly button widened, and his thick cock curved from that nest. It was paler than the rest of him, and the head was almost purple.

She gathered her courage, stood up, and closed the three steps between them. She remembered that he'd told her to begin with a kiss. Even on her tiptoes, she couldn't hope to reach his mouth, so she dropped to her knees and kissed the crown of his cock.

A shudder ran through him, and he put a warning hand on her head. "Honey, go slow. Take your time. It's okay to explore."

Like he'd done, taking the time to find out which pressures she liked and which spots made her cry out. She understood now. This was about learning his body and his tells. This was about making him hers.

She used her hands first, running her fingertips along his soft shaft and over the coarse hairs dotting his sac. She explored the ridge surrounding the head of his cock and the way the indent led directly to the tip. There was much more character present than the photos of the waxed and airbrushed models that seemed to be on every blog dedicated to romance. Every vein and ridge made him that much sexier.

In the periphery of her vision, she saw Everett's hands clench and unclench. He hissed and tried to control his breathing.

"Can you lie on the bed? I think this is going to take a while."

He laughed, but it was different from before. It held a hint of desperation. "I can assure you that it won't."

She looked up to find his eyes half-closed. The veins on his neck stood out, and he wore an expression of utter ecstasy. "Do you want me to stop?"

His eyes flew open, and he looked down at her. "I like your sense of humor, but I'd like it better if you said that with my dick in your mouth."

Her confidence in what she was doing grew immeasurably. She licked the underside of his cock like it was an ice-cream cone. His lids fluttered downward, and his breathing grew uneven. The smooth skin felt like velvet, so she decided to explore him with her tongue the same way she'd explored him with her fingers. He'd said to take her time.

He seemed to be holding it together until she got to his balls. She lapped at the thin line between his testicles, and he moaned loudly. Then she sucked one ball into her mouth, and he swore. She took that as a good sign. She couldn't stop the slight smile of pride from stretching her lips or the hum of satisfaction.

He tangled his fingers in her hair and grasped his cock with his other hand. "Playtime is over, honey. Open your mouth."

This change in dynamic shocked her a bit, but his commanding tone also made her wet. She opened her mouth, and he eased his cock inside. She had been nervous that she wouldn't be able to establish a rhythm he liked, but that ceased to be a concern. He took over, thrusting with his hips and dictating the rhythm. In essence, he fucked her mouth, and it was one of the hottest things she'd never imagined.

He took one of her hands from where she gripped his hips and wrapped it around the base of his cock. She was thankful he didn't expect her to take the whole thing. She'd choke on it, and that was not sexy.

"Touch my balls, honey. Cup them with your other hand."

It did not annoy her that he had taken over. She was vastly relieved that he was telling her what he wanted. She realized he'd asked her to do this for him the night before, and she hadn't really said anything. There had been no need. He'd been wonderful.

She rolled his sac gently in her palm, trying to get a feel for what he liked best. Just as she lost herself in the rhythm of the motion and the slide of his silky skin against her lips, she felt his fist tighten in her hair, pulling it in a way that made her eyes water and her pussy weep. Hot jets of semen spurted in her mouth. He pumped twice more before pulling out.

He backed away from her, and she looked up at him to see why, but his sated expression told her nothing. He grabbed two tissues from a box on his dresser and handed them to her.

"Here. Spit it out."

Mina felt heat climbing her neck. How had he known she hadn't swallowed? Did he mind? She accepted the tissue and used it. "Thanks. I just didn't want to—"

"That's fine. In the future, you don't have to hold it in your mouth. You can spit it into your hand until you get to a sink. I don't require you to swallow."

That was a relief. As much as she enjoyed the licking and sucking parts, she had no desire to swallow. His wording took her by surprise—how in the world could he "require" her to do anything?—but she chalked it up to postorgasmic bliss.

He took the wadded tissue from her and threw it in the small trash bin next to the dresser. Then he hefted her from the floor and tossed her onto the bed, which was only a few feet away. He followed her down, pinning her in place with his hips, and kissed her.

Mina felt engulfed, surrounded by Everett. His body pressed her into his messy bedding, and his scent cradled her from below. He touched her everywhere, caressing her and moving her clothes out of the way until nothing separated them. She felt his lips move over her skin as he kissed his way down her neck to linger at her breasts.

Surrendering to urgency, she let her hands roam his body, exploring his textures and lines and finding the places that made him kiss her a little more frantically. His cock hardened against her leg. She worked her hand between their bodies until she could enclose it in her palm. She meant to see what it took to make him moan, but to her surprise, she found it only partially hard.

In her hand, his cock swelled to its full length. She tightened her grip and slid her palm up and down as she marveled at the transformation. "I can't believe you're ready again."

He thrust his hips, fucking her hand. "You keep that up, and I'll come in your hand."

Perhaps he meant to gross her out, but the second he said that, an erotic image came to her of him kneeling over her, ejaculating on her stomach. He had that sultry, possessive look he wore so well. In her mini-fantasy, he smeared his semen over her breasts. If she didn't want to swallow, that was fine. She had other uses for his semen.

"I want that." She wanted more than that, but she wasn't at the point where she felt comfortable asking for it. He wanted to wait until he thought she was ready to have sex. He probably wouldn't think too highly of her if he knew she was having some lightly kinky thoughts.

She pumped her hand up and down his shaft. He regarded her with a mix of wonder and affection that had her completely willing to rethink her life plan. Really, what could she do in California that she couldn't do here?

Ever rolled them both suddenly, shoving her shorts and panties down while she was on top of him. He shifted her to the side so that she had a better angle to access his cock, and then he eased what felt like two fingers inside her.

"We'll come together. Then we'll make dinner, and I'll have you for dessert." He lifted his head, darting with predatory accuracy to capture her mouth for one of his soul-searing kisses.

She followed his rhythm. When he sped up, so did she. When he slowed down, so did she. And she realized that doing so delayed orgasm and prolonged pleasure. Each time he led her up that cliff, it got higher, and the precipice grew more dangerous. She didn't know how many times he changed directions; she only knew the coil tightening in her abdomen had become a fire that burned out of control.

Just when she thought she couldn't stand it anymore, he pushed her a little harder, and she fell down that chasm, screaming at the intensity of the pleasure and clinging to her anchor. Dimly, she heard his shout. He came, and warmth splashed onto her stomach as he fulfilled part of her unspoken wish.

Chapter Five

Mina clicked *Send* and sighed. This marked her fifty-seventh job application, and not a single one of them had panned out. She was either overqualified or unwilling to relocate. In the three months since she'd come home, her life had changed completely, and it was all due to Everett Burke.

He filled every moment of her life, even those he wasn't present for. She thought about him when she woke in the morning, alone in her bed. Though she'd spent a few nights at his place, he hadn't consented to more than oral sex.

She'd started taking birth control, going so far as to regularly take the little pill in front of him so he'd know she was ready and willing. She'd asked several times, but he'd merely reiterated that he wanted to make sure she wouldn't regret anything, and then he'd changed the subject.

He took her out a lot, even on weekend trips to New York, Boston, and Detroit. Most of those were work related, but he'd managed to wrangle an extra day or two of vacation. They hiked together. They picnicked on his property. He consulted her on the design options for his house.

She'd invited him to dinner to meet her mother, and his parents had them over regularly. Everybody in both their families and probably in the entire town assumed they were sleeping together, but everybody was wrong. Frustratingly wrong.

She'd fallen in love with him. Totally, irrevocably in love with a man who was driven to protect her and take care of her. This was not the type of man she'd ever thought she would fall for.

Tonight she would tell him she was in love with him, and then she would tell him she couldn't find a job in Vermont. It would test the strength of their relationship, but she felt like they were at a point where they needed to decide how they were going to move forward. Perhaps he knew she wasn't being entirely forthcoming with him, and that was why he refused to take their relationship to the next level. She couldn't stay in this limbo forever.

"Mina, should I wear the black shoes or the navy ones?"

She turned to face the door of her bedroom. Her mother held up two pairs of dress shoes, neither of them appropriate. Mina rose to her feet. "It's a Labor Day cookout, Mom. They're having hamburgers and playing ladder golf. Wear sandals."

Macy and Russ Burke had invited her and her mother to their annual event. It was the first time both families would be together socially.

"I need to look my best, Mina. Macy Burke always looks amazing." Jin Ae sat down on Mina's ottoman and considered the shoes in her hands.

"It's not a competition." From what little Mina knew about Macy Burke, she had the impression Ever's mother would be horrified if she found out how stressed Jin Ae was about the upcoming event. "Macy's not like that. She's actually a pleasant person. You said so yourself when you worked with her on the Fourth of July festival committee. Wear those red sandals I gave you for your birthday. They're comfortable, and they look nice."

Though her mother changed more times than Mina could count, they arrived at the party exactly on time. Jin Ae might be a stress ball, but she was never late.

They parked on the lawn at the end of a row of cars. Other people did the same thing, so Mina didn't feel like she was doing something she shouldn't. She followed the stream of people around to the backyard. The Burkes owned a huge spread of land near town, and they'd built a magnificent house in the middle of it.

The house Ever was planning wouldn't be as large. He had shaken his head at the opulence of it and asked her if she wanted to be the one who had to clean all the rooms. Mina knew Macy employed domestic help, but she also knew that Ever didn't want to deal with that kind of responsibility just yet. That was fine with her. She wasn't sure how she would feel about paying somebody to clean up after her.

Wilder greeted her once she made it to the party area. He slung his arm around her shoulders and kissed her cheek. Then he held his hand out to her mother. "You must be Mrs. Sung. I can see where Mina gets her good looks. I am Wilder Burke. Welcome to my parents' barbecue."

Color rose to her mother's cheeks at Wilder's compliment. "Thank you, young man. We are honored to be here."

Wilder took her mother's hands and kissed the backs of both of them, laying on the charm a bit thick. Then he straightened up and grinned at Mina. "Ever's helping over at the grill."

Mina returned his big smile. "They don't let you near that thing, do they?"

"Not if you want edible food. Look, there's Mom, the other culinarily deficient member of the family."

A stunning blonde woman slipped her arm through Wilder's and regarded Mina and Jin Ae with a welcoming smile. "Jin Ae, Mina, I'm so glad you could make it." She squeezed Wilder's arm affectionately, and then she enveloped Jin Ae in a hug.

Mina knew that her mother didn't care to be touched by very many people, and so she was surprised when Jin Ae didn't stiffen under Macy's demonstrative greeting. She actually hugged Ever's mother back.

Macy hugged Mina, but it was appropriately brief. Then she threaded her arm through Jin Ae's. "If you two will excuse us, I want to show Jin Ae my garden."

For years, Jin Ae's garden had been devoted to growing food, the only use of resources to which her father wouldn't object. In the past three years, Jin Ae had begun cultivating flowers. Of course, the Burkes had legions of professional-grade gardens.

There was no way Mina was going to get in the way of her mother enjoying this day. She smiled at Macy. "By all means. You two can talk about aphids."

As they walked off, Wilder took her by the arm. "Come on. I know you're dying to see Ever."

She blushed, but she didn't deny it. Seeing him would go a long way toward making the hopelessness of her wasted morning seem not so bad.

Wilder led her through the throng, stopping to greet some guests and introduce her around. People liked him, and many single women flirted, but he didn't seem to notice. She was dying to know the story behind why Wilder so rarely dated. She knew it was related to some woman, and she'd give anything to meet the person responsible for leaving Wilder to drift aimlessly.

Finally she caught sight of Ever. He nodded as he conversed with his father. Russ Burke gave her a picture of what Ever and Wilder would look like in thirty years, and she couldn't find a thing to complain about. The man was both attractive and fit. She knew he'd suffered a heart attack a few years before, but looking at him today, she'd never guess it.

"Is it done yet?" Likely the aroma seeping from the grill had prompted Wilder's question.

Ever and Russ glanced over, their conversation breaking off suddenly as Ever scooped her up in his arms and spun around. He stopped and smacked a loud kiss on her lips. Embarrassed heat traveled up her neck. She hadn't expected such an effusive display of affection in front of his father.

Instead of setting her down, he hugged her tighter. "I've missed you." He murmured his confession close to her ear, a private moment at a public event.

"I love you." It wasn't what she'd meant to say. She hadn't planned to blurt it out that way. In her head, she had pictured a romantic scene with just the two of them.

He set her down, but the intensity of his gaze held her just the same. He was pleased, happy, and a touch more arrogant. "I love you, too."

They'd served the last of the burgers. His father bent to make sure the grill was turned off, and Ever surveyed the crowded lawn. Mina was somewhere nearby, but search as he might, he couldn't find her in the throng.

A firm hand landed on his shoulder. He looked over to find his father regarding him with "that look" on his face. It was an expression Ever hadn't seen in quite a while. He tried to keep calm. Lifting his brows, he sent a silent query in his father's direction.

"You've found yourself a rare woman."

Even though his father's concerned expression didn't ease, Ever relaxed a little. "I know."

"You haven't told her, have you?"

He dropped his gaze, embarrassed and chagrined that his dad had read him so easily. He knew Wilder wouldn't have told their father things Ever had shared in confidence. "She's not ready to know."

"Bullshit. If this is the woman you want to spend the rest of your life with, you have to be honest. From the beginning. You're not getting off to a good start." Russ Burke regarded Ever fiercely. Ever struggled not to squirm.

"Don't worry. I have it under control. She's skittish. I mentioned spanking a few times and freaked her out. She needs me to ease her into it slowly." His face was growing warm. He hated being put in this position. He was twenty-five, for Christ's sake. He didn't like being second-guessed by anyone, much less his father, a man he'd spent his life idolizing.

Russ shook his head. "You need to talk to her, have an honest, open conversation. She's an intelligent woman. She won't appreciate this approach. It borders on condescending, and it's dishonest. You know where I stand on respect and honesty. Believe me when I say that if you don't drive her away like this, you're going to do irrevocable damage to the trust you're trying to build. No relationship can survive without trust, especially a D/s one."

She loved him. She'd uttered those sweet words hours before. Love would see them through a few difficult conversations. "She's submissive. I know she is. But *she* doesn't know she is. She can't embrace what she hasn't identified."

And he knew the concept would terrify her. Mina had a huge fear of having a man, even one who loved her with his whole heart and soul, in control of her life. He wanted her to feel comfortable and secure in his domination before he put the words to their actions.

But his father wasn't finished. "She's petite, not weak. Don't underestimate the power of a strong woman, especially when she finds out you've lied to her. Damn it. Some things can't be undone."

"I'm not lying to her. I'm waiting for the right time to have that conversation." He lifted his gaze and nailed his father with all the conviction in his heart. "I will tell her when the time is right. You don't know her like I do. She's stubborn, and she's still a little afraid of me." It was the reason he hadn't consummated their love, even though she'd waged one hell of a campaign to test his will.

"Women can always sense when they're being lied to."

He shrugged his father's hand from his shoulder. "I haven't lied to her. I would never lie to her. I just can't take the chance of timing this wrong and losing her."

Angry, and more than a little hurt by his father's lack of faith in his judgment, Ever stalked away. Each step closer to Mina drained the negative effects of the confrontation with his dad, and he focused on finding the woman who owned him, heart and soul.

The day flew. Extended family and friends welcomed her heartily, and whenever she tried to check on her mother, she found Jin Ae animatedly conversing with people from town and from Ever's family. Her plan to lure her mother to sunny California had definitely failed, but she couldn't find it in her heart to be unhappy about that. Perhaps this was the way things were meant to be. The universe's grand plan for her didn't involve leaving the town where she'd grown up.

Still, it was a little deflating to think about not being able to find a job nearby.

Her mother left the party before she did. Jin Ae no longer asked Mina what time she planned to be home. It was generally accepted that if she wasn't there by nine, she would be staying at Ever's apartment.

After the party ended, Ever held her hand as he drove her to his place. "Your mom and my mom really hit it off."

"They did, didn't they?" Remembering the way her mother's eyes seemed to glow the entire day, she smiled softly. "I'm glad. My mom needs friends."

Ever gave her a quick look, a slight furrow to his brow. "Your family isn't known for being very social. This isn't the first time my parents have invited your parents over for an event. It's just the first time anybody came."

That was news to Mina, but it didn't surprise her. "I never knew. My father didn't like to go places." Her mother probably hadn't known about the invitations either.

"What happened to your father?"

It was a valid question. She never talked about her father. This might have been the first time she'd brought him up. "When my mother divorced him, he moved back to where he grew up, somewhere near Cleveland."

"You don't talk to him?" Ever asked the question slowly. He had to know he was digging in sensitive territory.

"No. We weren't close."

"Why?"

She sighed. "He was a hard man to know. I don't really want to talk about him. He's gone, and I'm glad he's gone."

He glanced over at her, a movement she caught from the corner of her eye. She didn't turn her head, because she didn't want to have the conversation. Talking about him like he was a past event made the chains of the past feel a little less restrictive. Ever seemed to get the message, because he dropped the subject.

Jolo meowed insistently at them as soon as they arrived at Ever's apartment. She rubbed her face against Ever's leg, purring, and then she marked Mina the same way. The kitten was almost full-size now. She'd filled out, and her soft fur had grown much longer.

Ever lifted her smoothly and deposited her across his broad shoulders. The feline lay down, her front paws flexing as loud, rumbling purrs erupted from her throat.

Mina smiled, marveling at this gentle man. "You sure do know how to make a lady happy."

He grinned, probably at her unintended double entendre. "I hope so."

He headed to the kitchen, where he filled Jolo's feed bowl and brushed her while she ate. Sounds of contentment continued to pour from the kitten. Mina watched for a minute, wondering at his patient enjoyment of his pet. She'd always wanted a dog, some kind of companion that could hang out with her and listen as she shared her innermost thoughts. Part of her still longed for that kind of relationship, one based on blind trust and absolute loyalty. Another part of her stepped away in abject horror. She'd never even confided in a diary. How could she trust a pet or a lover?

Ever was many things to her, but he hadn't reached confidant status. She'd blurted out the three magic words earlier, and he'd returned the sentiment. But over the course of the day, she'd realized nothing had changed. While hearing that he had deep feelings for her made her giddy inside, it didn't make her feel closer to him. She felt no urge to tell him about her father or share the misery of her job search with him, though she knew she should.

Somehow, telling him those things would soil the purity of their relationship. Ever took great pains to make sure she was happy. He took care of her. He cherished her. He elevated her to a status she didn't deserve. Being a virgin didn't mean she'd waited for him in particular. It meant that nobody had struck her fancy until now.

She disappeared into the bathroom to brush her teeth and change for bed. It was late, and Ever had to get up in the morning for work. He and a colleague named Isla were scheduled to depart for Nebraska to set up a wish. Mina wasn't too sure about the kinds of wishes they fulfilled. She just knew they didn't deal with children or people suffering from life-threatening illnesses. Ever didn't talk about it too much, citing confidentiality agreements.

Perhaps it reflected badly on her that she didn't press him to talk more about what he did. Every time she thought about it, she backed away from the subject because she knew she would just end up feeling jealous that he had a job he liked while she couldn't seem to land a second interview unless she was willing to leave the state.

The night was warm, and Ever threw off amazing amounts of body heat, so she opted to sleep in a soft tank top and underwear. Ever came in while she was turning back the covers. He paused a few feet inside the doorway. She felt his gaze roaming her body, and she looked up to gauge the extent of his desire.

He almost never wanted to go right to sleep, but he wasn't looking at her as if he wanted to devour her. His hands were shoved into his pockets, and his somber expression made her tense. Ever had something to say. She waited, but he didn't speak.

"Ever? Is everything okay?"

His response was curious. He seemed to nod and shake his head at the same time. Then he pulled his hands from his pockets and folded them across his chest.

Mina abandoned the covers and rounded the bed, crossing to stand in front of him. She touched his wrist lightly. "Tell me what's wrong."

The expression on his face changed, softening as whatever worrisome thoughts had plagued him fled. He wrapped his arms around her waist and pulled her close. "Nothing's wrong, honey. With you in my arms, everything is stunningly right."

Though he spoke sweetly, tension stiffened the lines of his body, making his muscles even harder and more prominent against her. Something was different about the way he held her, as if a war was brewing inside him.

He lowered his head and brushed his lips across hers. It wasn't a kiss as much as a warning, and Mina's heart surged at the inherent promise. Ever was finally going to make love to her. He'd arrived at his decision. That explained the difference in his demeanor.

He cupped her face in his hands, skimming his fingertips over her cheeks before plunging them into her hair. In the gravity of the moment, her breath caught. He repeated the warning, sweeping his lips over her eyelids, her brow, and her cheeks.

"Ever." She whispered his name, a reverent plea.

"I'm a demanding lover." He traced her lower lip with the pad of his thumb. His ethereal gaze followed the path. "Possessive and controlling. Dominant. I can't change who I am, Mina. You must promise to use your safeword if I hurt you or it's just too much. And tell me when you're afraid."

She wasn't afraid of losing her virginity. In fact, she relished the idea. It was high time to get rid of that little inconvenience. She didn't think it would hurt. Ever had fingered her almost daily, and he approached oral sex like a junkie getting a fix. Though his cock was larger than the two or three fingers he usually used, she was more than ready to accommodate him.

After feathering her fingers over his jaw, she cupped his face the way he held hers. "I'm not afraid, Ever. I want very much for you to make love to me."

"Tell me your safeword."

"Oasis." No hesitation on her part, though she didn't see a need for a safeword. But if it made him feel better, then she would acknowledge it.

He closed his mouth over hers and devoured her with a kiss that made everything previous seem like lighthearted fun. The force of it immobilized her, and she understood a little why he'd voiced his warning. Ever had a reputation for being fun and laid-back. Though he'd been forceful when they'd played, he hadn't completely obliterated her concept of individuality.

This kiss made her feel like she was weightless and spinning, no longer an entity unto herself. At the same time, she felt heavy and grounded, an extension of him. He didn't bother with anything gentle or teasing. He explored her mouth with his tongue as if he was just confirming his territory. She'd never felt so overpowered before, and she had no choice but to let herself drown.

Then he broke the kiss and took a step back. She went to follow him, but he stopped her with the pressure of his fingertips on her stomach.

"Don't move, love." His eyes smoldered with patient danger.

He slid his hand around her midsection, keeping contact as he circled her body. He paused at her back with his hands on her waist. Slowly, he slipped them under her tank top and lifted it. The warmth of his hands brought chills to her flesh as he exposed her.

She'd been naked in front of him many times, but this seemed like the first time. Trembling, she struggled to stay still. She wanted to lean back until she felt the solid length of his chest, except she knew he needed to do this on his terms. Because she loved him, she could accept that condition.

He drew the shirt over her head and let it drop to the floor. Its gentle breeze fluttered down her leg. Never had throwing laundry on the floor felt so sensuous.

Pressing his palms flat, he roamed the exposed skin of her back, stomach, and breasts. He returned to them again and again, cupping them in his large hands and rolling her nipples until she mewed.

He wove a spell with the patterns and pressures of his endless caress. When he slipped his fingers into her pussy, she gasped and looked down. He'd removed her panties, and she hadn't noticed. He held her against his body, her back to his chest. She wanted to see him, touch him, taste him, but he didn't offer that option.

"You're so very wet, my love."

"I want to touch you." Her voice came out sounding breathy. She hadn't moved, but she was winded.

He played her clit expertly with one hand and grasped her chin with his other one. Turning her face to the side, he leaned down and kissed her tenderly. It was sweet and hot, and it set molten sensations free to riot through her body. Some of the tension of the day gathered in a tight ball. It coalesced, and she exploded when he released her lips.

"You'll get your wish eventually, honey, just not now." Withdrawing his arms from around her body, he stepped back. "Thank you for turning back the covers. Lie in the center of the bed, face up."

Mina started and turned to stare at him. It wasn't a new order. He frequently liked to tie her arms down when he ate her pussy. The light bondage thrilled her to no end, but she didn't expect him to bind her for their first time together.

He met her stare head-on, a stoic expression on his face as he waited for her to say or do something.

"You're going to tie me up?"

A slow smile spread his lips. "No, love. Not your first time. I'm just going to cuff your wrists and ankles."

In her world, that fit the definition of tying her up. She blinked at his patient explanation. Then she took a breath and turned toward the bed. He'd maintained for months that her first time should be memorable and special. She thought he'd meant for his presence to make for those conditions. It looked like he'd spent his time developing an elaborate plan. He was very good at planning. It was worthwhile to see how this would play out.

"All right."

He touched his lips to hers, and she had the feeling it was more a reward than a gesture of thanks. "That's my girl."

She took her position on the bed, extending her arms toward the bedposts as he'd taught her to do. He smiled as he buckled a leather cuff around her wrist. Then he bent down, and she heard a metallic *click*. The sound repeated as he secured a sturdy metal piece around a ring attached to the cuff. It looked like a stronger version of the device she used to secure her keys inside her backpack in college.

"I'm not going to blindfold you yet. I want you to see what's going on. It's important for you to know exactly how I've bound you. I won't always allow you this consideration."

His expression was on the somber side of grave. Mina was puzzled by how seriously he was taking this ritual. Then he slid a finger between the stiff leather cuff and her skin. The other times, he'd used ones made from a soft, bendy material.

"Wiggle your fingers."

She did, and he seemed satisfied with what he saw. He moved to the other side of the bed and secured her other wrist.

"These are a bit stiffer, less forgiving if you tug on them. Let me know if your circulation gets cut off so I can adjust you."

She had no problem informing him of any discomfort she might feel. "I will."

Then he moved to the end of the bed and bound her ankles to the posts there. She hadn't counted on that. Sure, he'd said that was what he was going to do, but he'd never done it before. When he finished, she was spread wide open, and she felt completely helpless.

He crawled on the bed, knelt between her legs, and came down on his hands to hover over her. "Tell me how you feel."

Though she'd blurted the words before, she meant them. Her heart softened, and she gave him a brilliant smile. "I love you."

He returned her smile and brushed a kiss over her lips. "I love you too, but that's not what I meant. I've bound you so that you can barely move. You're naked and at my mercy."

When he said it like that, it didn't sound half-bad. It felt different but still wonderful. Lifting her head, she smacked a kiss on his mouth. "I like being naked and at your mercy."

A deep satisfaction lit his eyes to a sparkling green. "Good, because I like having you this way."

From the back pocket of his shorts, he produced the sleeping mask he used as a blindfold. Mina tugged on her restraints, forgetting for a second that they weren't going to allow her to move. "No. I want to see you."

"You will. I promise. This is for foreplay only. Now, that climax I gave you was your only freebie tonight. If you want to climax again, you must ask for permission."

She blinked, not certain if she liked his audacity. He'd warned her that he was controlling, but she didn't think he would be so extreme. "Are you kidding?"

"Not even a little." He regarded her with an expression she couldn't read. "You belong to me, Mina. Your heart, your body, and your orgasms. You'll have them only with my permission, or there will be consequences."

At least he hadn't threatened to spank her. After those first few times, he hadn't mentioned it again.

He shifted, moving to sit next to her. "Now is the time to stop this, Mina. If it's not what you want, tell me. I'd never do anything you didn't want."

She marveled at his assertion. How could he possibly know what she wanted? "You didn't ask me if I wanted to be tied up."

Tracing a fingertip from her wrist to her hip, he pressed his lips together. "I gave you a safeword."

"So if I don't use it, you take that as permission?"

"Generally. I told you what I was going to do, you said, 'All right,' and then I did exactly what I said I was going to do."

He had her there. It was a convoluted logic that took permission to bind her as handing over control of her orgasms to him, but she really didn't want to argue. She could play this his way tonight and see where it got them.

She nodded. "All right. But when we make love for the first time, I want to hold you in my arms and see you with my eyes."

He grinned and kissed her cheek. "Don't forget to ask permission to climax. I'm not open for negotiation on that point."

She didn't feel that she'd negotiated anything. He slipped the mask over her eyes and stole her vision. Exhaling the breath she hadn't known she was holding, she coached her shoulders to relax. She was going to be sore tomorrow if she kept pulling on her restraints.

He kissed her foot. She felt the sure pressure of his strong lips along her instep. The sensation moved up her leg. It felt like he was using his hands and his lips. Any apprehension left over from their conversation drained from her. Uncertainty fled. She could handle being bound like this if he wanted to pamper her body with his hotly sensual caress.

By the time he made it to her arms, she had changed her mind. The relaxation that had spread through her body turned to a tension that wrung soft moans from deep in her throat. She wanted to writhe, but he'd drugged her body with the methodical way he'd marked every inch of it as his.

The only part of her he'd skipped was her pussy. It wept. The scent of her arousal diffused through the room, a desperate perfume she wished was more effective in motivating him to touch her tender pink folds.

"Please touch me. I ache."

He grazed his lips across hers, lingering there. She felt the insistent heat of his tongue demanding entrance, and she opened for him. He hovered over her, his shirt barely brushing her nipples as they strained upward. She arched her back the best she could and was rewarded with momentary physical contact.

Breaking away, he made his way down her body with wild, wet kisses. The ardent journey of exploration had ended, replaced with a voracious hunger. He stopped between her legs to feast, licking and sucking, massaging with his lips and scraping erotically with his teeth. Primed and ready, she quickly climbed the slope toward climax.

"I want to come." She congratulated herself for remembering.

He paused for a brief second. "No. Breathe through it." Then he dived back into his task, which now seemed to be torturing her instead of pleasuring her.

"Ever!" Energy coalesced in her core. She writhed, seeking to get away from his mouth and closer at the same time. His order to hold off conflicted with her body's driving need. "Please don't be cruel."

He mumbled something against her clit. The vibrations nearly did her in. She panted, quick little breaths that did nothing but highlight her need.

"Please, Ever. Please let me come. I need to come."

"Yes." He lifted away long enough to hiss permission.

Her orgasm flooded from deep within, a tide of endorphins releasing to riot through her bloodstream. She didn't cry out, because it stole her ability to vocalize.

The cuffs around her legs disappeared, and the cuffs binding her wrists followed. He slipped the mask from her eyes. She blinked in the soft light streaming from the lamps on either side of the bed, and she was able to focus in time to watch Ever undress.

He climbed on the bed and settled his body on top of hers, holding most of his weight on his elbows. She lifted a hand to caress his cheek. Her hand trembled, though she wasn't nervous.

He leaned into her caress, turning to kiss her palm after several seconds. "Last chance, honey."

Mina shook her head, refusing to change her mind. She'd waited too long for this. For him. "Make love to me, Everett Burke. Make me completely yours."

He went to roll away, but she grabbed at him desperately, holding on despite the tremors in her arms and hands. With a patient smile, he kissed her again. "I'm just getting a condom."

"No." She was on birth control, a fact he couldn't have missed. She knew he was clean, and he knew she was as well. "No condom. I want to feel you."

He hesitated briefly. "I've never had sex without a condom."

She lifted her knee, rubbing her inner thigh against his hip to invite him closer. "There's a first time for everything."

Chuckling softly, he kissed her again. It returned the serious tone to the situation. He deepened it, letting her know without words how precious she was to him. Then he lifted his hips and reached between them to position his cockhead at her entrance.

"I'm going to start slow. Let me know if it hurts or if you need me to go even slower."

She nodded. Though this was his first time with a virgin, she trusted him to know what he was doing.

He pushed forward. The sensation was different from when he used his fingers. She felt her tissues stretching to accommodate his size. Though his cock was long and thick, she didn't think it was too long or too thick.

Rocking his hips back and forth, he thrust shallowly, deepening each time. She kept expecting it to hurt, but the pinch and sting she'd read about never came. His rhythmic motions sent waves of pleasure through her body. "Yes," she whispered, encouraging him.

Then he stopped, and she recognized that he was fully seated and giving her time to adjust to the feel of having him inside her body.

She planted her feet on the mattress and lifted her hips. "Don't stop. Please don't stop. You feel so unbelievably good."

"So do you." He gasped, and she remembered that he hadn't climaxed yet today. "Put your hands on my shoulders, honey. Keep them there or on the bed."

She'd wanted to touch him, but she knew the fragile thread of his control might break. He wanted to make this good for her. She couldn't sabotage his intentions.

His skin burned beneath her palms, and his muscles rippled as he shifted slightly. Lifting his hips, he withdrew a little. He rocked into her body, watching her face. She didn't have time to analyze what he might be thinking, because the sated feeling of her last orgasm had fled. Having his cock inside her renewed her body's demand for another climax.

She wanted him to go faster, but he took his time. He varied his rhythm until he found the one that made her gasp. Mina felt her eyes roll back into her skull as her vision went gray. She arched closer and moved her hips to meet his thrusts, and she gripped his shoulders so hard it hurt her hands.

All control fled. She was a wild thing, a newly minted sexual being. A climax washed over her, bringing welcome relief. She cried out, but he didn't even slow down. His only acknowledgment was a grunt of warning. She'd come without permission.

The orgasm pulsed harder and harder. Unable to make her limbs respond, she slackened her grip, and her hands fell to rest on the pillow under her head. Ever nodded, a gleam of satisfaction competing with the predatory glint in his eyes. She felt the beginning flutters of her next orgasm, which promised to put the last one to shame.

"Oh no you don't." He reached down and closed his hand around her thigh and lifted it high on his hip. He altered his rhythm, opting for a circular motion that teased her sweet spot.

It kept her where she was, on the verge of something earth-shattering. The feelings of pleasure neither increased nor decreased, which drove her to a desperate place. She wanted to move, to meet his thrusts, but he'd pinned her with his hips and the position of her leg, and she didn't have enough energy to fight him.

"Ever, please. Oh please."

He dipped his head and took her lips in a soft kiss, communicating that he was in control of his body and her pleasure. "I could make love to you for hours. You're so sweet and sexy, utterly irresistible. You deserve to be thoroughly loved, worshipped, used."

With that, he increased the pace of his thrusts. She cried out at the sudden change and the way her greedy pussy seemed to beg for more. Being used didn't fit with her idea of being loved or worshipped, but she wasn't going to argue. She didn't necessarily want to be worshipped, and she loved the way he was using her.

In moments, they climbed the sheer face of that rock. Delicious heat pooled like lava everywhere he touched her. "Ever, please let me come."

"Yes." He thrust in short, fast, hard motions, knocking her into flight.

The orgasm pounded her body, thumping between her legs in time to the sound of her heartbeat that echoed in her ears. She shouted half syllables, each word meaningless as soon as she abandoned it.

Several thrusts later, he followed. His entire body convulsed as his cry melded with hers. She felt the hot jets of his semen bathing her cervix. He thrust once more and collapsed on top of her, the whole idea of supporting his weight on his arms forgotten.

When she could, Mina wrapped her arms around his neck and held him close. She'd never felt so much a part of another person before. Ever had been right to hold off, to celebrate the sanctity of their first time together. Her first time having sex involved a level of love and care that left her exposed and vulnerable. In the safety of his arms, she could accept and embrace laying herself bare like this.

Limbs and bodies entwined, they trembled together.

Ever woke suddenly in the middle of the night. Cocooned safely in his arms, Mina didn't stir. His heart thundered as the weight of what he'd done settled over him. After months of waiting, he'd finally claimed Mina, body and soul. He didn't regret waiting. That had been necessary. He never wanted her to look back at their first time together with remorse.

But that wasn't the weight that crushed him now. He finally understood what his father had been trying to tell him: he'd lied to Mina. He'd made love to her without letting her know exactly what love meant to him. She'd consented to the act under a false notion that he'd nurtured by not correcting it.

At the moment when it had mattered the most, he'd betrayed her by not being honest. Perhaps she wouldn't regret their first time together, but he would never be able to treasure it. He had to make it up to her.

He had to be the man she thought he was.

The next day, after she'd returned home, he purchased a steamer trunk. He placed it in his bedroom, on the floor under the window. It was out of the way but still present in the room, a physical reminder of what needed to be done.

He still didn't think she was ready to hear the truth, and perhaps part of him was afraid he would lose her if he came clean too quickly. Until he could be utterly honest, he vowed not to dominate her again. No more bondage. No blindfolds. No insisting she ask before climaxing. He would do none of those things again without her permission—no, without her insistence.

He lined the bottom of the trunk with a blanket. The first layer consisted of canes and crops, implements he'd kept hidden in closets and drawers. Another blanket went in next, separating the floggers and ropes. Next he packed various dildos and vibrators into clean plastic bags. Lastly he added the restraints and blindfolds he'd been using on her.

At last he closed the lid, promising himself that it wasn't a final act. One day, he and Mina would open that trunk, and together, they'd explore the contents.

Chapter Six

Pale timber rose from the ground, stretching upward in a dizzying design that seemed both larger and smaller than it had on the plans. The rough frame for Everett's house was nearly complete. With a loan from his parents, he was making his dream come true ahead of schedule. Mina could make out the bones of the massive great room, and she could appreciate how it flowed into the dining area and kitchen.

It was vacant today, a barren structure that seemed to have been abandoned before it could reach its full potential. Much like her career aspirations.

In the distance, she could hear the sounds of men working on Wilder's house. It was a few days further along, courtesy of Ever's generous heart. They were using the same workers, and Ever had agreed to let them finish framing Wild's house first.

It amazed her how different the two houses would be. Wild had chosen an A-frame model that would feature a lot of wood and stone. Ever, with her blessing, had gone a more contemporary route. The house would be spacious but modern. No elk heads would ever grace the walls, not that they would at Wild's place either. Well, unless they were photographs. Wilder had an amazing skill with a camera.

Arms slipped around her waist. "It'll be finished next summer. Will that be enough time?" Ever strung a line of kisses along her neck.

She leaned into his embrace and closed her eyes to enjoy the tingles that shot down her spine. "Mmmm. Time for what?"

"Time for you to move in with me."

Those tingles turned a little cold. She couldn't afford even half of a place like this. She had no job and no fucking prospects for one.

Ever didn't seem to notice. He continued explaining. "I figure that would be enough time for your mother to be comfortable with us moving forward in our relationship. I want you to meet with the designer and start choosing the paint colors and furniture."

Mina wanted nothing more than to stay where they were in their relationship. It was a good place. They loved each other. They spent a lot of time together, even traveling for weekend getaways. They made love frequently. But they didn't talk about settling down or anything serious like that.

At times, though, it seemed like Ever was hiding something. After the first night he'd made love to her, things had altered. He no longer tied her up or blindfolded her when they played.

She couldn't complain about the quality of his lovemaking. He was sweet and generous, always making sure she had an orgasm. Sometimes when she was about to climax, she would catch him with a certain look on his face, as if he was fighting an internal battle. But the expression would disappear quickly. He'd do something incredible with his lips or his fingers or his dick, and she would forget everything but the way he made her feel.

Other times he seemed to want to say something to her, but he didn't. She didn't know why he was guarding his feelings, but since she was also hiding stuff from him, she didn't pry. If she did, then she might find herself explaining about things she'd rather not discuss. Like the concept of moving in with him.

"Okay." It was easier to agree than to explain why she didn't want to meet with a designer. Ever always demanded answers. He wanted to know how her job search was going, if she was looking at all, if she had decided against engineering, and why she refused to talk about her father.

He didn't interrogate her or push for responses. Instead, he peppered casual questions into other conversations. *You look lovely in that dress you made. You could be a fashion designer.* Behind every comment, she heard the underlying questions he never voiced, but that he must surely be thinking. *You graduated five months ago. Why aren't you employed?*

She inhaled deeply, letting the crispness of the early fall weather fill her lungs, and then she let it out slowly, trying to exhale away the stress.

Was he looking for a housewife? He'd never indicated what he wanted one way or the other. Knowing him, he would probably love it if she stayed at home to take care of his house and children. He'd come home every night to a hot meal, spend the evening talking or making love, and not worry about whether his laundry was clean.

"What's wrong?"

She should have expected the question. Ever seemed to spend all his free time studying her, analyzing her actions and reactions. She frequently felt self-conscious, though she knew he didn't intend to make her feel that way. It was just that when he focused on her with that laser-like intensity, she had the feeling he could see into her head and her heart.

"Nothing's wrong."

Convincing him of the truth of that statement would be nearly impossible. He was too perceptive.

"Mina, my love, you're getting tense, and you didn't answer my question."

"I said I'd meet with your designer."

Given the way his apartment looked, Mina had been under the impression that Ever had good taste in decor and furnishings. Then he'd blown her assumption to shreds when he'd laughingly told her that his mother and older sister had handled all those details.

"You didn't say whether you'd want to live here."

She had begun taking for granted that he wanted her to live there with him. Otherwise, why ask her to approve the blueprints and work with a designer?

"Is your hesitation related to your job search? Have you heard back from anybody?" He turned her to face him, and he held her captive with his penetrating green stare. His expression was gentle, inquisitive, and entirely too probing.

After applying for over one hundred jobs, she'd hit a wall. A week ago, she'd stopped sending out résumés. She shook her head, not wanting to talk about her failure. He'd only found out about her fruitless efforts at finding a job by accident. He'd shown up unexpectedly one afternoon when she'd been on the phone doing a long-distance interview with a company near Santa Monica that she really wanted to work for. They'd offered her a position, but not one that would enable her to stay in Vermont and work from home. She hadn't accepted, because it would take her three thousand miles from Ever.

She'd fibbed and told him she was waiting for a callback about a second interview. She'd refused to tell him the name or location of the company, but he was smart enough to know it wasn't local. He'd spent much of the evening frowning or lost in thought.

The last thing she needed was to let him think about that topic again. Not only would it just upset him; it was none of his business. She loved him desperately, and that scared the crap out of her. Her father had been controlling, and although Ever wasn't, she still had a hard time trusting him. She didn't want to end up stuck like her mother had been.

Rolling her eyes angrily, she broke his hold and headed toward his Jeep. She didn't really want to answer either question.

Ever followed, making his presence known as he reached around her for the door handle. He insisted on opening doors for her all the time. Her mother thought it was courteous.

Instead of opening her door, he caged her against the car. "That was exceptionally rude. I don't deserve to be treated like that."

"Then stop being so nosy. If I had news, I'd tell you." She pushed as much disgust and condescension into her tone as would fit.

"I'm not so sure about that. You're touchy about certain subjects. You keep me locked out, Mina, and I don't like the distance it puts between us."

Right then, she hit her limit for dealing with him. She tried to whirl, to face him head-on and make him back down, but he kept her locked in his cage, immobile. She braced her hands against his truck and pushed back as hard as she could. That move got her nowhere. "I'm not going to put up with this shit today."

"Mina." He growled the warning. "That's not fair. I asked you to move in with me. If that's not what you want, then you just need to say so."

As if he wouldn't push.

Actually, he probably wouldn't, and that realization deflated her ire. He wasn't the same man who'd bought her two baskets of flowers even after she'd told him not to. He wasn't the man who'd kissed her on the first date, turning her rules around so that he followed the letter of them instead of the spirit—and she'd loved it.

She missed that man. She'd fallen in love with him, and then he'd disappeared.

She elbowed him sharply in the ribs. From the way he exhaled, she knew she'd landed her blow in a prime spot. "I want to know what happened to you. I want to know why you've changed."

He stepped back, releasing her. She turned to find his gaze averted, his emerald eyes clouded with something that looked a lot like shame.

"I haven't changed."

Now that she had the upper hand, she wasn't going to let it go. "You have. There's at least one time every day when you look at me and you don't say what you're thinking. Sometimes when we talk or argue, you stop and weigh your words first. You used to just talk to me."

"Mina." It was a plea.

She'd never heard him sound so upset. Lifting her arms, she moved forward to comfort him, but he moved away. "Ever, don't be upset. I just... You used to tie me up and blindfold me, and...I miss that. I miss..."

She didn't miss everything. Some of the high-handed ways he'd handled her had been too reminiscent of her father. That was another taboo topic.

He stared at her, appraising her with a calculating look she hadn't seen in far too long. A shiver of apprehension ran through her. She hadn't realized how much she'd missed the thrill of not knowing what he was going to do, but knowing that she would come out of it writhing with pleasures she'd never imagined.

"You're saying you want me to tie you up and blindfold you?" For once, he stood totally still.

She nodded once. In the back of her mind, she congratulated herself for successfully changing the topic.

"And that you want me to stop censoring my thoughts and actions?"

"Yes." Well, that might not have been the absolute truth, but she wasn't going to qualify it right now. The timing was wrong.

"Then I have to tell you, Mina, that I'd like to know why you refused to answer my question. Do you want to move in with me when the house is finished or not?"

Her temper exploded, mostly because her tactic hadn't worked. "Damn it! Why do you have to be so pushy? Why can't you and your fucking one-track mind follow a simple conversation?"

He stepped closer, caging her against the car once again. "As I recall, you asked me to stop censoring my thoughts and actions."

She snorted and pounded on his chest with her fists. "Move it, you fucking Neanderthal."

A shutter dropped over his expression, rendering it stony and hard to read. "There are consequences for this kind of disrespect."

She shivered at his implication, but she didn't know whether it indicated nerves or anticipation. It had been so long since he'd behaved this way. He'd never spanked her. Part of her, the reckless part, wanted him to just do it. Perhaps it would break the power he had over her and she would be able to think clearly when he was around. Perhaps she could better evaluate the offer from the California company that wanted to send her a plane ticket.

But other than those first few times, he hadn't used that threat again. She had no idea what consequences he meant. Would he take her home and deny her the pleasure of his company? Would he break up with her?

He waited several long seconds, and she knew he was gauging her reaction. She didn't really have one. She wasn't afraid he would hurt her physically, and if he wanted to be childish, then she wasn't going to hang around for it.

When enough time had passed, and she didn't know how he decided on that, he opened the door and helped her up into his vehicle. They made it to his apartment. He locked the door, threw the mail he'd grabbed on the way up onto his dining room table, and regarded her with his hands on his hips.

"Strip."

Without bothering to see if she was going to comply, he snagged a dining room chair and dragged it into his bedroom. Curious, she followed him to see what he planned to do with it.

He kicked aside his clothes from the night before and placed the chair near the foot of his bed. Turning, he lifted his eyebrows expectantly. "Remove your clothes."

Used to him being more romantic, or at least kissing her first, Mina shrugged out of her shirt and shorts. Her panties and bra followed, landing in the heap he'd created when he'd pushed his clothes out of the middle of the floor.

He watched without revealing the level of interest he usually displayed. She could have been rearranging his throw pillows for all he cared. Once she finished, he spread his hand toward the chair. "Sit."

From the steamer trunk on the other side of the room, he extracted a length of rope. In less than five minutes, he had tied her to the chair, securing normal places like her wrists and ankles, but also wrapping it around her waist and shoulders. The coating on the wooden chair grew sticky against her back, and she couldn't lean forward to find a more comfortable position.

Her legs, of course, were spread, exposing her pussy the way he liked.

"No blindfold."

Since she had no idea what he planned, she had no idea if that was the consequence of rolling her eyes, calling him names, and elbowing him in the ribs. If so, she could live with that paltry punishment. While she liked being blindfolded, she was used to going without it.

"What's the safeword?" The tone he used sent a chill down her spine. She didn't know if he meant to be imposing, but the fun, easygoing lover she'd come to know had vanished. For the first time in months, Ever made her uneasy.

Not uneasy enough to forget the word he'd used before. "O-Oasis."

98

With that, he buried his face between her legs and worked his magic. Everything was forgotten as the tide of pleasure swept Mina away. He knew exactly how to touch her to drive her to the brink.

"Oh, Ever, yes. You have an incredible tongue. I love what you do to me." She moaned and murmured to him, knowing that he loved it when she vocalized her thoughts and feelings. She couldn't share her failings with him, but she could let him know how good he made her feel.

He mumbled something, but she only felt the hum against her pussy. It was all she needed.

"Please let me come." She didn't know why she asked, but he used to insist on this.

He lifted his face away and sat back on his heels. "No."

She thought he might resume his activities, but he made no move to do so. Instead, he held up something in his hand. It was a round red rubber ball with straps coming off either side.

Pressing it to her mouth, he said, "Open up."

She wanted to ask him what he was up to, but the moment she opened her mouth, he forced the ball between her lips. Shocked, she opened the rest of the way. He wedged it between her teeth and secured the straps behind her head. Now she couldn't say anything. Her protest was muffled.

He reached for her hand and arranged her thumb and forefinger into the shape of an O. "Safe signal, since you're gagged and all."

He grabbed his e-reader, opened it up, and flopped onto his bed, reading before he landed. Since he hadn't immobilized her head, she had no trouble turning it to see him. For several moments, she watched him, wondering at his game. She was tied to a chair with a gag in her mouth. Her pussy throbbed with need, and he ignored her.

This was not what she'd been asking for when she'd told him she missed being tied up. She tried to get his attention, but the gag pressed against her tongue. Any sounds originated in the back of her throat, so she screeched at him a few times. Nothing. He pretended he didn't hear her.

Her pussy cooled. She figured this was some kind of punishment, and she gave up trying to get his attention. Now she was pissed. Who the hell did he think he was, treating her this way?

After a time, he put his e-reader on his dresser and knelt in front of her. She expected him to remove her gag, but he only held up the largest vibrator she'd ever seen. They'd played with several different vibrators. Ever liked to run them all over her body, tease her before slipping his choice inside her.

This vibrator wasn't one they'd used before. The head was large and round, easily the size of a softball. There was no way in hell that thing was going to fit inside her. She struggled against her bonds, trying to warn him not to get that thing near her.

He took note of her panic. "There's no need to be afraid. I'm not going to hurt you."

That didn't exactly reassure her, but she calmed down enough to realize he knew it wouldn't fit. He pressed the bulbous head into her soft tissues and flicked a switch on the handle. Strong vibrations rocked her core, awakening the abandoned climax.

Her breath caught, and her moan remained partially lodged in her throat. When she was close, the vibrations morphed into a pulsing pattern that had a long rest between each burst. She threw her head back and whimpered with frustration. All this because she'd refused to answer his question?

For the next half hour, she watched his digital clock, vacillating between wanting to grovel and wanting to beat the hell out of him. Time and again, he drove her so close to orgasm only to stop just before she could climax. By the time he removed her gag, frustrated tears streamed down her face. He untied her arms and legs and shifted her to the bed before leaving the room.

He returned with a cool cloth, which he used to clean her juices from her pussy and thighs. Then he covered her with a soft sheet. She watched listlessly as he moved around the room, cleaning off the chair and clearing away the implements of torture he'd used on her.

Though it was only early evening, she was too tired to get up. She wanted to get dressed and go home, to leave his apartment so she could lick her wounds and analyze the complex emotions tearing through her with gale force.

He lay down on the bed, not touching but not letting her scoot away from him. "Well, Mina, what do you have to say for yourself?"

She stared at him with more than a little incredulity. "I can't believe you did that to me."

"Punishment is never fun. I much prefer to give you an orgasm than to deny you."

Sitting up, she pulled the blanket with her. "If you were upset about me rolling my eyes or calling you a Neanderthal or elbowing you, then you could have just said so." She conveniently omitted any mention of the big question he'd posed.

"I could have, but it wouldn't have changed your behavior."

"Ever, this isn't right. I don't like this at all." She was lying. She had liked it, and that scared her. For most of her life, she'd spent her time

100

trying to blend into the shadows, trying to avoid any kind of attention from men.

She was used to feeling certain things, not a whirlwind of confusion. That was what she didn't like. She wasn't sure she was supposed to let her boyfriend punish her for a disrespectful action. That was wrong. Wasn't it?

"I just wish you would have talked to me about it. Maybe asked why I did it or something."

He sat up and cocked his head to the side. "Why did you do it?"

"Because I...I..." She sputtered and stalled. Revealing her fears and failings wasn't something she wanted to do. "You keep asking about things I don't want to talk about."

"Why didn't you just tell me that?"

That was a perfectly good question. "Because I didn't want to hurt your feelings. You seem to open up to me very easily. You tell me everything that's on your mind, and I know you expect me to do the same. I can't do that."

"Not yet." He regarded her somberly, and she had no idea what kinds of thoughts were going through his head. "Sometimes the truth hurts, but in the long run, it's always the better course of action."

His eyes held such sadness that she slipped her arms around him. He pulled her close, holding her with his whole body.

She basked in his embrace for a little while. As he relaxed against her, she looked up at him. "Ever? Punishing me isn't going to change my behavior. You don't get to tell me what I can and can't do."

"No?" From the tone of his question, she didn't think he'd changed his stance on the issue.

"No."

"We'll see." Before she could argue, he pressed his finger to her lips. "Let's make dinner, honey. I'm hungry, and so are you. I won't press you to talk to me about things you don't want to talk about, but next time, just tell me it's too much, too soon. Okay?"

She didn't want to admit she was hiding anything, so agreeing to his proposal was out of the question. "We need to talk about how domineering you are."

Ever nodded. "I know, but now is not the time. You're upset. I'm not too happy with myself. We're both stubborn, and neither one of us is in the mood to be all that reasonable."

In the end, it seemed he got his way. She wasn't sure how she felt about that.

The next morning, Mina drove Ever and Wild to the airport. He could tell she was a little relieved to get rid of him. After last night's punishment fiasco, he needed some time to put his head on straight again. He knew he'd messed up. He knew he shouldn't have punished her. It was long past time they had an honest talk. In retrospect, he could see the wisdom of his father's advice. The stubborn part of him held the view that things would work out just fine. They'd both been upset last night, and that definitely wasn't the time to have the kind of discussion they needed to have.

Time apart would do them both some good, though part of Everett wondered if leaving before they had a chance to clear the air was the better course of action. He and Mina needed to have a tough conversation.

Wilder waited until their flight touched down in San Francisco before he questioned Everett's quietness. As the passengers around them scrambled to grab their carry-on bags, Wild folded his hands across his stomach and threw his query at Everett. "So what's going on with you and Mina?"

Ever shrugged and tried to stand, but Wild had the aisle seat, and he showed no signs of wanting to join the masses.

"Come on. Who do you think you're fooling? She might have given you a really nice good-bye kiss, but she practically pushed you onto the plane."

Outside the window, Ever spied trees with green leaves. The fall colors in Vermont were breathtakingly beautiful, but that season didn't seem to exist in Southern California. "I'm going to ask her to marry me."

"That's not a bad thing." Wild peered at him, his crystal eyes turning cloudy with confusion.

Mina had been a little abrupt with him, but he didn't think it was due to having received her first punishment. After they'd talked about it, she'd let the matter drop. They'd made dinner together, coordinating their culinary efforts flawlessly, and then he'd made love to her. Joining their bodies and hearts bonded them more every time they had sex. Since he knew he wouldn't be seeing her for a few days, he couldn't pass up the chance to make sure she knew exactly how much she meant to him.

Still, she had issues confiding in him. The element of complete trust hadn't quite developed between them, but they were making progress. The fact that she'd asked him to stop being so vanilla was telling. She was a true submissive, and she needed him to dominate her.

Getting engaged would prove to her that he was fully invested in their relationship. "No, but I think she suspects, and I think she's nervous about it."

"Why would she be nervous?"

Everett shrugged. "I'm not sure. I don't think her parents had the best relationship."

Wild chuckled. "They're divorced, so probably not."

It was more than that. She didn't talk about her father at all. "I think her dad was abusive. I'm not sure exactly how, but I think it's made her a little gun-shy. We're still working on building trust. I asked her to think about moving in with me when the house was finished."

That wasn't news to his brother. Wilder usually knew what he was thinking. None of his family had been surprised to learn that he'd changed the design of the house based on her preferences.

"And she said?"

She hadn't answered. Everett shrugged. "She didn't say yes, but she didn't say no either."

"Ahhh, I get it. She wasn't jazzed that you wanted to live together, so by proposing, you aim to show her that you're serious."

He knew Wild would understand. While he wasn't in a rush to get married, he recognized that Mina would be his bride someday. There was no reason not to start planning the inevitable event. The more he thought about having his ring on her finger, the better he liked the idea. "I love her. She might have some reservations, but I'm going to set all her fears to rest."

Wilder looked at him like he was nuts. "You're going to set her fear of having an abusive husband to rest by dominating her without her informed consent? That's not going to build trust. Ever, what the hell is wrong with you?"

Ever swatted his brother's arm. He didn't appreciate Wild's disparaging summation. "Get up, you asshole, before the flight attendants call security to carry us out."

Wild narrowed his eyes, his expression glacial, but he waited until they were at the baggage carousel before bringing it up again. "That's not why she was pushing you onto the tarmac."

"What?" Ever snagged Wilder's bag and kept an eye out for his own.

"If she suspects you're going to pop the question, she's not going to push you away. No, she's not happy with you. You had a fight?" Wilder snagged Ever's bag, and they exchanged suitcases.

He didn't want to discuss the mistake he'd made, but if anybody was going to understand, it was his brother. Everett matched his stride to Wilder's, and they headed for the bus that would take them to their rental car.

It wasn't until they were alone in the car that he answered Wilder's question. "She got mad at me, rolled her eyes, called me some names, elbowed me in the ribs. Hard. She hits damn hard."

"Awww. Do you have a little bruise?" Wilder cut off someone in the right lane in order to make their turn.

He did have a bruise. "Fuck you."

"Wimp."

They weren't going to get anywhere like this. Ever let it go. "I punished her."

Wilder was silent. Ever glanced over to find his brother navigating heavy traffic with his lips pressed together. Finally Wild exhaled a sigh. "I love you, man. You're my brother and my best friend, so please don't take this the wrong way. I've never seen you be so epically stupid. You've had months to talk to her, and you haven't done it yet. You can't punish your sub when she's not your sub. She's not submitting to you because she wants to. Right now she's accommodating you, trying to make you happy, and it's not working for her. And you can't punish someone who hasn't agreed to terms. We do this all the time for other people. What makes you think it works differently for you?"

"I've been vanilla with her for the past two months." As vanilla as he could be. His alpha nature was difficult to suppress, but he'd done it because he loved her. No matter what anyone said, Mina was different. She was special—delicate and deserving of adoration. He had to protect her, make sure she was ready to hear the truth about him.

Wilder snorted. "How's that working for you?"

"She asked me to go back to the way things were. She wants me to dominate her. She asked for bondage and sensory deprivation. I gave her what she asked for."

"Did she ask you to dominate her, or did she ask for a little bit of kinky play?"

"It's the same thing."

"Not to her, it isn't."

The bondage in which they'd engaged was very tame, especially by his brother's standards. However, he disagreed with Wilder's assessment. His brother was wrong. Mina wanted him to be her master.

104

She might not know the proper terms, but she felt an undeniable need to submit to him.

Ever didn't feel like arguing.

"I plan to tell her after I ask her to marry me."

Wilder didn't say anything, but the look he gave Ever spoke volumes.

Mina stared at the barren dirt in the flowerpot. In this crisp October weather, there was nothing to be done with it. She was supposed to be putting the hanging baskets in the storage shed so her mother could bring them out next year and plant new flowers.

But she was lost in thought, remembering the day Ever had purchased the pot. Flowers had flowed from it, hanging over the sides in a glorious shade of red. He'd asked her to dinner. She'd been nervous and excited to go on a date with a man who had the audacity to kiss her just because she'd agreed to see him.

He'd been gone for one whole day, and she didn't miss him. No, that was a lie. She missed the feel of his arms around her. She missed the way he smelled. She missed his laugh. She missed hearing his voice, though she'd let her phone go to voice mail when he had called to let her know he'd made it safely to California. She wanted to tell him she wasn't sure whether she was more angry or hurt at what he'd done to her, but she couldn't decide, and she couldn't figure out why she felt so betrayed.

She loved Everett Burke with her entire body and soul, yet she felt like she was stuck in a relationship that was going to suck the life from her. She'd asked him to tie her up during sex, and he'd done exactly that, only it hadn't been what she'd expected. A small part of her had hated the loss of control, but a tiny piece of her argued that he'd done it because he cared. He hadn't been callous or cruel. She'd called him domineering, and that was an apt description. She just couldn't figure out whether she could have a life with a man who nurtured that kind of tendency. It was all very confusing, because a larger part of her hadn't hated it one bit.

Speaking of life, she had promised to sleep at his apartment so that Jolo wouldn't be alone. She forced herself to finish this last gardening task, and then she packed a bag.

Jin Ae handed her a plastic storage bowl as she came into the kitchen to bid her mother good night. "Breakfast. You don't eat enough."

Mina smiled in a weak show of gratitude. She hadn't been very hungry today, a side effect of the emotional upheaval. "Ever left plenty of food for me."

He'd stocked up on her favorites before his trip, taking care of her even when he wasn't there.

In Ever's apartment, Jolo meowed loudly and wrapped her body around Mina's ankles. Mina dropped her bag in the entryway and scooped up the cat. They bumped foreheads. Jolo purred, though she did make it clear that she would prefer to be on Mina's shoulders.

Setting her on a window seat, Mina petted her. "No, Jolo. We've been over this. My shoulders are not wide enough for you. There's sliding and slipping, and then it ends with your claws in my back. I'm not into pain or injury."

Though Jolo's owner did seem to be causing Mina some pain and heartache. She didn't like that either. Ever was the first man for whom she'd had feelings. She'd never been in love before. This first disagreement weighed heavily on her. She wasn't proud of her behavior. She shouldn't have hit him like that. She'd seen the deep purple bruise when he'd showered that morning.

He'd always been careful not to leave bruises on her.

The idea of telling him that she was a loser who couldn't get a job made her feel ill.

Remembering the odd way he'd "punished" her also made her feel ill. What gave him the right to do that to her? Why hadn't she called the safeword or formed the safe signal? What if doing so meant their relationship was over?

For several hours, she wandered around his apartment. The television provided a soundtrack, though she barely listened to the home improvement show that featured the foibles of ordinary homeowners trying to renovate their own homes. To Mina it seemed like a cheap way to film a show, though she had to admit it was sometimes funny to see what kinds of stupid things people did.

She fired up her computer to see if any new job offers were on the horizon. The company in California that had offered her a plane ticket had contacted her again, this time with a proposal that promised more money.

Mina desperately wanted to accept the offer, but given how Ever wanted her to move in with him next spring, she couldn't seriously entertain that option. Still, she put off sending a refusal.

On a whim, she searched for Oasis. It was a band, a college, a dating service for people over fifty, a restaurant chain, and a clothing store, among other things. Too many options, so she narrowed her search by adding "Vermont" and "wishes."

One result came up over and over, so she clicked on it.

The home page was graced by a photograph of a naked woman bound to a chair with a thick rope. Her legs were open, though her pussy was turned away from the camera. In her mouth was a ball gag, similar to what Ever had used on her the night before. A man stood behind her, his hands cupping her breasts. Instruments of torture lay scattered on the floor around them. The model's eyes were widened in a combination of fear and ecstasy. The caption read *This slave is ready to please her master.*

Mina couldn't tear her eyes from the site, and when she found a sample questionnaire, she nearly had a heart attack. It asked questions about sex—oral, vaginal, and anal—that used words she'd never encountered. It asked about bondage and submission. As she read, she realized why she'd been so unsettled and confused about what Ever had done to her. He'd delivered a master's punishment for his slave without asking her permission or telling her what he was really doing.

All this time, he'd been a Dom treating her like a submissive slave. A slave—a role she'd promised herself she'd play for no man. Her life belonged to her, and she was not going to give anyone the power to trample all over her dreams. Flashes of Ever replayed in her memory. At the beginning of their relationship, he'd made her ask to have an orgasm. He'd controlled every aspect of their sex life, and she'd let him. Perhaps he hadn't been as dominating as the descriptions indicated, but he'd known damn well what he was doing, and he hadn't once asked her about it. She felt betrayed and used on the most basic level.

She wasn't going to stay here and make the same mistake her mother had made all those years ago. Everett's lies hurt. Pieces of her heart clenched painfully, but it was better to find out now, before she compounded the problem by moving in with him.

Picking up the phone, she called the California firm that wanted to hire her and made arrangements for a flight.

The entire display case sparkled. Ever bent down to get a closer look at the complex designs and the different configurations of gems. He huffed out a breath.

"How the hell am I supposed to pick from all these? She barely wears jewelry, and what she does wear is tasteful and understated." Mina's accessories accented her beauty. They didn't upstage it.

Wilder chuckled. He had yet to give the contents more than a casual glance. "Then look for something simple. She's marrying you, not the ring."

Behind the counter, the salesperson gave a dainty snort.

Ever eyed the woman, noting the high-quality cut of her power suit. He estimated her age to be somewhere in the early seventies. "You disagree?"

She favored him with a small, elegant smile. "The ring is a symbol of your relationship, but it's also a test. How well do you really know her? This ring will tell her what she means to you."

"She's petite, so I don't want anything too big. I'd like some rubies because she looks great in red." He thought for a minute, considering the changes she'd made in the design of the house. "It needs to be classic. Tasteful. Platinum. Symmetrical."

Wilder's lip curled, a precursor to a rare smile. "Symmetrical?"

"She likes balance. I wanted five bathrooms, but she insisted on four or six. Same thing with the burners on the stove. She moved the fireplace so that it was equidistant from either wall in the family room. She thinks like an OCD engineer." He wished she would talk about her job search. He knew she was looking, but she refused to apprise him of her progress. He wasn't stupid; there weren't many computer engineering jobs in Vermont.

His job at Oasis could be done from anywhere in the country, especially if they wanted to grow the business. If she would just talk to him, they could work out a different solution to their living situation. Perhaps the Vermont house would become their vacation and retirement residence.

But every time he brought up the topic, she became angry and withdrawn. The punishment had been an ill-advised, desperate attempt to break through to her. He just wanted her to trust him enough to let him in, to confide in him, to know that he would always be there for her, no matter where life took them. He hadn't accomplished that at all.

Just then, he spied the perfect ring. It had a good-sized rock in a nest of diamond and ruby chips. He knew immediately that she would love it. He made arrangements to have it inscribed and sized. It would be delivered to his apartment when it was ready.

On the way out, his cell rang. He grinned as he recognized Mina's ringtone, and he winked at Wilder. "Looks like the future Mrs. Everett Burke can't wait until tonight to talk to me."

She hadn't picked up the phone when he'd called the night before or earlier that day, so he had been a little worried.

Wild shook his head, but he smiled too, so Ever knew his brother was happy for him.

"Hey, gorgeous, what's up?"

She was silent for a second, almost as if she was surprised he'd answered. Then her words came out in a rush. "This isn't going to work out. I can't see you anymore."

The meaning didn't penetrate. A confused buzzing started in his ears. "What?"

"It's over. I'm sorry."

She was crying. He heard the hiccup of her sob, though she tried to mask it. "Honey, tell me what's wrong."

"It's all wrong. We don't belong together."

"Mina—" He tried to say more, but she'd ended the call. Immediately he redialed, but she didn't pick up.

Next to him, Wilder waited, his eyebrows pinched together in concern. "What's wrong?"

Ever shook his head. The buzzing in his ears grew louder, and the moment took on a surreal quality. "She broke up with me."

The shock on Wilder's face mirrored what Ever felt inside. "We'll get the next flight home."

Numbly, Ever nodded. He let Wilder handle the arrangements. They made it to town just before midnight and headed straight to Elmhurst. It was the location of their first date, and Isla had called Wilder to inform him that Mina was there with a man.

Rock music blared from speakers set up near the makeshift stage. A local band played their rendition of something he couldn't identify. It didn't matter anyway. Tables had been cleared away for dancing, and the floor was packed with bodies.

He zeroed in on them right away. His shock morphed to anger, tingeing the world in red. He plowed through the crowd, knocking people aside. Behind him, he dimly heard Wilder apologizing for him.

He slapped a hand on her date's shoulder, whirled the smaller man around, and punched him in the face. The man stumbled backward, falling against several people nearby. A huge circle opened up around them. Mina regarded him with wide eyes. Fear blazed from every line of her body.

He wrapped his hand around her wrist and pulled her closer. "You're coming home with me, and you're going to explain what the fuck is going on."

She tried to break his hold. Her eyes were even wider now, and her chest heaved with the force of her exertion. He'd never seen her look so terrified. Part of him wanted her to be afraid. She'd messed up badly, and she needed to know there were severe consequences for playing games like these.

Her mouth moved, forming words of protest that he ignored. Her date stepped between them and tried to break Everett's hold on Mina's arm. Ever tightened his grip, not caring if he left bruises, and punched the man squarely in the stomach with his other hand. The blow wasn't as forceful. The man bent forward and grunted, but he didn't give up.

"Let go of her."

Some words made it through the haze of rage fogging his mind, but they only pissed him off even more. Nobody told him how to handle his woman. Letting go of Mina, he cocked his arm to take another swing at her date, but Wilder hooked his arm through Everett's, halting him before he could get any forward momentum going.

Wilder's voice sounded in his ear. "It's not his fault, bro. You'd do the same thing to defend your date if some asshole showed up and tried to cart her away."

The words of wisdom did little to eradicate his anger. He looked at Mina, but she wouldn't return his gaze. "Mina, can't we talk about this?"

She shook her head. He tried to go for her again, but Wilder held him back.

"Let's go home, Ever. This wasn't the best idea we've had."

Micah appeared on his other side. His childhood buddy had recently joined him and Wild in working for Oasis. He was a little taller and bulkier than both Everett and Wilder, and he'd never lost a contest of physical strength against either brother.

Wordlessly, his brother and his friend escorted Everett into the cool night air. Isla and Eva, two other friends and Oasis employees, joined them.

Nobody asked questions, and he was grateful for that. He had a gaping hole where his heart had once been. He couldn't think straight. Her words and the image of her with another man's hands on her hips wouldn't stop replaying in his mind.

A small set of hands cupped his face, but they belonged to the wrong petite woman. Isla was ten years his senior. She'd worked for

Oasis since he was a teenager. At one point he'd harbored a small crush on her. Then he'd realized she was a Domme.

She gave him a sad, watery smile. "I have a lot of alcohol at my house. Let's get drunk and strategize."

Strategy proved to be pointless. By the next morning, Mina had moved, and her mother refused to say where she'd gone.

Chapter Seven

Mina's snug little car hugged the mountain curve tightly. The early-morning light filtered through the trees to glare briefly on her windshield. It reflected from the surface of the early snowfall, intensifying the brightness. She winced and felt in her purse, searching for her sunglasses. It was second nature to wear them at home in the California sun. Late November in Vermont didn't seem so bright by comparison, yet she felt the need to protect her eyes.

For the second time in six years, she'd come back to the little town where she'd grown up, this time to celebrate Thanksgiving with her mother. Because the warm weather in winter was such a novelty to her mother, Mina usually flew Jin Ae to Santa Monica for the holidays. She'd long ago given up trying to convince her mother to abandon Vermont. After floundering for a few years, her mother had finally integrated into the little town where she lived, and now she operated a popular breakfast café.

The café was closed this morning. Her mother had thought to get an early start on the main course this year. She'd begun cooking last night. Twenty minutes ago, she'd burst into Mina's room, hysterical because the turkey was burned and they were out of milk. To calm her, Mina had agreed to go buy another one. Only nothing was open in small-town Vermont. It wasn't like California with its abundance of stores that stayed open on all holidays.

The last time she'd visited home, which had been a little over a month ago, she'd brought her boyfriend, John. It was the first time she'd brought him with her to Vermont. He was a decent guy, and she wanted her mother's opinion before she consented to taking things to the next level. They'd dated for three years, and she'd moved in with him eighteen months ago.

Jin Ae hadn't been impressed, but she hadn't disliked him either. She'd merely shrugged. "You know I'm not the best judge of character were men are concerned."

And so she'd flown home with John and spent the intervening time rethinking the relationship. If she pretended that her mother's less-than-enthusiastic reception had played a part in her decision, she would be lying. The fault lay squarely at the feet of one Everett Burke, grade-A jerk.

As camouflage for his deviant personality, he was exceptionally handsome. Tall, about six feet, which meant he towered over her five-foot frame. Broad shoulders. Athletic. His defined muscles hadn't diminished now that he was turning thirty-one. When he had barreled into John on the dance floor, she'd known instantly that he was just as strong as he'd been when they'd dated, and every bit as ruthless as those photos and "toys" had indicated.

He'd met her gaze for one brief moment, an icy chill to those warm green depths, and then he'd glowered at John. Mina hadn't been terrified because they were in public and Ever's friends had been nearby. The last time Everett had been pissed off by her choice of companions, Wilder had dragged Everett away before Ever could break something on her companion's face. The poor man had only asked her to dance. Wanting to think about anything but Everett, she'd thrown herself into the arms of another man.

This latest incident had passed without anything further happening, mostly because she'd pulled John closer and made him leave.

John hadn't protested. He never went against anything she told him to do. Sometimes it was tiring to have to instruct him all the time. *Take out the trash. Stop rubbing my clit in that one spot; it's not a magic button. Call the satellite company because we're not getting a signal.*

Seeing Everett had made her reflect, with more than a little touch of bitterness, that she'd never had to tell him what to do. He'd unerringly found her erogenous zones because he'd taken the time to actually look for them. He'd watched her reactions to make sure she was enjoying his attention the way he wanted her to. In other areas, he wasn't the kind of man who took orders. He gave them. She could ask for things, sure. When she did, he tried everything in his power to make it happen. It might not always be in the manner she anticipated, but it was always wonderful.

Seeing Ever always made her long for a lover who could make her feel the incredible things he'd made her feel. He'd set the bar high well before the night he'd taken her virginity, before she knew what kind of man he was, and she had yet to find another man who could show her those heights again. Not even her vibrator, which was more competent than John, could mimic Ever's skill.

With a small twinge of guilt, Mina thought about all the times she'd closed her eyes and pretended that John was Ever. Since seeing him last month, even that had ceased to work. It only highlighted all the ways in which Ever had made her happy that never occurred to John to try. Sex wasn't the only area where John—all the men she'd dated, really—fell short. Ever was kind and thoughtful and intelligent. He had a wicked charm and a great sense of humor. He found her stubborn side amusing instead of exasperating.

His smile always made her heart beat faster, and she loved the way his lips frequently turned up in a half smile that always looked a bit mischievous.

The son of a bitch had been perfect in every way but one. She'd be damned if she'd settle for the kind of life her mother had.

Another flash of light through the evergreen forest had her digging deeper in her purse for those sunglasses. Her sense of touch turned up nothing. Glancing over, she saw where she'd gone wrong. She readjusted her aim and put her eyes back on the road. Only, the road wasn't where she'd left it. Her car skidded sideways. She steered into the skid, but it was too late. Something hit her passenger side door. She felt weightless for a moment, and then the world went black.

Everett slowed significantly to take the next curve. His common sense told him he probably didn't need to be that careful, but he couldn't help it. Nearly a year ago, his father had hit a patch of ice and lost control on this very stretch of highway. The road wasn't as slippery today as it had been when his father had last driven. Though they'd had some snowfall, the past few days had been sunny enough to keep the asphalt mostly dry. He kept a watchful eye for those occasional patches of black ice.

In the passenger seat next to him, Lydia glanced over, concern etched in her dark eyes, but she didn't say anything. His sister-in-law-to-be was a beautiful woman. She was short, and she had a curvy build his brother positively loved. Kindness always sparkled from her eyes, and that just made her even prettier.

"You drive like an old man." Trust Wilder to make the insensitive remark.

"This is where Dad went off the road, asshole."

Lydia turned to peer into the backseat, likely giving Wilder a warning look. "It's all right. We have plenty of time before we have to be at your mother's house."

"The food's going to get cold."

Everett caught the teasing in his brother's tone, but Lydia didn't. Wilder was trying to take his mind off the tragedy that had claimed the man both of them did their best to emulate. They'd both worshipped and loved their father, and both of them led their lives guided by the principles he'd modeled.

She frowned, the motion pulling all her features down. "It'll be fine. I packed the dishes in those insulated food carriers you got for me."

Normally, Everett would say something to fan the flames, because Wilder and Lydia were a lot of fun, but a flash on the side of the road caught his attention. It was near the same spot where his father's car had spun out, so he slowed even more and pulled over.

Lydia was indulgent on most days, but her sharp frown indicated she was nearing the end of her patience. "What's wrong?"

The low bank of snow on the shoulder was melting. Water ran over the road, though it had iced over in a few shady places. The sun glinted from the nearest bank, penetrating through his sunglasses. He shook his head. "I'm not sure."

Wilder leaned forward and put a hand on Everett's shoulder. "Ever, today is not the day to lose it. Marielle and Danica flew home for this. Mom needs us. This is her first Thanksgiving without Dad."

It was the first Thanksgiving without Dad for all of them. They'd all taken his sudden death very hard, but none of them had been as affected as their mother. She'd lost her husband, her best friend, and her master.

Everett pushed the release for his seat belt. "Just give me a minute to check it out." He opened the door and leaped from his Jeep before either of them could say anything more.

Dirt and rocks marred a section of the clean snow on the shoulder. They'd put up a guardrail since last winter, but it only covered the curve in the road. The tracks, fresh from the looks of them, began after the railing ended. He followed them to the edge and peered over the side. It was a short drop, only a few feet, but a car had gone off the road and hit a tree on the passenger side.

Ever jumped down, not caring about his dress shoes or pants, and hurried to the vehicle. The land sloped down after the drop, a gradual decline that nonetheless made the car impossible to see from the road. As he got closer, he noted the rental plates and stickers on the bumper. A form was bent over the steering wheel. Someone from out of town was in there.

"Wild! Someone's down here! Call for help!"

115

The driver's door had come open in the crash. He looked inside, ready to use his rudimentary medical skills. Slumped behind the wheel was the woman with whom he'd once thought he'd spend the rest of his life. Blood ran down her face, and her skin was far too pale. Her eyes were closed, and she wasn't moving or making a sound.

Reaching out, he touched her back. She made a quiet whimpering sound, the sweetest noise he'd ever heard. "Mina, honey, wake up. Can you talk to me?"

Her eyes fluttered open. She stared at him blankly, her pupils large and unfocused.

He pushed her hair away from her face to find the origin of the blood. "Tell me where you're hurt."

She tried to sit up. She made it a few inches before she tilted toward him. He reached out, steadying her without pulling her from the car. At least she was alone. He wasn't sure he'd try to help whatever son of a bitch she was seeing now.

"Don't move. Wild's calling for an ambulance."

"My head." She lifted a hand to the other side. It came away bloody.

"Let me see."

She turned her head, and he saw the gash on her forehead. "I feel like I'm going to throw up. I need to get up."

The pigheaded woman lurched from the car, stumbling and tripping into him. Mina generally did what she aimed to do. He caught her before she went too far, mostly by virtue of being in her way. She bent over and lost her breakfast on his shoes. Pivoting to stand behind her, he banded his arm around her chest, just under her shoulders, to hold her weight because he knew her legs weren't working properly.

She was in shock, and she probably had a concussion. As he held her, he was relieved to find no further damage. However, when she finished vomiting, she cried out.

"Mina?"

"I think I broke my arm."

"Which one?"

"Right one. I was reaching for my sunglasses, and the road moved."

That she could identify her right arm and that she remembered what happened prior to the accident were good signs. Still, he wasn't going to wait for an ambulance. It could take forty minutes to get here. By that time he could have her to Burlington General.

He took off his jacket and fashioned a sling for her arm, tying the sleeves around her neck to hold it in place.

Wilder called down from the road. "Ever! I have the police on the phone. How many people are down there?"

"One. Tell them we'll take her to the hospital."

Mina stared at him as if she'd never seen him before. Mindful of her hurt arm, he scooped her up and began navigating the incline.

"I can wait for the ambulance."

Anything to avoid being with him. Ever felt his temper flaring. Six years later, it shouldn't matter anymore. She'd abandoned him, relocating to the other side of the country to get away. She'd moved on with her life. He needed to do the same.

Just thinking about it made his blood pressure rise. He channeled that energy into climbing the steep part of the drop with her in his arms.

"Ever, put me down. I can walk."

"Are you insane?" He'd made it to the road.

Wilder regarded them with a stoic mask, though Everett knew his brother was both wary and concerned.

Everett looked down at Mina, assessing her injuries once again. "Stupid question. Why would you do anything that makes sense? You're in shock, so I'm going to disregard anything crazy you say."

Wilder gestured over his shoulder this thumb. "You sit in the back. I'll drive. We'll make it before she bleeds out."

He ignored Wild's dig and headed to his Jeep. Sliding into the backseat, he was careful not to jostle her too much.

"Do you need me back there?" Lydia stared with wide eyes at the cut on Mina's head. "Is there a first-aid kit in the back?"

Everett shook his head and put that on his shopping list. He'd get one for everybody. Perhaps Oasis should purchase them for all employees. His mother would support the expenditure. "We'll be okay. I promise not to throw her out the window. There are some napkins in the glove compartment."

Lydia handed those to him. Keeping Mina on his lap, he dabbed at the blood on her face and neck. Wilder turned the car around and headed for the freeway.

Mina sputtered, most likely objecting to the way he dismissed her concerns. She'd always walked the line with tolerating his high-handedness. "This is kidnapping."

She was trying his patience. He exhaled a long stream of air and struggled to remember she was hurt. "Yes. Picking up somebody who's just been in a car accident and taking her to the hospital definitely falls under that heading."

"Sometimes you're funny, but this isn't one of those times." She squirmed in his arms, fighting his hold.

He wasn't doing more than supporting her shoulders and providing a place for her to lean against as she sat on his lap. She pushed at him with her hurt arm. Blood drained from her already pale face, and she squeezed her almond-shaped eyes shut.

"See what happens when you lose your temper?" He did see the irony in his statement. Mina had always been far more patient than him, but she also kept her emotions to herself. Perhaps he did fly off the handle and yell rather easily, but at least he got his emotions out and moved on. Mina let things fester.

Where she was concerned, Everett also let things fester. She'd denied him a final fight, an argument, a discussion, a chance to talk some sense into her.

He took another deep breath and stowed his feelings. Mina buried her face in his shoulder and wrapped her unhurt hand around his wrist so tightly she was cutting off his circulation. He tried not to think about how good it felt to have her in his arms.

If she had been a stranger, he would have put her in the seat next to him. Except for his sudden masochistic streak, there was no reason to keep her in his lap.

He lifted his hand and stroked her hair. It was shorter now, falling just above her shoulders instead of halfway down her back. He liked her new look. She huffed out an uneven breath and loosened her grip on his wrist.

"I don't understand why you still care."

He'd never stopped caring. "Neither do I."

"I got blood all over your sweater." She released his wrist and ran her palm over his chest. "It's a nice sweater. You didn't have to take me to the hospital."

If she kept touching him like that, he wasn't going to be responsible for his actions. He captured her hand, kissed her palm, and then he set it on her thigh. "Shut up, Mina. We're fifteen minutes from the hospital. Just shut up for fifteen minutes."

His command, though rude, lacked heat. For the first time since she'd known him, he sounded defeated. Exhausted, she rested her cheek against his chest and closed her eyes.

The cold air roused her. She opened her eyes to find Ever setting her onto a gurney. A huge red-and-blue sign on the building read EMERGENCY. This was the point when they parted ways. Fine, sharp points of panic poked at her stomach and made it difficult to breathe.

Ever was talking to the nurses, but his words didn't make sense. His voice soothed her, and she was so afraid he'd leave. She clutched at him, and she cried out at the burning pain in her arm.

Hands pushed her back onto the gurney. Ever peered down at her, his bright eyes swimming in and out of focus.

"Don't leave me alone." She sounded desperate. She was desperate, but she didn't know why.

He held the hand that didn't hurt and brushed his thumb under her eye. "I'll stay until your mother gets here."

He straightened up and said something to Wilder and the attractive woman holding Wilder's hand. She recognized the woman from Elmhurst the month before. Mina had been dancing with John, and Ever had been crouched down with his arm around that woman's shoulders, having a private conversation with his mouth so close to her ear. It made Mina strangely happy to know the woman belonged to Wilder.

Then Wilder and the woman got into the car. The nurses wheeled her into the building and parked her in a curtained room. Ever stood off to the side as they shined lights into her eyes and probed her limbs for more damage.

She focused on Ever, on the strength emanating from him, and she felt her senses return to normal.

"You called my mother?"

"Lydia did."

Lydia must be the name of Wilder's girlfriend. "Can you thank her for me?"

"Yeah." He shoved his hand in his pocket and shifted uncomfortably.

"Thank you for bringing me here."

John would probably come with her mother, but she knew better than to mention it. When she'd wondered at the fact that he still cared, the flash of pain in his eyes had cut deep.

That was why she'd broken off their relationship over the phone. She'd told herself she was afraid of his temper, but she also knew she couldn't handle hurting him. If she'd faced his grief, she would have crumbled the second he asked how they could work it out. Ever was a big believer in working out problems. Mina was a big believer in running from them.

Yeah, she was a chicken. The nurses left, and Mina became a nervous chicken. They were alone, sort of. The curtains cut down the ambient noise and provided some privacy, but people were nearby.

"Thank you for staying with me." She disliked hospitals. A few times her father had beaten her mother to the point where she needed medical attention. It was never anything that couldn't be easily explained away—a kitchen accident, a fall down the stairs—but it seemed nobody ever noticed or cared that her mother was being mistreated.

"Stop." He approached the bed, firm resolve stamped in the harsh slant of his mouth. "We don't have to do this. Small talk isn't necessary. We don't have to pretend to be friends. I'm okay with sitting in silence."

Unable to face him and the shame she felt, she looked away. She couldn't go on second-guessing herself. Thanks to her move, she had the job she'd always wanted. She hadn't compromised her dreams or ended up with a man who had no compunction about hitting a woman.

She'd asked her mother once what she had seen in a man like Jong-Kyu Sung. Her mother had said he had been handsome and charming when they first met. He'd been exciting, and they had so much in common. She had given up her dreams and her dignity for him.

John was the all-around safer choice.

The curtain parted, and a nurse came inside. She beamed a smile at Mina as she hung a bag of saline on the IV stand. "I have you booked with X-ray for your arm, but the doctors want to run some tests on your head first. I'm going to take some blood and start an IV."

As she spoke, she extracted things from the containers on the shelf and put them on a nearby tray. Mina looked away from that side of her body. She could handle having blood taken and an IV tube put in, but she couldn't watch it.

Having to turn her head in that direction put Ever in her sight line. He leaned against the sturdy partition separating this room from the next. His dark slacks were rumpled. His soft sweater stretched across his shoulders and accented his firm chest. The pleasing shape of the shirt on his body didn't draw her attention away from the smears of blood that lent a macabre pattern to the solid design.

Dark drops stained his pants, and she'd thrown up on his shoes. Yet he didn't seem to notice any of it. Concern etched lines around his mouth and eyes, and his gaze didn't waver from her.

The nurse finished her tasks, assured Mina that her turn in radiology was close, and left.

She was alone with Ever for the long wait. Her head throbbed, but she was feeling better. She should tell him he didn't have to stay.

"If you send me the bill, I'll pay for having your clothes cleaned."

He blinked, staring at her as if her suggestion was preposterous.

It didn't take long for her to realize why he was looking at her that way. "You have to get over this whole 'not letting women pay for things' problem you have."

Something dark and dangerous glittered from his eyes, and the lines around his mouth turned harsh. "Even if I were so inclined, I don't have your address. It's one of those things you neglected to leave behind when you tossed me aside and fled the state."

He made her sound heartless, completely callous, and a little criminal. She huffed, and the move made her aware of some of the bruises forming on her chest. "I didn't toss you aside. You lied to me, Ever. Big, fat lies."

Pressing his lips together, he glared at the ceiling. Then he muttered under his breath. "I didn't lie to you."

"You're a Dom. The only way you could have failed to bring that up in five months is because you meant to keep it from me." Aches throbbed in her ribs and shoulder. She didn't want to fight with him when she could barely keep her wits about her.

She didn't want to fight with him at all.

"I might not have used that word, but I was pretty explicit about the kind of man I am. You didn't have a problem with it. You had a problem when I tried to go vanilla, so get off your high horse." He clenched his fists, but he didn't otherwise alter the casualness of his pose. "Damn it, Mina. It's been six years, and that's all you have to say to me?"

Shock coursed through her system, combining with whatever was already there. "What did you expect?"

He looked away, pushing off the wall and turning his back to her, but not before she saw the raw pain in his expression. The pain echoed in her heart.

"Nothing. I expect nothing from you."

She wanted to slip her arms around him, to soothe his pain and hers, but she lacked the strength to get out of bed. "Ever."

"You left, Mina. You left without talking to me, without yelling or screaming or giving me a chance to respond. I would have done anything to make you happy. Anything at all."

She had to strain to hear the low rumble of his voice. Silence ticked away the seconds. He took one step toward the curtain, and she panicked.

"I was afraid. I couldn't find a job here, and I knew you wouldn't leave. I knew you would talk me into giving up. And then finding out what you are...what you do... It was too much. I couldn't stay and let you destroy my dreams."

"Jesus, Mina." He took a ragged breath, but he didn't turn to face her. "It's a good thing you left. If you thought so poorly of me, then you didn't know me at all."

With that, he did the leaving. She didn't call him back. Her brain was too muddled to process everything he'd said.

Several hours later, after she'd broken up with John and sent her mother to drive him to the airport, she slept in her private room. She sported a short cast for her broken wrist, and bandages covered four stitches. They'd admitted her for observation, probably because she couldn't stop crying.

She wanted Ever to come back. She wanted him to hold her in his arms and tell her that everything would be okay, that he forgave her for the way she'd left.

In her fantasy, he explained his reasons for keeping such an important secret.

In reality, the soft knock on her door led to a visitor she hadn't expected. A petite lady stood at the threshold, her blonde hair swept up elegantly and her coat belted in a way that emphasized her slim waist.

"Macy?"

Mina hadn't seen Everett's mother in years. She'd once enjoyed an amiable relationship with the woman, and she knew her mother had maintained a close friendship with Macy Burke. However, she'd never anticipated having to face the mother of the man who still suffered from having been with her.

"Hello, Mina. I hear you've had a rough day."

Her mind raced, trying to figure out what Macy was doing there. She gave a weak smile. "Not one of my ten best."

Macy closed the door to the hall and pulled a chair to sit next to the bed. She switched on her tablet computer. "Darling, I know Everett hasn't been terribly forthcoming in regard to what we do at Oasis."

In point of fact, he'd never said a word. Mina shook her head, agreeing with Macy's statement.

"We are firm believers in happy endings, my dear. We make wishes come true. We help soul mates take steps that will lead them to spiritual harmony. Sometimes, when things go horribly wrong, they need an outside force to set everything right."

Mina stared at Macy. Perhaps she'd hit her head harder than she thought.

"Mina, you are a sweet submissive, delicate and charming. There's nothing wrong with letting a loving Dom take care of you. It doesn't make you less of a woman, and it doesn't take away your independence. Submission makes you stronger. After all, as a submissive, you call all the shots. The Doms have the harder job. They have to take care of us."

She smiled dreamily, though Mina didn't make the mistake of thinking that Macy had lost her marbles. The things she said made sense on a level Mina desperately wanted to understand. Everett had always taken care of her. Even today, he'd seen to her care when he could have left it up to the medical professionals.

Macy's expression turned sad. "My son found his soul mate years ago, but he failed to follow some really solid advice from his father and his brother, and he lost the only woman he was destined to love."

A knot of emotions squeezed Mina's insides. "Macy, Ever is finished with me. He doesn't want me back."

Macy's smile turned indulgent and the tiniest bit devious. "He might not be in a place to admit that, but that's a small hurdle. Let's start with your wish, darling. We have a lot of paperwork to get filled out, some permissions to be signed, things like that. It's going to take a few hours. You must not be shy with me. Ask questions about anything, and I'll give you my best answers."

The knot loosened, shaking free hope and a lingering reluctance to talk to this woman about intimate matters. She couldn't speak frankly to Macy Burke about her son. That would be far too awkward.

As if she could read Mina's mind, Macy stood. "I know. We're not there yet. But you must work with someone on staff. Isla is in the hall, waiting. She said I might need backup. I'll leave you two alone. Remember: be honest. It's the only way this can work."

Chapter Eight

Case 5-E

Give me two days to prove I can be Ever's submissive.

"No. Fuck no." Everett paced the length of his mother's office, shaking his head vehemently. He jabbed his finger in the air, pointing to the thick folder on Macy's desk. "Reject it. Throw it out."

She remained seated behind her large oak desk, her hands folded sedately in front of her. "Ever, darling, I'm not going to throw it out. It is within our power to make her dreams come true."

"At what cost?" He thundered the question and slammed his fist on the file folder. "I can't do this, Mom, and I can't let anybody else do it either."

Micah followed the volley of the conversation, wisely keeping his mouth shut. One of Ever's oldest friends, Micah had been there the night he'd confronted Mina while she was on a date with another man.

His temper had never ruffled his mother's feathers, or Micah's for that matter. He was mostly bluster and wind. She gazed at him through calm blue eyes, her expression firm. "Darling, you've spent six years torturing yourself over this woman. Don't you think it's time for some closure?"

Oasis didn't operate on the basis of looking for closure. His parents had built this business on the philosophy that sometimes people needed to set up the right circumstances to make a couple seize their chance at happiness.

"She's spent three years living with a guy." It killed him to think about her with anybody else. "Now she suddenly wants to give being submissive a try?"

A brilliant smile lit her face, an expression he hadn't seen too often in the year since his father's car accident. "Isn't that what you've been waiting for? You can't force someone to be submissive. They have to want it. The timing is finally right."

Weary, he sank into the chair next to Micah's. "I haven't forgiven her for what she did to me."

"I know." Macy came around the desk and perched on the arm of his chair. She put her arm around his shoulders. "But you weren't exactly in the right either, my stubborn, stubborn boy. You must get to know her all over again, have honest conversations about painful topics, and finally learn to communicate with each other."

He wanted nothing more, but Mina had run from him last time. "I couldn't survive losing her again."

Macy kissed him on the forehead. "We'll have to make sure that doesn't happen."

Ever didn't know how they were going to manage that, but he knew it all hinged on how he handled the details of her wish.

Macy patted his shoulder and went back to her desk. She scooped up the folder and held it out. "Micah, sweetheart, set this up."

Standing, Micah towered over Macy. He was a few inches taller than Ever. His shoulders were broader, and he boasted more muscle than anybody Ever knew, even Micah's younger brother, Jude.

Doubt clouded Micah's dark eyes. "Macy, are you completely sure about this? I know Ever wants another shot with her, but do we know why she's suddenly asking to spend time as a submissive? Didn't she get a concussion when her car went off the road?"

"Yes." Macy's smile grew. "Sometimes life smacks you hard to force you to see what's right in front of your face. Valentine's Day falls on a Monday this year. Start the wish the Friday before, and give it the weekend. Ever, darling, I found the perfect Valentine's gift for you two. I'm having it delivered to your house. I hope it shows up in time."

As he and Micah returned to their end of the building where the security offices were located, the thoughts zooming through Ever's head made him dizzy. Did Mina honestly know what she was getting into? She'd had plenty of time to research D/s relationships, but had she really? Underlining all that was dread. He knew they were in for one knock-down, drag-out argument. He hated arguing with Mina. She was as stubborn as the day was long, and he could only lock her in the stocks so many times.

"This was your wish." Micah's quiet observation brought him out of his head. They'd reached the hallway in front of their offices.

A couple years ago, his group of friends had made wishes. Eva's had come true almost immediately. Wilder's had happened just a few months ago. That left him, Micah, Jude, Isla, and Jessalyn.

Isla, the tiny blonde Domme who was also the oldest member of their group, poked her head into the hall and lifted one finely sculpted brow. "You accepted Mina's wish?"

Ever nodded. Now that it was on tap to happen, he couldn't seem to settle on an emotion. Wilder had been a mess from the time he found out about Lydia's wish until she took matters into her hands. Eva's romance had been fairly straightforward. One look at Pete and she'd never looked away.

"I want to have a play party that weekend." He glanced around at his dominant friends. "Tell Pete and Eva, Wilder and Lydia, Jude, Sara, Sydney, and Jessalyn. I want her to meet other submissives. They'll be able to give her insights I can't."

Micah's mouth twisted with an ironic smile. "And it reestablishes her with your group of friends. This time nobody will have to hide who they really are."

The times he'd brought Mina around before, he'd asked his friends to refrain from discussing dominance and submission. She'd been so naive where relationships and sex were concerned that he hadn't wanted to shock her.

"Yeah," he said. "I'm done handling her with kid gloves. She's going to get one hell of an education."

Isla pursed her lips. "Are you sure about this? Your friends are awfully protective of you, and I can't imagine everybody welcoming Mina with open arms. Not after what she's done to you."

They'd all seen the way he'd grieved her loss. But they were his friends. How could they be anything but sympathetic? If he wanted Mina, then they would support his efforts to win her back.

"Maybe not at first, but they'll warm up to her."

Micah and Isla exchanged glances and shrugged. Micah clapped his hand on Ever's shoulder. "If that's what you want, then I'll make it happen."

Chapter Nine

Ever spooned one more dollop of his creamy Greek yogurt over the bowl of fresh fruit. Mina would be down any moment now. He'd awakened her half an hour earlier by pushing her legs apart and satisfying the needs of his morning erection. She'd climaxed, though her pleasure hadn't been his goal.

He was a tad nervous, because as he'd shouted his release when he'd taken her in the middle of the night, he'd heard her softly spoken declaration of love. It should have warmed his heart, sent him soaring as it had the first time she'd told him that she loved him. But it didn't. Instead he was apprehensive. Part of him didn't believe she knew the difference between feelings of love and the euphoria of sexual release.

The fact that she was here, and that she'd agreed to the majority of his terms, was a testament to her good intentions. Still, he'd been burned by her once, and he was finding it difficult to trust her again.

He carried both bowls to the sunny breakfast nook nestled in a curved bank of windows on the far side of the kitchen. It was a modification Mina had suggested, a dreamy gleam in her eyes as she envisioned them sharing the first meal of the day. Since the house had been completed, he'd taken most of his meals there, fighting the thoughts of what could have been that assailed him.

She came through the kitchen, her bare feet treading silently along the patterned tile. He'd originally planned for hardwood, but she'd wanted tile. The February weather was cold, and he'd turned on the heated floor so his naked slave wouldn't get chilly. He spread a soft towel over the cushion on her chair. "Sit. Eat breakfast."

Hot coffee steamed next to the bowl of fruit. She inhaled deeply, and a satisfied smile settled on her lips. "Thank you, Master. You make the best coffee."

He waited until she was halfway through her meal before he asked a necessary question. "Tell me about last night. What worked for you, and what didn't?"

She froze, staring at the contents of her bowl. "I...I...I'm not sure."

Processing her first night as a submissive in one chunk might be overwhelming. Ever decided to help her. "We established that you have trouble masturbating. Was that your first time, or your first time with an audience?"

"My first time with somebody watching." She nearly whispered her response. Ruddy undertones rose to the surface of her cheeks and neck. It was sexy as hell.

"How did you feel about that?"

Though the blush stayed, it didn't spread. She stabbed at her fruit as she considered his question. Finally, she nodded. "It was hot. I think what I liked best was seeing your face, knowing that you were enjoying what I was doing. When you tied me up and wrapped me in plastic wrap, I think half of what got me off was watching you. I loved it when you came on me. I've had that fantasy for a long time now."

Her admission surprised Ever with what it revealed about her true need for submission. "Good," he said. "Because it will happen again."

She shifted in her seat, squeezing her legs together. It seemed talk of it turned her on.

"Spread your legs, slave. If I happen to drop my napkin, I want an eyeful when I reach down to pick it up." He grinned as he gave the order, loving the way her blush deepened.

"Yes, Master."

He heard the telltale slide of her flesh over the fluffy towel. "Good girl. Now, let's discuss your punishments."

She started. Though she sat across the table from him, it was a small affair. He lifted his foot and put it on the edge of the chair between her legs, knowing that the touchy subject would drive her to instinctively draw her legs together. They hit his foot and moved apart.

"Sorry, Master." She lowered her gaze demurely, waiting for him to accept.

"You were afraid of the spanking, yet you agreed to it. Even...before you left...the mention of it made the blood drain from your face. Why?"

She put her fork down and pushed her food away. The intense sorrow in her expression clutched at his heart. "My father used to beat my mother. Nobody knew about it, and I trust you to not tell anybody. She stayed with him until I went to college because she couldn't take the chance that I'd be alone with him. He didn't touch me, not even for a hug or anything, but she thought if she wasn't there to be his punching bag, then he'd take it out on me."

Ever felt sick. He dropped his fork into his bowl and reached across the table. She hesitated for a few seconds before giving her hand. "I'm so sorry, Mina. I never knew."

"Well, I never told you. I've never told anyone."

He felt the weight of her shame and fear. He wished she'd told him this all those years ago. Perhaps the wounds had been too fresh, too raw for her to confront. It explained so many things. "Thank you for telling me."

She nodded, a tiny movement that betrayed her fear.

"That explains why you've forbidden impact play, but it doesn't explain why you agreed to spanking as a punishment. It doesn't have to be a punishment, honey. It can actually be quite pleasurable. And as you learned last night, there are other ways to punish your transgressions."

The fear morphed to bafflement. "I don't see how spanking can ever feel good, and I know there are other ways to punish me. I still have nightmares about the time you tied me to a chair and wouldn't let me come. I thought a spanking would be quick and easy, and I was right about it being quick. I think it'll get easier as I get used to it. And if that whole forcing-me-to-orgasm thing was a punishment, it was very ineffective. I'd sign up for that ride again and again."

Ever struggled to keep a tight rein on the gamut of emotions her analysis produced. He noted forced orgasming wasn't a punishment, which worked fine for him. The gift his mother had purchased, a forced orgasm tower, had arrived the day before. He planned to use it.

But the part about her having nightmares... He'd considered that a light punishment. He hadn't even denied her a few hours later when he'd taken her to bed. He blinked. "Nightmares? Why?"

She removed her hand from his grip and looked away. "Too much, too soon."

He'd known punishing her had been a mistake, but he'd never realized the extent of the damage he'd done.

"I know I said I wouldn't push, but this is important. Nothing we do together should give you nightmares." He wanted to reach for her hand again, but he also didn't want to overwhelm her.

Vulnerable and lost, she stared at her breakfast. "I didn't understand how you could do something like that to someone you professed to love. Finding out the way I did only made it worse."

Ever chewed his lower lip, uncertain whether he should follow through with his plans for the weekend. "Mina, why are you really here? What do you hope to gain from this weekend?"

"Gain?" She echoed his word with a frown. "I'm not sure. I only know that I wanted to see if things could have worked out between us."

He picked at his napkin, unraveling the stitching bit by bit. He'd wondered the same thing himself. The years spent without her hadn't been bad, but they hadn't been great either. He'd dated, had relationships, but he'd never met anyone with whom he felt a connection that came close to the one he felt with Mina.

Carefully, he put a feeler out there. "Your wish expires tomorrow. Do you really think two days is enough time to know definitively whether or not it would have worked out?"

Her brow wrinkled as she considered his question. "I don't know. How different is this from the way things would be if I'd moved in with you?"

Ever shook his head. There was no way of knowing that for sure. "We would have negotiated terms, worked out the kinks. I've never lived with a submissive before. I didn't quite know what to expect."

He still didn't, but he wasn't going to reveal that to her.

"Would you keep me naked all the time?"

"Hell yes." He grinned to soften that blow. "Unless there was something specific I wanted you to wear or you negotiated terms for being dressed. I'd let you wear clothes when we had company, though you'd probably end up naked at a play party."

It was her turn to blink. "Play party? Like one of those parties where the Doms all play with each other's subs?"

"It depends on the limits each master, mistress, and submissive sets. For example, at tonight's party, I won't let anybody have sex with you. That's your limit and mine. I will, however, let some of them touch you. In those instances, it will be at my direction, and you will treat those hands as extensions of mine."

The color drained from her face. No doubt she was imagining who he'd invite to a play party. She was familiar with most of his friends already, though she would meet a few more tonight.

She attempted to speak, but nothing came out. He let her gather her wits, watching as she swallowed several times and strived to control her breathing.

"And so that means you would touch other subs?"

That wasn't the question he'd expected. If she'd objected to being touched by other people, he would have negotiated the details of that limit. However, she'd seemed to accept his terms, showing concern only that he would pay attention to other subs.

"Yes. Sometimes I help out with other people's scenes."

She sat silently, staring out the window. The vista before them was magnificent. The barren trees were draped with snow. In the window behind him, the mountain dropped away to reveal the green-and-white valley below.

"Mina? Does that bother you?"

The question seemed to bring her back to the present. "I don't know. It depends on whether you're throwing it in my face or..." She scrunched her brows together, and her eyes moved with the speed of her thoughts.

"Or?" he prompted.

She swallowed. "Is it wrong for me to want to be bound or kneeling by your side, not part of the scene, but not excluded?"

"Not at all. I encourage you to voice your wants and needs to me. Being a submissive doesn't mean you exist to serve me. As a Dom, I have an intrinsic desire to see to your needs."

Her breath caught. "You've said that before."

"Yes, and I meant it. Think back, Mina. Was there one time I didn't make every attempt to see to your needs? Even when you refused to confide in me, I tried my damnedest to make sure you were fulfilled and that you were happy."

She shook her head, agreeing with him, though he knew he'd failed her in the end. There was more she wasn't telling him, but it would come out in time. He couldn't force her to reveal everything until she was ready. Patience had never been his strong suit, but if he wanted a future with Mina, he had to dig deep.

He stood. "Put away the dishes, and tidy up the kitchen. When you're finished, go into the great room and kneel on the cushion in front of the fireplace."

Sounds traveled up the large, curved staircase leading down to the lower level. Mina knelt on the oversize throw pillow he'd left for her in front of the massive stone fireplace and listened, trying to discern what he might be doing down there.

She rested her bottom on her heels, keeping her back straight, knees wide, and arms clasped behind her back. She wasn't sure where she was supposed to face, but the stairs let out in the hallway near the kitchen, so she wouldn't be able to see him when he came up anyway.

She wasn't upset that he'd made her clean up the breakfast mess. He'd cooked the meal, and she'd cleaned up his kitchen before. She was a little on edge about the idea of a play party, and of other men being allowed to touch her. The old Everett would never have allowed anybody that liberty. She wondered how friendly he would get with the

131

other submissives at the party. Though she'd put on a good face earlier, the idea didn't sit too well with her.

Nearly twenty minutes had passed before she heard the quiet sounds of him coming up the stairs. He breezed into the room with a bundle in his arms. It was a cloth, which he unrolled onto an accent table next to an upholstered chair. He draped a towel over the seat and motioned her closer.

"Come sit. Keep your legs apart."

She sank into the plush upholstery, noting how much easier it was on her delicate bottom than her heels. At the last moment, she spread her knees until they were stopped by the arms of the chair. It was comfortable, but it seemed so unladylike.

Ever sat across from her on the sofa. He wedged himself in the corner and rested his arms along the back and side, easily dominating the space. "Attending a play party requires trust and negotiation. That wasn't in our original agreement. If you have an issue with it, now is the time to speak up."

She didn't want to voice her misgivings, but he'd asked. "I don't really know what happens at a play party. You said you wouldn't let anybody have sex with me, but you would let them touch me. I'd like to know who and how. Also, will I be naked?"

His gaze traveled slowly over her body. "No. I'll dress you appropriately, though you won't be wearing much. For tonight, you'll wear my collar, and that signifies anybody who wants to talk to you must have my permission. You should remain by my side with your eyes demurely lowered. If somebody speaks to you, you must look to me for permission to speak."

On the plus side, she didn't have to make small talk with anybody. On the negative side, he hadn't addressed her main concern. "I'm not sure how I feel about having other people touch me, even with your permission and supervision."

He nodded thoughtfully. "That's where this whole idea of trust comes in. If you're ever going to submit to me, then you need to trust me completely, in all ways."

Being here with him showed a hell of a lot of trust. "I trust you. I don't trust anybody else." She knew she could call that as a hard limit, but it wasn't a hard limit. It was a soft limit. An exceedingly soft limit.

"You're not required to trust anyone else. I'm responsible for you. That should be enough." His expression remained neutral, which she found surprising. Normally he was pretty reactive. She thought he'd at least scowl at her argument.

She had to press the issue. "So you'd let another Dom touch my pussy?"

"Perhaps. I might let a sub touch your pussy."

The idea of a woman's hands there made Mina shiver, but she wasn't sure whether it appealed to her. "Would you let them finger me?"

He shrugged. "It depends on whether I think you can take it."

"Isn't that the opposite of possessive?" This revelation didn't fit with her picture of him.

"You still couldn't come without my permission. I own your orgasms. I control your pleasure. That hasn't changed." He lifted the corner of his mouth in a crooked smile. "I can see you're very interested in this idea."

She shifted, and then she shifted back when she realized she'd altered the position he'd ordered her to assume. "I wouldn't like to see you finger another submissive."

He laughed, and she didn't see what was so amusing. When his humor died down, he nodded. "Do you have an objection to me holding the vibrator while her master flogs her?"

Mina scowled. "I'm not sure."

"Then it's something to think about." He wiggled his knee, showing a bit of impatience. That was the man she knew, always on the go. "Play with your pussy."

He'd warned her about this the night before, that he would expect her to masturbate by herself.

She wet the tip of her finger in her mouth and put it on her clit. Looking at Ever, she saw that she had his complete attention, and the swell in his jeans was growing. So she lifted one leg and slung it over the arm of the chair and pushed her hips forward to give him a better view of her pussy.

He grinned in approval. "That's it. Make it good for your master, and you might earn a reward."

She wasn't sure what constituted a reward, but she'd always been motivated by positive reinforcement. Tracing her finger around her clit, she tempted him with slow circles. The friction and his expression acted in concert to heat her passion. She rubbed and played, taking the time to get to know her pussy the way she'd discovered exactly how he liked his cock sucked.

Soon she was breathing hard. In the back of her mind, she knew he wasn't going to let her get off easily. He wanted a show, so she moved away from her clit and slipped two fingers inside her body. She'd never done this before. It felt different from when he did it. The

133

pressure of her fingers was less confident and firm. Though it generated an enjoyable sensation, she felt a little cheated. She preferred him.

"I want to watch you come." He gestured to the table next to her chair. "Use one of those."

She turned her head to peruse the selection arrayed on the cloth. Though she'd seen many of the toys in sex shops, she had no idea what some of them were. Vibrators, she understood. Ditto for clitoral stimulators. But she didn't know what to do with the ones that had extra arms and projections. Was she supposed to ride with a buddy?

Gingerly, she selected a vibrator that looked a lot like the one she had at home. Simple and powerful. She played it over her clit and around her labia before slipping it into her pussy. Closing her eyes, she gave herself over to the wonderful sensations. When she masturbated at home, she often imagined him watching her. There was no sweeter bliss than to have this fantasy come true.

"Open your eyes, honey. Look at me."

In her fantasies, he never interrupted with commands. He told her she was beautiful and sexy, but that was all. The order came as a bit of a shock, distracting her from her impending climax, but she welcomed the warm vibrancy of his voice.

She opened her eyes. He pinned her in place with the force of his gaze. She understood that she wasn't masturbating. Her hands and the vibrator were a proxy for his hands and his cock. He wasn't just watching; he was fucking her. That knowledge excited her even more.

"Master, please may I come?"

"You may."

Waves buffeted her, and she surrendered to them. To him.

A few moments later, he rose from the sofa and held a hand out to her. "Come downstairs with me. You can keep me company while I set up for the party."

She took his hand and followed him down the wide, curving stairs. The lower level contained the dungeon. Huge windows along one wall let sunlight stream through. She gaped at the spectacular view. It was so like what she'd seen the last time she'd been to the building site, the day Ever asked her to consider moving in with him. And then he'd punished her. She shivered in remembrance.

"The windows are reflective. If you're outside, you can't see in. At night, I have blackout curtains that we'll draw over them." He stood next to her, giving her a moment to take it all in.

The room was large. Last night when she'd arrived at his house, he'd led her downstairs immediately, but the lights hadn't been on, and the dungeon was in the other direction. This part at the back of the house consisted of one large living area. To the left and right, matching sectional sofas and accent tables created a stunning symmetry in the room. It struck a chord deep inside her and filled her with a sense of calm satisfaction.

At that moment, she realized he'd never fallen out of love with her. Perhaps he hadn't said the words, but he'd built the house the way she'd wanted and arranged the furniture in a way he knew she'd like.

Looking up at him, she didn't try to hide her emotions. She wanted to say so many things, but like always, her feelings jumbled up inside until she couldn't pick out the threads. One word came out. "Ever."

Releasing her hand, he enclosed her in his arms. "It's all right. You don't have to hide from me."

She basked in his scent and the feel of him surrounding her. She wore nothing at all, but she didn't feel exposed. She felt safe. "I don't want to hide from you."

He cupped the back of her head with his hand and urged her to face him. "In the next day and a half, I'm going to demand everything from you, Mina. You're going to give me things you never knew you could give, and you're going to understand, with every fiber of your being, what it means to belong to me."

Searching his eyes, she found comfort in his sincerity. The idea of submitting, of allowing another person to take over her body and soul, didn't terrify her the way it used to. His intentions were good, and he was dedicated to taking care of her. He always had been.

"I want to belong to you. I want you to show me how to give you the parts of me that I can't even give to myself." For so long, she'd kept her emotions buried. She'd never truly opened up to anybody, not even the only man she'd ever loved.

He inhaled sharply, and the weight of the moment settled on them both. "I need you to be honest. I need you to tell me if this is just a fantasy for you."

The threat of tears hovered behind her eyes, and emotion welled in her chest. "When I opened my eyes after the accident and saw you standing above me, I thought I'd died and all my wishes had come true. Later I realized I'd been shown a light, and I needed to take this chance."

The hand behind her neck squeezed, pulling her hair in a little warning. "Mina."

"No, Master. This isn't just a fantasy for me. I've been with my company for long enough that they'll let me work remotely. I want to know if we have a chance together."

He pressed his forehead to hers and clenched his fist in her hair. "So do I."

She smiled and offered her lips to him.

He availed himself of that offer, ravishing her mouth with his brand of love. "Tonight isn't going to be easy, love. I'm going to push you hard."

"I know." She needed to be pushed.

He nodded in the direction of a configuration of metal and padding. It looked like the outline of a box with a T sticking out of the top from two points. "Hop on that bench. We need to see if I have it sized correctly."

He led her closer. The contraption didn't make sense until he instructed her to place her elbows on one set of pads and her knees on the other. The T-shaped bar supported her abdomen, though she couldn't really rest her weight against it unless she wanted to feel it pressing into her tender tissues.

She supposed it could be used for spanking or flogging or any number of activities she'd forbidden. As Ever secured the metal brackets around her wrists, neck, and ankles, she realized he could stick a gag into her mouth and do anything to her he wanted, her limits be damned. But she knew he wouldn't. She trusted him to push her limits, not break through them.

When he made another circuit around her body, he wrapped the neoprene straps around her arms below the elbows and her legs below the knees. She was well and truly stuck into place.

"This is called a punishment bench, but I don't plan to punish you right now."

The neck collar forced her to hold her head up, which put his stomach squarely in front of her. He released the neck cuff, adjusted it down, and locked her in again. Now his cock was in the perfect position.

He bent over and smacked a kiss on her lips. "You look incredibly sexy right now, Mina. I could do so many things to you, including leave you here, bound tightly for no other reason than because I want to see you like this."

The idea caused a little thrill to run through her. If he enjoyed seeing her like this, then she wanted to remain here. "Yes, Master."

He straightened up, and she saw the swell of his cock against his jeans. She licked her lips in anticipation.

"And if I decide to put you here at the party, to allow my guests to witness this beauty, will you resist?"

She'd never been comfortable with being nude in front of anybody except for Ever. Would she allow Everett's friends—his brother among them—to see her naked and exposed? Yes, she would. "No, Master. If this is what you want, then it's what I want."

Ever froze, and she figured she'd surprised him with her answer. He disappeared from her view, but she knew exactly where he was as he walked the length of her body. He kept his hand on her, tracing a path over her shoulder and down her back. He plunged one finger, two at the most, into her pussy.

"If I finger you?" He curved his finger and hit her sweet spot. "Will you come for me?"

She didn't know if she could do that with everybody watching, though with Ever's skill, that might only be a matter of time. "Yes, Master." Her answer was breathy because his motions felt so good.

"If I licked you?"

He didn't lick her, but he did circle his thumb around her clit.

"Yes, Master. For you. Anything for you."

He withdrew his fingers and circled her anus, smearing her juices where nobody had ever touched her before. She flinched and tried to move away, but the restraints proved effective. "This bench has an arm that will hold a dildo or a vibrator. If I put a dildo on it and slid it into your virgin ass, would you stop me?"

Anal play was on her list of soft limits. She had no way of knowing whether she'd like it, so she'd put it firmly in the "you'll have to convince me" column. Right now, it didn't seem like she'd deny him anything. His finger circled the tight muscle guarding her back entrance, massaging it with light strokes. It felt foreign and strange, dark and forbidden. She wanted to be a little bit wicked.

"Would it hurt?"

"Only if I wanted."

That didn't provide the reassurance she sought. "Would you want it to hurt?"

She felt the tip of his finger press her hole, followed by the curious sensation of him sawing in and out. Slow tingles made their way up her spine.

"No, honey. I want to make you come, remember? With everybody watching, cheering you on, perhaps even offering to help."

He withdrew his finger from her ass, which was good because she was too startled by his newest revelation to keep herself relaxed.

"Help?" It took her three tries to get the question out. Even then it wasn't adequate enough to communicate everything she was asking.

"First answer my question, Mina. Would you let me fuck your ass in front of everybody until you had an orgasm?"

She trusted him, so the melting of her reluctance came naturally. "Yes, but—"

His cock filled her pussy, stemming the flow of her thoughts. He gripped her hips and thrust, fast and hard. Her orgasm hovered nearby, and she struggled to breathe through it. She knew he wasn't that close.

As soon as he dug his fingers into her flesh, she asked for permission to come. He denied her, and his semen bathed her insides. She barely managed to hold off until he withdrew from her body.

She shook with the force of unreleased tension. If he so much as breathed on her clit, she would shatter.

Luckily, he didn't feel the need to clean her up immediately. He came back around to her front, his jeans fastened and a wet wipe in his hand. He tossed the wipe toward a wire basket and made the shot. Mina swallowed a comment about it being due to luck rather than skill. He hadn't let her climax, and she very much needed to come.

He released the bracket around her neck first. By the time he'd completely untied her, the need to climax had receded, and she could trust her legs to hold her up. She stood next to the punishment bench, understanding that he could choose to punish her by withholding orgasm. Since she hadn't done anything wrong, she figured this was his way of keeping her horny and therefore submissive. Dependent on him.

"But what?"

She peered up at him, not understanding the question. It took her several seconds to realize she'd been about to put a condition on her consent to anal sex. "But I would prefer that my first time not be in front of an audience."

He gave her a crooked grin, but he nodded his acceptance.

"Also, what do you mean by saying that people would ask to help? Help how?" Sliding that extra question in there might be against protocol, but she didn't care.

Ever shrugged. "However I want. Whatever fits into your limits."

She hadn't specified terms for anybody other than him. Earlier he'd said that others would touch her, that she was to treat those hands as extensions of his, but could she really do that? She didn't want to let him down. He'd said he would push her limits, but she didn't know how much she could take. "I didn't answer questions with anybody but you in mind."

"Don't worry; we'll talk about that later. You and I will need to set up our betting cards for poker."

She wondered about that, but he was already pushing her toward another contraption. This one had a base large enough for her to stand on. He guided her into position and locked her ankles into place. A spreader bar was bolted into the base, making her stand with her legs slightly more than shoulder-width apart.

The long pole in back had metal brackets to lock her wrists behind her, and it had another that banded around her neck. Ever adjusted the heights until she was comfortably bound. Then he slipped a blindfold over her eyes.

"You're going to be here for a while, honey. For the entire time you're stuck here, you don't have to ask to come. You might also use this time to think about whether it matters who is holding the magic wand, especially when you can't see anything."

With that, she heard a clink and several popping sounds right in front of her. A motor whirred to life, and a huge, curved vibrator was nestled against her pussy. It stimulated the entire area, sending such powerful vibrations that she felt them inside as well.

"Ever?"

"Hmm?"

"Would you want to watch somebody else get me off?"

He brushed his lips over hers. "It depends on the circumstances. I told you: sometimes I like a little help from my friends." Then he deepened the kiss, massaging her mouth as he plunged his tongue inside. When it ended, he stepped away, taking the soft heat of his body with him. "Now, let's talk about some safety precautions. If you feel like you're losing consciousness at any time, call for me. I may not always be in the room, but I'll be within earshot. If you're being chafed and you need something adjusted, call for me. Do you understand?"

"Yes, Master."

She wanted to ask how long he planned to leave her like that, but she sensed he was gone. It didn't take long for the climax simmering just below the surface to bloom. Waves of pleasure shook through her body, urged on by the power of the vibrations between her legs.

It didn't stop. Ever didn't pause the machine to let her catch her breath. As a result, she didn't come down from her orgasm. The next one built immediately, breaking so hard that she cried out and tried to move her pussy away from the device. Her bindings held, and she wasn't able to do more than press her pussy slightly harder against the vibrator.

139

She longed for completion to hover just out of reach, for this contraption to hold her on the edge, but it didn't. Over and over, it forced her to climax. She lost control of everything as pleasure took over. He'd told her to think about something, but she couldn't remember what, and then she forgot how.

Tears streamed from her eyes, and she was sure she drooled more than she would ever admit. Her cunt dripped juices down her thighs, and her throat became raw from crying out.

She had no idea how many climaxes had taken her or how long he'd left her there when the vibrations stopped. Her pussy pulsed as if that little device were still pressed against her intimate tissues. The blindfold came off. As he released her neck, feet, and hands, she slowly opened her eyes, letting them acclimate to the brightness.

He helped her take one step forward so that she no longer stood on the platform. He pressed a glass of water to her lips and held it while she drank. "You may thank me."

"Thank you, Master."

"That was for the water." He smiled wickedly and set the glass down on a large round table in the center of the room that hadn't been there when he'd put her on the orgasm machine. Then he opened his jeans. "Now thank me for all those spectacular orgasms."

Understanding what he wanted, she dropped to her knees. Her body felt liquid, and it took strength of will to lift her arms. She grasped his shaft with both hands, giving it a gentle squeeze as she looped the thumb and forefinger of each hand around him. Then she moved her hands apart, pulling up with her right hand and pushing down with her left. When she made it to the tip, she gave him a little twist. With her left hand, she continued down until she found the indent marking his perineum.

He sucked in a ragged breath, and she hadn't even put her mouth on him. She pumped his shaft a few more times. By the time she closed her lips around his purpled head, he was close. It didn't take long before she felt the hot spurt of his ejaculate against the back of her throat.

She sat back, and he handed her a tissue. A fresh tear pricked behind her eye. She spit out his semen and smiled up at him. "You remembered."

"Yeah. I remembered." He touched her forehead. "You have one hour off to clean up and attend to personal matters. At the end of that time, I'll bring you the outfit I want you to wear, and we'll discuss what will and won't happen at the party tonight."

Chapter Ten

Ever stared at Mina and marveled at her calm demeanor. He'd handed her a menu of prizes for poker. She'd sat down with it on the sofa in his bedroom, wearing the lacy electric blue teddy he'd chosen. It was sheer everywhere except for her breasts and crotch. In the back, it was little more than a thong as it arched high on her delectable ass, so if she were to spread her legs, something was going to show.

Right now her legs were crossed. As she read, she kicked one foot. The speed varied, and he wondered at the correlation between her anxiety level and how furiously or slowly her foot moved. Her expression revealed nothing except that she was concentrating. Sometimes she pointed her toe or rotated her ankle. No matter what, she kept her legs firmly crossed, and he couldn't catch a glimpse of her pussy.

Watching her come so many times had been hell on his self-control, yet he'd managed to set up for the poker game and make a few appetizers. From the kitchen, he couldn't see her, but he could definitely hear her. Her siren's call of moans and orgasmic cries had done nothing to lessen the ache in his balls. The blowjob had dulled the edge, but the effects were diminishing now that he was back in her presence.

"You can ask questions."

She pursed her lips and frowned. "I understand that the chips are worth points instead of money and that you can redeem them for prizes, but how do you know where you can spend them? I mean, let's say I got enough chips to cash them in for oral sex. How do you go about choosing who is going to do the honors?"

This game had evolved over time. The problem Mina outlined was one of the first they faced. He handed her a stack of chips. "I wrote your initials on these. Before anyone could cash these in to get one of your prizes, they would have to win them from you. If you collected enough chips from say, Jude, you would cash them in with him. But you also get to choose whether you want to give or receive."

He let that one sink in for several moments. Their rounds of Texas Hold'em began with light prizes, like a kiss, foot rub, or nail painting. They progressed to a second stage where players could win a light spanking, minor bondage, two minutes of having their face buried in a body part of their choice, nudity, or a full-body massage. The last round could include impact play, strict restraint, oral sex, mutual masturbation, or toy play. Participants offered the prizes they were comfortable giving, and refusals were always honored.

Mina studied the chips, which he'd already labeled for her, with a troubled expression on her face. "Ever—Master—would you really be comfortable with me offering something like that?"

He didn't make the mistake of confusing the events of a party game for a relationship. "These are my closest friends. I trust them more than anybody in the world. If that's what you want to offer, then I'm okay with it."

She stared at him, and he wished he could tell what she was thinking. After a long time, she looked away.

"Mina, don't hide from me. Now is the time to say what's on your mind."

"I don't want to offer that as a prize. Some of the other things... Until today, I'd never masturbated in front of another person. I'm just not sure I'd be willing to do any of the things on this last list."

Ever shrugged. "It's not a big deal. If you play, it's all voluntary. You can opt to spend the evening sitting at my feet and watching. Or you can play a round or two and sit out the ones you don't like. Not everybody will play the last round, and not everybody offers sex acts as prizes."

She gave him a wry smile. "I know, but I don't know how to tie anybody up or flog them, so sex is all I have."

"Not really. You can offer to clean a house, spend a day as a personal shopper, or debug a computer. Though I'll warn you that you're not the only one who'll offer that last one, and most of them require partial nudity. Sara offers housecleaning wearing a French maid's outfit and no underwear. Isla offers flogging lessons, so you could learn to flog somebody."

She lifted the blank menu card in her hand, flipping it over to look at each side. "How do you know who is offering what?"

"Everybody will bring their menu cards. You'll take them when they get here and photocopy them. I have a copier in my office."

Her chest expanded as she took a deep breath. "I'm curious enough to play. I guess we'll see how it goes."

Ever was also unsure how the evening would progress. Part of him questioned his wisdom in introducing her to the atmosphere at a play party on her second day as a submissive. He shoved away his reservations. Either she would rise to the occasion or she would prove she'd been right in fleeing from him six years ago.

"Stand up and turn around."

142

Mina set the game directions on the sofa beside her and followed his order. The darker blue of the hem curved upward to highlight each shapely cheek of her ass. He longed to imprint the outline of his hand on each one, but he had to accept the fact it would never happen. After what she'd revealed about her father, he couldn't justify using corporal punishment. If he wanted a life with her, he had to adjust the vision of his future he'd come to take for granted.

"Bend over and brace your hands on the cushion."

She did, and he let her remain that way for nearly a minute before he moved to stand behind her. He speculated at what thoughts ran through her head. Did she know how much he liked looking at her? Or perhaps she was trying to figure out what he was doing. He reached between her legs and released the delicate snaps holding the fabric together. She didn't flinch or quiver at the unexpected contact, but the string was drenched. Had the position or the conversation turned her on?

Either way, it eased the road for him to take what he wanted. He flipped the material up and opened his jeans. His cock had been begging for this the entire time they'd talked. He remembered when they were first together, the number of times she'd pleaded with him to take her. It had been a continual test of will to turn her down, but he couldn't justify taking her virginity just because they were both horny. He'd wanted more for her. He'd wanted it to be an act of love. The first time she'd popped a birth control pill in front of him, he'd nearly forgotten how to breathe.

With the memory of her passionate kisses and the feel of her soft body pressed to his, he slid his cock into her wetness. She widened her stance, bracing herself to take whatever he chose to dish out. He fucked her slowly, drawing out each stroke until she made tiny cries from the back of her throat.

Her body fit him so well, encasing him in satiny warmth. Electricity zinged up his spine, and love swelled his heart. He couldn't say the words just yet, but he couldn't keep from showing her how he felt.

"Do you want to come?" His voice came out in a growl, all he could manage in the face of the incredible feelings she generated in him.

"Yes please, Master," she whispered, her tone tight with passion.

"Then come for me, honey."

Her walls convulsed around him, sucking an orgasm that weakened his knees and paralyzed his vocal cords. He thrust twice more before twisting to fall on the sofa next to her. He grabbed her hips, taking her with him so that she ended up in his lap.

She leaned her head back against his shoulder, her chest heaving in time with his. After several long moments, she ran her palms down the sides of his thighs where his jeans had fallen as he'd taken her.

"Ever?"

It bothered him less and less that she forgot his title. She remembered it often enough, but when she dropped it, he knew she did so because she felt connected to him.

"Yeah?"

"I'm sorry."

The unexpected apology wrapped in a melancholy tone perked him up, and not in a good way. "Sorry?"

"Yes. I'm sorry I ran away. I should have stayed. I should have talked to you, given you a chance to explain why you treated me like a submissive without first asking if I wanted to be one."

That hit him like dual arrows in the head and chest, which made it impossible to think. She shifted, easing away from his softened cock. He tightened his grip on her hips, holding her in place. They needed to talk, badly.

The soft chime of his doorbell traveled through the house. Their first guests had arrived. A huge part of him wanted to ignore it, but another part of him argued that he needed time to think, to figure out how to atone for such a large sin. All those years ago, he'd stubbornly clung to the idea he knew what was best for her. He'd resisted his father's warnings and faced the man's disapproval because he'd been so convinced he had been right. But he hadn't.

He'd broken the first rule of being in a D/s relationship: open, honest communication. Mina didn't owe him an apology. He was the one who'd fucked up. He owed her more than a hasty reply.

"Clean yourself up," he said, his voice scratchy from all the feelings caught in his throat. "And meet me downstairs. You're playing hostess."

Mina pressed a cool cloth between her legs. He hadn't taken her hard, but the swelling hadn't quite gone down from the time she'd spent strapped to the pleasure tower. If this was life as a submissive, she might just quit her job and live as Ever's sex slave. Why had she run from this all those years ago?

Oh yeah, because she hadn't trusted him after she'd found out that he'd been lying to her. She hadn't known what she was running from, exactly, but she'd known what she was running to—a career, a future, a chance to gain some self-esteem, and the first taste of the freedom of self-reliance.

She'd grown up in her time away from Everett Burke, enough not to regret leaving, but that didn't mean she wasn't sorry for the way things had turned out. In the past six years, she'd become her own woman. She'd explored life, and she knew what she wanted—another chance with Ever. She'd run from fate once before; now she was ready to accept her destiny.

As she snapped the crotch of her teddy together, she studied the menu of options and decided what to put down on her card. She had some dirty little fantasies too, and this play party seemed like the perfect venue for exploring them.

She hadn't decided yet if she'd play the final round. The first round was dubbed "Playful" on the card. It seemed like a more intimate version of an icebreaker. She supposed for a tight-knit group of friends, it wouldn't be such a big deal. The second round upped the ante, so to speak. It was called "A Little Naughty." The final round, for which she did put down a couple of offerings, just in case she decided to play, went by the title "Down and Dirty."

When she put down that she'd be willing to give a handjob or engage in oral sex, part of her hoped somebody besides Ever would cash it in. She wanted to see his face as he watched her pleasure somebody else. The devious side of her really wanted to test the level of his possessiveness. And she wanted to see how close this group of friends truly was. After all, she'd known none of the submissives when she and Ever had first been together, and she'd only met Jude the one time.

An inquisitive trill captured her attention. Looking toward the door, she spied a tawny mass of fur. Ever's kitten had grown up. Until that moment, she hadn't remembered he had a cat. She crouched down and held out her hand. "Jolo?"

The cat bounded into the room, shaking loose a few excited vocalizations, and stopped just out of reach. She sat down and blinked. Her fur had grown long and thick, and it gleamed as though it had been brushed recently. Ever had always pampered the cat. It looked like he had spent at least some of the time he wasn't with her in grooming Jolo.

Mina took a step forward, careful to move slowly, and ran her fingertips over the soft fur on Jolo's head. The cat bumped her head up, demanding a more substantial show of affection. Mina obliged, murmuring nonsense syllables as she crouched down for a better angle. After a few minutes, Jolo fell to her side and presented her belly, purring madly the whole time.

"You're still in here." Ever's tone held a note of reproof. "Our guests are arriving. I need you downstairs by my side where you belong."

Mina stood, and Jolo let loose a trill of protest. "Sorry."

Ever smiled. "Are you talking to me or her?"

She gave him a sheepish grin. "Both?"

He scooped up Jolo and set her across his shoulders. She settled in and resumed purring. Then he snagged Mina's hand. His abrupt manner would have given her pause if she hadn't spied the amused curl of his lips that he tried to hide.

"Come on, ladies," he said. "Time to play some poker."

She watched, amazed at how comfortable Jolo looked perched on his shoulders. "I didn't realize you still had her."

He frowned, glancing at her as he led her down the hall to the stairs. "Why wouldn't I?"

Lots of things could happen, but she didn't want to list a bunch of depressing possibilities. "I just meant that I haven't seen her." It had only been a day, but the cat had never been the kind to hide from company.

"I don't let her in the playroom. She was in bed with us for a little while last night, but she took off when we woke up."

Mina had been sound asleep and hadn't noticed. When she'd awoken, she hadn't paid attention to anything but Ever. "She's still very sweet."

He squeezed her hand. "She's always liked you."

At the bottom of the stairs, Jolo leaped onto a table and sat down to groom herself. Voices came from the direction of the living room. Mina recognized Wilder's distinctive tone and Isla's answering laugh. Now that other people were present, she wasn't sure about wandering around in lacy lingerie.

Ever released her hand and gestured toward the kitchen. "Go help Lydia and Jessalyn bring the food downstairs. We'll start playing as soon as everybody gets here."

"Yes, Master." Mina hurried through the foyer, walking quickly past the opening that led into the living room where the group was gathered. Just a few hours ago, she'd masturbated there for the first time in front of another living soul.

146

In the kitchen, the layout of which she'd had significant input into, she found two women arranging finger foods onto trays. They both looked up when she came in.

"Hi." The pretty black woman smiled, revealing an even row of teeth in a way that didn't look very different from a growl. Her dark eyes shone with barely concealed distaste. "I'm Lydia. This is Jessalyn. You must be Mina."

Mina stopped, hovering several feet away. Lydia was Wilder's fiancée. According to the police account, she'd been the one who'd driven Mina to the hospital after the accident that had reunited Mina with Ever. Now that she was seeing her in person, Mina recognized her as the woman who'd been the focus of Ever's attention last fall when she'd brought John home to meet her mother for the first time. She'd wanted to leave the moment Ever had walked into Elmhurst, but John had wanted to stay for one more dance. Watching him speak to that table of women hadn't been pleasant. She'd spent the rest of the night wondering if Ever was seeing one of them.

Mina forced herself to give a polite smile. "I am. It's nice to meet you."

Just from the way she stood at the counter, Jessalyn seemed like one of those people with too much energy and not enough to keep her occupied. She shifted back and forth, her movements as loose as her long, dark hair and as leonine as the print on her corset. Either glad to witness Mina's discomfort or just happy to be there, she grinned, and it lit her entire face. "Wild said you'd be polite."

"He said standoffish." Lydia corrected her friend. "And she is. Look how far she's standing off."

Jessalyn snorted. "That's because you look like you're going to eat her. You know you have to get Wilder and Everett's permission first."

Heat rose up Mina's neck and parked in her cheeks. When she'd envisioned having oral sex with somebody besides Ever, she'd pictured other men, like Micah or Jude. She tried to stammer out a response even though she knew it would be inadequate. "I don't think Ever would go for something like that."

Both women laughed at her, openly delighting in the comment.

Lydia recovered first. "You must not know him very well, then."

"Yeah. No man is going to turn down the chance to see two women together, especially if they get to tie you up and make you do exactly what they say." Jessalyn picked up a tray and headed toward the door, still chuckling.

Lydia scooped up another and nodded to the last one. She attempted to rein in her smirk, but she wasn't too successful. "Grab that."

It was full of diced fruits and vegetables with two kinds of dip in the center. Mina picked up the heavy glass serving tray and lumbered after the women. She wasn't sure she liked either one of them. Not only had they both been comfortable in lingerie, and they'd both been very attractive, but they hadn't even given her a chance to prove herself.

She'd known that Ever's family and friends wouldn't be as forgiving as him, but she hadn't expected them to be so openly hostile. She took the tray downstairs and put it on a side table set up near the poker table. Somebody had already put out ice and drinks. Soda, water, some kind of dark beer, and wine were neatly arranged at one end of the table. Thank goodness there was wine. She might need a glass or two.

Jessalyn and Lydia fussed with the layout for a few minutes. Mina watched silently, waiting in the background instead of directing the action as a true hostess should. Once, this would have been her house, and she would have taken the lead in things like this. Now she was just another guest. Lydia had more right to the title of hostess than she did. As Wild's fiancée, she was practically family.

Mina shook away the melancholy. She could get through this. She could prove herself worthy of Ever, and she would gain acceptance in his circle of friends.

Pasting on her best smile, she clasped her hands together. "Is there more? This doesn't seem like enough to feed twelve people."

Lydia frowned. "You're right. Let's check the fridge down here."

Mina hadn't known Ever kept a refrigerator on the lower level. Again, she felt one step behind as Lydia took charge. She followed the woman through a door that led to a kitchenette, berating herself for not asking Ever to give her a tour of the house. This hadn't been part of the original design.

"Yep. Here's the rest." She glanced up, flashing a genuine smile at Mina. "Subs. How fitting."

Jessalyn came into the room, her musical laugher filling the smaller space. "Good one. Are they homemade? Everett makes the best sandwiches."

Though she'd been tied to the pleasure tower, she knew that Ever had spent a lot of time preparing food. She wished he'd ordered her to help him. Now that she was here as a submissive, she missed being a larger part of his life. "They are. Let's get them set out."

148

As they moved the massive array of submarine sandwiches, Mina decided to take a chance. It wasn't something she would normally do, but she was getting a little desperate. She knew this night was another test. If she couldn't fit in with this group, she had no chance of reviving her relationship with Ever.

"Lydia? Can I ask you a question?"

The taller woman lifted her shoulders in a gesture that invited the query but didn't encourage it.

"Do the Doms eat first? And do the submissives serve them?" In the past, Ever had always taken care of her, and they'd always dined together.

Lydia considered this, a faint frown marring her forehead. "Sometimes. It depends on who is calling the shots. Ever doesn't usually care to be waited on, but Sir likes it. It's your job to know what Ever wants and give it to him."

That was the problem; Mina didn't know what Ever wanted. This was another conversation they'd failed to have.

"Unattached Doms can order the unattached subs around." Jessalyn finished setting out the vegetable subs. "But they usually ask instead of order. We wouldn't refuse, but that's more a product of friendship and less a response to their dominance."

Grateful they'd both taken her question seriously, Mina nodded. "Thank you. I'll ask Ever what he prefers."

She wanted to ask Lydia if she always referred to Wilder as "Sir," but she didn't feel comfortable digging into the other woman's business. Yet. One day they would be friends.

Upstairs, the size of the gathering had swelled. She recognized Wilder, Micah, Isla, and Eva. Jude had filled out since she'd last seen him, but his strawberry-blond curls were easy to pick out. She filed into the room after Lydia and Jessalyn. Following Lydia's cue, she took her place kneeling at Ever's feet.

He glanced down at her, his brows lifted in an expression of mild surprise and pleasure. Wordlessly he stroked her hair, a reward for behaving appropriately. The conversation continued around them. Mina followed it the best she could, trying to fill in the pieces she'd missed while they'd been setting up the food.

The doorbell rang. Ever shifted to get up, but Wild held up his hand. "I'm closer."

When he returned, a petite woman trailed him. She wore a black bustier that left her midriff bare and a matching skirt that fell to midthigh. Her long blonde tresses fell down her back and over her shoulders. The cold had reddened her cheeks a little, giving her a healthy, slightly ethereal quality.

"Sara's here," Wilder announced.

"Late as always." Jude's comment hovered between fond and snide, an unexpected tone given his neutral expression.

"Bite me, O'Connor." Sara flashed a smile at everyone but Jude. He got daggers. "You were supposed to pick me up."

"I never said I'd pick you up." The heat in his icy glare dared her to argue.

Ever rose to his feet, interrupting what was turning into an uncomfortable moment. "We're glad you made it, Sara. It wouldn't be the same without you. Let's go over the rules before we head downstairs."

"Sounds like a great idea." Micah sat forward, his hands clasped loosely together and his elbows resting on his thighs. He frowned in Mina's direction. "I also think you should introduce your new submissive. Not everybody has met her yet."

Ever motioned for Mina to stand. She took her place by his side, a refuge in this sea of hostile strangers. Starting to his left, he made a circuit of the room, introducing her to everybody. None of them stepped forward to shake her hand or greet her. They merely nodded, most of them curtly, as Ever said their names. Pete was new to her, as were Sydney and Sara. She'd met Lydia and Jessalyn already, and she'd known Eva, Isla, and Micah from before. She'd expected a little more of an acknowledgment from Wilder, but he didn't do more than appraise her with a cool look.

Afterward, Ever went through the rules quickly, noting that anybody could refuse to redeem any prize. It seemed even the stated offerings were subject to approval. Mina understood it would be bad form to offer a prize and not follow through, though nobody vocalized that stipulation.

When he finished, Ever gestured toward the stairs leading to the lower level. "Go on down and start eating."

She waited for him to follow his guests, but as the room cleared out, he clasped her hand and pulled her closer. Though the air was warm, she welcomed the solid feel of physical contact and the surety of his scent.

He lowered his head to ensure the privacy of their conversation. "I'm sorry to put you in this position. This kind of tension wasn't meant to be part of your wish. I'll understand if you want to bow out for the night. We can begin again in the morning."

"They're your friends," she said, trying to keep a lightness to her tone that she didn't feel. "Of course they're going to be wary of me. You're still wary of me."

"No. I'm not. Not anymore."

His confession warmed her inside and out. This might be all she got from him, but she would take it for now. She lowered her gaze, submitting to him because she felt it in her soul.

"Mina, you and I need to talk."

The rawness of his tone sent her heart soaring. "I know."

"You don't have to go down there. I'll never require you to put yourself in such an uncomfortable position."

She heard so much more than what he was saying. "I want to be by your side, Master. Always."

He bit his lip as if he was holding back the urge to order her to her room. Finally he nodded. "I've got your back, honey. They're my friends, but I won't allow them to treat you badly, especially since it's my fault you left me in the first place. If you want out of the game at any time, just tell me. I'll take care of you."

She wasn't certain how much control he had over his friends, particularly when he wasn't in the room. Besides, she didn't want to have to rely on him to fight her battles. She'd broken his heart and left him. That was all they'd see until they knew her better. Only then would they acknowledge Everett's fault in the matter.

The thought behind his assurance made her feel better. She paused at the top of the stairs. "Did you still want me to copy everybody's preference cards?"

Eleven people squeezed in around the large card table. Ever willed his knee to stop wiggling back and forth before somebody noticed as he waited for Mina to join them in the basement. She wasn't taking too long, but Lydia had also gone upstairs on an errand for Wilder. After the frosty reception earlier, he didn't like the idea of her being exposed to his friends without him around. Mina was trying very hard to behave tonight. He wasn't sure she'd defend herself, not that she should have to do it in the first place. He'd put her in this situation. She needed protecting.

"You think she's going to take off again?" Wilder's soft question pulled Ever's mind away from worrying about Mina.

He scowled at his brother. "No."

Wild scowled back, mocking him. "It's not an unreasonable question."

Ever thought about her apology, how she'd revealed the real reason she'd run from him. He had messed up badly by not being upfront with her. She hadn't a clue what it meant to date a Dom, and he'd abdicated his responsibility to make sure she made an informed decision.

"It's my fault she ran the first time. I won't make the same mistake twice."

Wilder's frown turned real. "I told you to be honest with her. *Dad* told you to be honest with her."

Ever matched his brother's expression. He was all too aware of his mistakes. "It's a miracle she's here at all. Be nice to her. I can't lose her again."

Conversations around them were dying down as their friends began to sense a problem. Ever wanted to table the discussion, because he needed to talk this out with Mina first.

Wilder didn't seem to notice. His brother's eyes clouded over with concern. "You weren't the only one holding back. Twenty-four hours with her and you're ready to whip out that ring?"

He'd never returned the engagement ring he'd chosen for her. It sat in a drawer, nestled behind things he rarely touched. "Just trust me on this. I need you on my side."

A stack of papers appeared in front of him, and Mina took the seat he'd saved for her. She didn't lean toward him or try to interrupt his exchange with Wilder, and she didn't attempt to make eye contact with anyone else.

When he'd suggested a play party, he hadn't counted on the complication of never having fallen out of love with her. This was supposed to provide closure for him, prove she wasn't meant to be his submissive. Instead, it bothered him that she was the object of hostility. He wanted everyone to see in her what he saw—her kind, vulnerable heart; her sweet, giving nature; and her quick, intelligent mind.

He'd spent so many years setting them against her when he'd committed the graver sin, and now it was going to take a mountain to change their minds. He needed Wilder's help.

Wilder leaned back in his chair, slinging his arm out to the side so it rested along the back of Lydia's chair. He played his fingertips along her shoulder, but he kept his attention on Ever. At last he nodded, a promise of support. It was all Ever needed. Once Micah, Jude, and Isla figured out Wilder was going to give Mina a chance, they'd follow his lead.

The submissives in the group would be a tougher sell. Because they had all been properly trained, they wouldn't empathize with Mina's reasons for abandonment so easily, and they'd likely downplay the significance of Ever's responsibility in alienating her. Sometimes his friends gave him too much credit.

He reached across the small space separating them and closed his hand over hers. Though he'd made sure the temperature in the room was warm—submissives didn't wear much clothing in the first place, and the game would entail losing more of it—her skin was icy. Checking the temperature of her skin with an unhurried caress, he found her core warm. Only her hands were cold.

"Sydney, I believe you're dealing first." Wilder pushed a fresh deck of cards toward their friend. Like Mina, Sydney wore a blue teddy. Unlike Mina, Sydney also wore a skirt and a loose blouse.

Ever went into the kitchenette and made a mug of tea, which he placed in front of Mina. Even if she didn't drink it, the warmth of the ceramic would feel good on her hands.

Though she looked surprised, she smiled her thanks and inclined her head toward his cards. "It's your turn to ante up."

He had a three and a four, but they were both hearts, so that was something. He threw in the required amount of chips and turned to Mina. "Are you cold?"

She shook her head and curled her hands around the mug. "Just my hands, and you've taken care of them nicely."

"So, Mina, how long are you back in town?" Eva's smile was a cross between syrup and a poisoned apple.

Ever shot her a warning look, which Eva promptly ignored.

"A few days, maybe longer. Things are up in the air right now." Mina frowned at her cards, but she increased her bet.

"Really?" Jessalyn's gaze remained on her plate. She picked at the remnants of her sub and dropped a sliver of red pepper into her mouth. "What happened with that guy we saw you with at Elmhurst a few months ago? Wasn't he here with you when you got into your car accident?"

Ever remembered that night clearly. Lydia had been Wilder's submissive, but they had both been madly committed to keeping the romance out of their relationship. Isla had invited Lydia out to Elmhurst for karaoke and to get to know the other members of their group of friends. Mina had been there with her then-boyfriend.

Blood drained from Mina's face, leaving her looking a little sallow. She shifted uncomfortably, and he knew she wanted to move closer to him, to let him protect her, but she didn't want to risk his rejection.

Ever didn't lose his temper easily, and he was dangerously close to exploding. That was a topic he hadn't broached with Mina, though when he'd done the background check, Jude had found out Mina had ended her relationship with John Westerberg soon after the accident. Jessalyn had no right to bring that up. It was none of her business.

Wilder put his hand on Ever's shoulder, bringing him back into the moment. "She's with Everett now, so it doesn't matter."

Jessalyn threw her cards into the pile, folding her hand. Her green eyes darkened. "I think I speak for almost everyone when I say that it does matter."

Mina exhaled heavily. "Then you'll agree it's none of your business."

Ever stared at her, shocked and impressed that she'd said anything. She'd even managed to make the set-down sound polite.

"Yes," Wilder added. "It's between them. If Ever's satisfied with her apology and she's satisfied with his, then that's the end of it."

Jessalyn drew her brows together and leaned forward, but Isla put a restraining hand on her arm. It always amazed Ever at how submissives responded to a firm presence, whether or not attraction was present. It was part of what he loved about being a Dom.

"You know what?" Isla tossed her head, sending her long blonde hair back over one shoulder. "I have discovered that you can put pretty much any word in front of 'waffle' and it makes for a good curse."

Everybody stared at her in silence. Ever didn't know what the hell she was talking about, but he was grateful to her for derailing Jessalyn's destructive line of questioning.

Finally, Mina broke the quiet. "You mean like if somebody is giving you a hard time, you can call them a douche waffle?"

Jude inclined his head thoughtfully. "Pussy waffle."

"Dick waffle," Sara shot back. It appeared she hadn't forgiven Jude for not picking her up. Ever wasn't sure whether those two actually hated each other. Sometimes they seemed ten seconds from falling into bed together.

"Jizz waffle," Sydney added.

"Scrotum waffle," Eva supplied. Her husband, Pete, leaned back and tried to look at her cards. She pressed them to her breasts where her corset pushed them up. "Shithead waffle."

154

"Calling your Master names isn't in your best interest, my dear." Pete reached under her cards. From her yelp, Ever deduced that he also made it under her clothes to pinch her nipple.

"Ass waffle," Micah contributed with a nod, proud of his suggestion.

"Penis waffle." From the way Lydia smiled at Wilder, neither of them considered it a negative epithet.

Wilder leaned over and kissed her. "If you're lucky."

Her grin grew. "When you're around, I'm always lucky."

"I think 'biscuit' would work as well." Micah drummed his fingers on the table. "Ass biscuit. Yep. It works."

Jessalyn made a gagging sound. "That just sounds gross."

Ever caught Isla's eye from across the table and mouthed his thanks. She'd effectively diverted the topic away from Mina. Next to him, Mina visibly relaxed, and she made several more suggestions for creative curses.

Chapter Eleven

The end of the first round took Mina by surprise. While she hadn't done too badly, she'd lost almost a third of her chips. Many of them had been replaced by other people's chips. She wasn't sure whether it was a better strategy to bet her chips or the ones she'd won. In the end, she'd hoarded as many of her chips as possible. When Micah directed everybody to count up their winnings and figure out how they were going to spend their loot, uncertainty kicked in.

Mina studied the cards of those from whom she'd won enough to redeem her chips. All of a sudden she didn't have enough courage to demand a hand or foot massage from anybody. Though they'd all been nicer to her after Isla had changed the course of the conversation, she still wasn't certain about her place with this group.

She leaned close to Ever so that she could speak to him without being overheard. "Do we have to cash them in?"

"No. You can save them up for the next round." He brushed a kiss across her lips, taking some of her tension away with him.

Eva, another of the pretty blondes at the table, gave Mina a conspiratorial wink. "Are you saving up for a light spanking? We have a pretty adept crew here. Just don't pick Sydney. She's as much of a sadist as she is a masochist."

Her husband looked like he had spent his formative years in the Marines. Pete was tall and broad-shouldered, and he seemed menacing, even when he was studying his cards. He narrowed his eyes at Eva. "My dear, if you want a spanking, just ask. I'm always happy to oblige. Anytime, anywhere."

Eva turned a flirtatious smile to Pete, which Mina couldn't understand. He really didn't seem like the kind of man with whom one would flirt. Even his term of endearment had sounded harsh. "I'm saving up for a tit massage, and I'm not going to tell you from who."

Pete growled, and Mina drew back. Was that the kind of treatment she could come to expect from Ever?

"Come here." Ever tugged at her arm and issued his order in a stern tone.

Mina was uncertain she wanted to go anywhere, but she found herself obeying. She situated herself on his lap. He put his arms around her and held her against his chest.

156

"What's wrong?" He spoke into the curve of her neck, his hot breath fanning the sensitive skin there.

"Nothing."

"Liar. You look like you're about to run and hide. Does Pete scare you?"

"A little." She wasn't sure whether Pete scared her or if she found the idea of Ever behaving that way scary.

"You'll get used to him. Eva's a bratty sub. She likes to push him until he punishes her. It works for them." He rubbed his hand up and down her arm in a soothing pattern. "That kind of dynamic wouldn't work for us. I like that you're a sweet submissive."

Mina didn't consider herself particularly sweet, but she couldn't see goading Ever like that. She nodded her agreement.

Ever pushed a pile of chips from his stack to hers. "I want you to go sit on Pete's lap."

His volume was sufficiently loud that everybody heard. Eva lifted a brow, but she didn't appear otherwise concerned that Ever had just told Mina to go sit on her husband's lap.

Mina opened and closed her mouth, apprehension coursing through her veins. "That's not on my list."

"I know," he said. "But as your Master, I'm taking the liberty of putting it there. Do you have a problem with it, sub?"

She did have a problem with it, but she didn't see a way out of this that didn't include calling her safeword, which she perversely didn't want to do, or getting a spanking for disobeying him. She knew Ever had a good reason for giving that order. She shook her head. "Now?"

"Yes." He patted her knee and pushed her off his lap.

Mina trudged around the huge table, heading toward Pete. He pushed back his chair and held out his arm, inviting her closer. She glanced at Eva several times, wondering if Eva had an opinion on this development. In a cruel twist of fate, Eva also had a small stack of chips belonging to Mina.

She sat on Pete's lap, perching as close to the edge of his knees as she could without falling off.

Pete slung his arm around her and scooted her closer to his torso. His touch was surprisingly gentle. He grinned at her and winked. "Don't worry. I've had my shots."

"Shots?"

Eva laughed. "He's kidding." She pushed her stack of chips with Mina's initials on them toward Mina's pile. "I'll take a hand massage. I gave Master one hell of a handjob on the way over here."

She extended her hand, parking it on Mina's lap. Mina had only ever given her mother a hand massage before. Eva's fingers were long and slender, mirroring her build. Mina turned Eva's hand so that the palm faced upward, threaded her fingers through Eva's to stretch the tendons, and set to work on the fleshy parts first.

Eva closed her eyes and moaned. "Damn, that feels good."

After a few moments, the demands around the table picked up. The next thing she knew, shoulders, hands, and feet were being massaged. Some people moved to sit on the sofa in order to be more comfortable. Ever stood behind Sydney's chair, brushing her hair. He glanced over at Mina and winked. She thought she might feel jealous, but she didn't. For the first time that night, she felt like part of the group.

Mina relaxed on Pete's lap as she concentrated on Eva.

The perky blonde rolled her eyes in ecstasy and made a quiet, high-pitched noise in the back of her throat. "Damn, girl. You are seriously good at this."

"Yeah," Pete agreed. "She usually only makes those sounds for me."

Mina stiffened a little until she realized they were joking with her. She smiled up at Pete. "Maybe next time I'll have to put 'tit massage' down as one of my second-round offerings. We'll see what kinds of sounds she makes then."

From the look on Pete's face, he was already picturing it in his head.

"All right, everybody. We'll take a break and get some food. Round two begins in twenty minutes." Ever's announcement interrupted anything Pete might have said, and for that, Mina was glad. She wasn't adept at playful banter. Already she was out of her league with Pete and Eva.

Ever handed Sydney her brush and crossed over to where Mina was just getting up from Pete's lap. He scooped her up and kissed her hungrily. She melted into his embrace and opened to his questing tongue.

People flowed around them, heading to the food table, the bathroom, or over to where Ever had arranged the two L-shaped sofas so that they faced each other in a loose square. It ruined the symmetry of the room, but it allowed for the large card table to take up half the space.

When he released her, Mina buried her face in his neck. He played his fingers through her hair and down her spine.

"You okay?"

158

Reluctant to remove herself from him, she nodded.

He pulled her head back and searched her eyes, a slight frown marring his chin. "Really okay?"

"Yeah. You're right. Pete's not so bad, and Eva's pretty nice." She was glad Jessalyn hadn't chosen her for anything. The woman had lost badly, and she'd ended up giving more than one massage and painting Isla's toenails. It was karma biting her on the ass for being so hostile toward Mina. It made Mina feel a little better.

The second round had a more playful tone. Most of the group warmed up to Mina, especially since she proved herself to be a graceful loser. The cards had worked against her, and almost everybody had some of her chips. She hoped they'd been spread around thinly so that fewer people could cash them in for favors.

Ever eyed her tiny pile of chips. "You are not a good poker player."

It wasn't her first time. John had liked to have their friends over for games every now and again. She shrugged. "Sometimes lady luck is good to me, and sometimes she's a bitch. Hopefully I'll do better next round."

He lifted his brows. "You don't have to play it, you know. I'll understand if you want to bow out. It's probable that Wild and Lydia won't play. Pete and Eva won't either."

That was likely because Eva had been running off at the mouth, testing out the waffle and biscuit theories. In the last ten minutes alone, she'd called Pete a whore biscuit and a twat waffle. The way he'd growled at her when she'd called him a vagina waffle had cemented the certainty of her punishment.

Mina wondered whether he'd wait until they got home or if he'd do it in front of everybody. She thought back to the spanking Ever had given her and decided she didn't want to witness Eva's punishment. She would be mortified if Ever did that in front of an audience, and she would be mortified for Eva if Pete were to turn her over his knee right now.

"I don't see the harm," she said. "Perhaps you'll win enough of my chips to put me in a masturbation race."

He pursed his lips. "Or somebody else will."

There was no way she could win the race, no matter who cashed in that prize. However, she couldn't dismiss his concern. "I won't play if you don't want me to."

Ever shook his head, refusing to commit to a preference. "This is your decision. I just don't want you to feel pressured to do something you don't want to do."

She still had a lot to prove if she wanted to be accepted by his friends, and she needed their approval if she had any chance of a future with him. Besides, she was having fun. "I want to. It's been enjoyable so far."

Micah pushed a huge pile of chips into the center of the table, and he kept his hard gaze glued to Jessalyn. "Bondage for a round, babe. Let's see how well you play when you can't move."

Her eyes bugged out a little. Sara patted her hand. "Don't worry. I'll help you out."

Jessalyn swallowed, and for the first time that night, her entire demeanor mellowed. "You're doing the rigging?"

Micah grinned.

"Nothing uncomfortable. And I get to have one hand free so I can still play."

Micah rose from his chair and disappeared into the playroom. "Ever, I'm going to borrow some rope."

"Help yourself." Ever shuffled the piles of chips in front of him. Mina noticed he had a significant number of Sydney's and Sara's. He pushed them toward the center of the table. "Ladies, it's time to get naked."

Mina started, staring at Ever as if she'd never seen him. She wanted to demand an explanation, but she didn't think that would go over well. He ignored her.

Both of the women stood up. Sydney stripped away her teddy in two moves, revealed every inch of her curvy body. Mina watched, fascinated, as Sydney drank in the attention she garnered. Sara followed suit, though Mina noticed that she only seemed to be paying attention to Jude's reaction.

Pete shoved a pile forward containing chips from Lydia and Wilder. "Wilder spanks Lydia."

Jude played his chips next. "Sara, since you're already naked, I'm going to flog your breasts." He raised his voice to shout through the open door to the playroom. "Micah, grab a flogger."

Lydia went next. She had a huge pile in front of her, though Mina noted that she seemed to have more chips than had been there a few minutes beforehand. Wilder had fewer. She scooted them toward Mina. "You get a breast massage. Everett will do the honors or designate someone else."

Micah returned with a coil of thick rope. He tossed a flogger to his brother on the way. The corners of Sara's mouth turned down, and Mina's heart went out to the woman. Though if she hadn't wanted to be flogged, she probably shouldn't have put it down on her card.

Ever patted his knee. "Come on over here, honey. I promise I'll do a good job."

She tried to sit so that she was turned toward him as much as possible without straddling him, but he turned her so her back was against his chest. He pushed the straps holding her teddy on her shoulders down. The stretchy material didn't protest as he extracted her arms and folded down the top to expose her breasts.

"You know, Isla, it occurs to me that Eva is still wearing clothes." Ever made his casual observation in the same tone he might use to point out that the lines on the sides of a road had been repainted.

Isla shook her head. "We can't have that. No subs should remain clothed for the third round. It just seems wrong somehow. Unnatural."

She shoved a small pile forward. "This should do it. Eva, why don't you give your Master your clothes? I'm sure he can find a more fitting use for them."

Mina hadn't recalled Jessalyn or Lydia being told to expose themselves, but as she watched, Micah peeled away Jessalyn's corset and hose. Wilder placed a pile of towels in the center of the table. Mina hadn't noticed him leaving or returning.

One by one, the subs took towels and put them down on their seats. Micah began looping rope around Jessalyn, binding her at the ankles, knees, and waist first.

Ever's hands closed over her breasts, bringing his brand of sweet heat. Until then, Mina had forgotten that her breasts were exposed. Now that every submissive except Lydia was naked, she didn't feel so self-conscious.

He squashed her breasts against her chest until she sucked in a breath. It didn't hurt, but it did make her nipples pucker into hard little points. Then he moved his hands and began kneading the muscles around her breasts. It felt so good that Mina couldn't suppress a moan.

Next to them, Wilder had scooted his chair back. He directed Lydia to bend over his legs and brace her hands on the floor. Mina knew some people really liked this kind of thing, and for the life of her, she couldn't figure out why they would find it appealing enough to try in the first place.

Ever cupped his hands around her rib cage, rubbing there in a way that managed to be both relaxing and erotic. Her breasts felt swollen, and her pebbled nipples begged for attention.

Wilder flipped Lydia's skirt up and ran his palms over her bare, chocolate cheeks. He raised his hand, and Mina looked away. She wondered if his handprint would show up on her dark skin.

In the other direction, Micah had finished binding Jessalyn. Ropes covered much of her body, but her breasts bulged from between strands left deliberately wide enough to keep them exposed. As Mina watched, Isla rolled one nipple between her thumb and forefinger. Jessalyn whimpered as the Domme pulled and pinched.

Next to her, Sara sat in a chair, her hands tied behind it. Jude had turned her so that she faced outward, and Mina could only see the back of her. He swung the flogger, and she dropped her head back with a groan of pleasure. From Mina's vantage point, it appeared as if she had spread her legs as well. From the gleam in his eyes, Jude looked like he was enjoying the show.

A loud smack sounded from her other side. The sound of a spanking was louder and harsher than the soft swish of the flogger sailing through the air. Mina couldn't stop herself from looking back at Lydia.

Wilder didn't spank her quickly. He paused between each one and ran his palm over the area he'd just abused. Lydia moaned loudly. Sara made several short, high-pitched noises. Mina swung her head back and forth, barely aware of Ever's hands until she felt his fingers parting the lips of her pussy.

Her waist was still below the level of the table. Though this wasn't part of the prize, she didn't protest. Not only did she have trouble denying Ever anything he wanted, but she didn't think anybody was paying attention to her. Between Sara and Lydia, the demonstrations were turning pretty erotic.

Sara muttered something over and over that sounded like "please." Lydia thanked Wilder for each spank. She even lifted her ass for more. Though it was turned away, Mina swore that many of his blows landed on her pussy.

Between her legs, Ever eased two fingers into her vagina. He pumped them in and out, assuming a leisurely pace. Soon the noises in the room—pleas, moans, smacks, and slaps—melted together. Mina rested her head back against Ever's shoulder.

"Please, Master. Let me come."

Abruptly, everything in the room stopped. Ever withdrew his fingers and licked them clean. Wilder set Lydia on her seat, where she had already placed a towel. Jude turned Sara back to face the table, her reddened breasts bearing evidence of her payment.

"Beautiful," Pete said. He folded his hands on the table and nodded his approval. "Just enough to make them desperate. Will there be a third round?"

"I'm in. Who's dealing?" Mina looked around the room, but everyone seemed preoccupied.

On the other side of the table, Eva smiled. She had dealt the second round. She pushed the cards toward Mina. "Why don't you take a turn? I think Pete and I will sit this one out."

Pete got to his feet. "I'll sit. You won't be able to."

Ever shook his head. "Ten-minute break."

Upstairs, Mina took an ice cube from the freezer and put it in her mouth. She knew Ever had turned the heat up. She'd expected to be warm, not hot. Thanks to his extra-special massage, she was burning up. If he came into the room, bent her over the counter, and fucked her hard, she would be very happy.

Lydia came into the room instead. "We're about to get started. Generally, we stay downstairs until the party is over. And subs should always be available to their masters."

She turned to go, probably expecting Mina to follow her. Mina reached out and grabbed Lydia's arm. "Wait. I have to know. Does it hurt?"

Slowly, Lydia turned back. Her brows were drawn together, creased with confusion. "Does what hurt?"

"Your..." Mina looked in the general direction of Lydia's rear end.

"My ass? Pleasantly so. Hasn't Ever spanked you yet?" She cocked her head to one side.

Mina shook her head. "We don't do any of that. Just bondage and bossiness. He spanked me once for disobeying him. I don't understand how you could ever enjoy something like that." Yet Lydia had been obvious in her pleasure.

"Punishment is different. It's meant to hurt. What Wilder did was meant to feel good. If he'd just done it a few more times, I probably would have come." Lydia gave Mina a reassuring smile. "Don't knock it until you try it. Now come on before we both get into trouble. I didn't tell Wilder I was coming to look for you. If he thinks I'm masturbating, I won't get to come at all for a whole day."

Mina had gone longer than that between orgasms. She didn't see the big deal until she imagined being away from Ever for twenty-four hours. The idea caused a pain in her chest that hadn't subsided by the time they made it to the lower level.

Ever pulled out her chair and frowned. "What's wrong, honey? It's okay if you've changed your mind."

She kissed his cheek. "I haven't."

For this round, she'd cavalierly consented to oral sex, forced orgasm, and toy fucking. Part of her wondered if Ever would let anyone

163

besides him redeem these prizes. She wanted to go down on Ever in front of them all, proving at last that she belonged to him. At least that was the way it played out in her head.

In reality, the round went on for a very long time. A few hands in, she watched in awe as Pete loaded a naked Eva onto the extreme punishment bench. The tableau of the beautiful, bound submissive made her pussy clench in envy. It gave her an idea of what she had looked like when Ever had bound her onto the thing earlier.

Pete showed no signs of dropping his pants, even though his erection made a huge bulge in the front of his jeans. He secured the restraints and opened up a bag that had been sitting near the sliding door that led to the backyard. He pulled out a ball gag, which he promptly pressed to Eva's lips. She opened her mouth eagerly.

Ever tugged at her wrist. "You might not want to watch."

She realized she'd been holding up the game. After all, she was the dealer. "Sorry."

She tried to tune out what was going on behind her. It was difficult, especially when she heard Eva's muffled noises of protest and a soft whir. It wasn't the frantic-quick sound of a vibrator, more like the slow churning of a motor. After a little while, all she heard were quiet whimpers.

Somehow, she managed to win a good amount of chips. It might have had something to do with the distracted manner in which everybody else played the game. Because she couldn't turn around, Mina was in a position to catch the hurried tells that many of them forgot to hide.

While she hadn't won many of her chips back, she did have enough of other people's to ask for several prizes. She planned to use her winnings to get back at the Doms for stripping clothing away from the submissives. In particular, Mina thought Jude had been very cruel to Sara. The woman deserved some kind of reward for putting on such a good show.

Nobody made a move to cash in. Several stretched languidly. Mina scooted her first pile forward. Micah and Isla exchanged glances. Jessalyn lifted her brows. Lydia leaned closer, fascination parting her lips. Mina forced her face to remain neutral. With her being new to the group, this might be considered a bold move, but it was what the round was for, wasn't it? They didn't have to hold back because she was there. If things worked out with Ever, then she wasn't going anywhere, and they would need to get used to having her in the mix. "Oral sex. Jude licks Sara."

Jude started, and Sara's eyes widened. He sat forward. "Are you serious?"

If Sara protested, Mina would just say she had been kidding. Though Sara kept her gaze downcast, she appeared to be hiding a desperate bit of hope.

"Yes. I'm serious. Are you refusing? Ever said everything had to be consensual."

A muscle flexed in Jude's jaw, and his strawberry-blond goatee seemed to shimmer in the light. "I'm not refusing."

"Good." Mina pushed another pile forward. "And Sara will suck your cock."

Now Jude blanched. Had she gone too far? She was making her choices based on what they'd put on their menu cards. Mina looked to Ever to see what she should do, but he was no help. He appeared to be biting his lip in an attempt to hold back laughter.

"Unless she says no." Mina had to add that in. Sara had a right to refuse.

"I'm in," Sara mumbled.

The raspy sound of chips scraping across the table drew Mina's attention to her right. Lydia beamed as she sought to redeem her chips. "Micah and Ever will flog me, double Florentine style."

Mina didn't know what that was, but she was amazed Lydia would want to be flogged after she'd been spanked.

Ever looked to Wilder for permission. Micah did the same. Wilder shrugged. "She likes a heavy hand, which I'm sure you'll figure out before your arms fall off."

Eva was still strapped to that machine. Pete had attached some menacing clamps to her nipples. Weights dangled from the ends, pulling her skin taut. Mina shivered, but the expression of ecstasy and pain on Eva's face was more than a little amazing.

Pete flipped a switch, and the slow whir of the motor, which had become part of the background noise, ceased. Eva let out soft shouts of pain as he released her nipples. He massaged them, which seemed only to make her squirm and cry out more.

Jude shoved forward a small pile of chips. "Mina is bound and blindfolded, and everybody who chips in gets to fuck her with the toys on her list. Orgasm not guaranteed."

Shocked silence greeted his proposal. From the size of the stack in front of him, Jude didn't have enough to request all that. Mina looked to Ever for guidance.

Her master's sea-foam eyes glinted hard. "Nobody touches my sub without my permission. I'll put her on the pleasure tower. She'll endure it until you and Sara finish. Then you're even."

Jude set his jaw and glared at Ever. The tension in the room was so palpable most of the submissives around the table squirmed. For several long moments, Eva's whimpers were the only sounds.

"Bend her over the punishment bench. Choose the slimmest vibrator you have and set it to the slowest speed." Jude growled his counterproposal. His fists were clenched and on the table.

Ever scratched his chin, seemingly unaffected by his buddy's threatening pose. Finally he nodded, accepting Jude's amendment. Mina didn't understand what had happened. She only knew she'd crossed a line she hadn't known was there. She wanted to take it back, but now that Ever had spoken, not following through seemed like it wouldn't help the situation.

"Give me ten minutes to wash it down. We'll take a break." Ever stood. He took her hand and led her to the contraption that Eva had recently vacated. She scurried after him, trying to keep up with his longer stride.

"Ever?" She whispered, trying to keep the conversation between them. "Did I do something wrong?"

If he heard her, it wasn't evident in his bearing. He didn't respond as he wiped down the wicked-looking piece of equipment. It hadn't seemed so menacing earlier.

"Ever, please. I didn't mean to upset anybody. I thought they would like it."

He looked up from what he was doing. "I'm sure they will." The soft baritone of his voice sent shivers down her spine. He kept his voice as low as his tone. "Not that either of them will admit it. You called them out on whatever the hell is or isn't going on between them. You did what none of us have had the courage to do. You'll need that courage now, honey. Make me proud."

At least he wasn't angry with her. "Am I allowed to come?"

"If you can. Either way, I'll take care of you later." He guided her onto the bench. Then he bent down and secured her arms and legs. "I'm impressed, though taking on a Dom like that will never end well, even if your intentions are good."

She understood that to mean Jude had to save face. He didn't want to fulfill the terms of the bet, but he wouldn't step down. It would go against every macho standard he held dear.

Jude hadn't specified that she be tied down, so she figured the bondage was to satisfy Ever's need for control. He checked the restraints before locking the collar around her neck and placing a gag in her mouth. When he moved behind her, Jude took his place.

He leaned forward, appearing to check the lock on the collar. "If you think either Sara or I will thank you for this, you're wrong. And if you think Everett didn't set you up with this whole night, you are much too naive to last with him. He wanted to see you fail. He wanted to see you squirm, and you're definitely living down to his expectations."

She felt Ever probing the opening of her vagina, which had been wet earlier but had dried at Jude's harsh statement. Nothing Ever had said or done had hinted at the deep dislike apparent in Jude's tone and words. Did he still harbor a deep resentment of her? Doubts assailed her. When she'd told him that she loved him, he hadn't responded at all. Was this his revenge?

The pressure of Ever's fingers left, only to return with the wet glide of lubricating gel. Jude moved away, and Mina remained still, reeling too much to protest or call a halt to everything. A slim dildo penetrated her, but she felt nothing. The quiet sounds of a motor whirring to life barely registered in her consciousness. She noted the feel of the dildo sliding in and out of her, a violation she forced herself to endure.

Perhaps this was retribution for the way she'd run out on him, but she'd be damned if she'd give him the satisfaction of a reaction.

Chapter Twelve

Everett watched Mina's face for signs of distress or enjoyment, but he was unable to discern anything. As far as he could tell, she seemed to have accepted this as the consequence of betting and offering toy fucking as her prize.

Jude clasped his hand around Sara's wrist and led her into the playroom. He closed the door behind him. Normally Ever would object to anyone using the room without his permission, but these weren't normal circumstances.

He hadn't expected Mina to play that last round. The prizes were out of her realm of experience, things she would shyly give him if he asked, not things she would perform or endure in front of an audience.

He knew Isla, as she frequently did, had been ready to call an end by suggesting they move on to another activity. From the look in his eyes, Wilder had been seconds away from taking Lydia home, which would have prevented her from spending her chips. Jude might have tried to extract the promise of having his house cleaned from Sydney, but he wouldn't have forced the issue if she'd declined. Or Sydney would have traded that responsibility to Sara.

After four hours of eating and playing cards, Ever had truly expected his friends to start making their excuses. Mina had derailed all that by cashing in her bet. Knowing her, she'd picked up on the unresolved sexual tension between Sara and Jude, and she'd wanted to help them.

But Jude's relationship with Sara was complicated by a history neither of them was willing to share with the group. Though Ever had known Sara just as long as Jude—Ever had been the one to hire her—nobody knew exactly what had gone on the night she'd shaved stripes into his eyebrow. Since that time, the pair had vacillated between friendly and veiled hostility.

In response to Jude's disappearance, Micah raised one dark brow at Everett and Wilder. Both brothers shrugged. None of them were going to point out that all prizes were to be publicly awarded. Mina's back was to the playroom door, so she wouldn't know what was going on anyway.

Sydney stretched. Her long, dark hair fell back over her shoulders. Ever noticed that she'd put her clothes back on. Looking around, he observed that everyone had dressed.

With a loud yawn, Sydney said, "Look at the time. I need to get to bed. I have an early morning tomorrow."

Pete slapped Eva on the ass. She flinched and smiled. Stepping closer, he put his arms around her. "Yeah, us too. We have a late night ahead of us."

Ever let Wilder escort their friends to the door. Not only did he refuse to leave Mina; he wanted to make sure Sara was all right. He liked that his friends knew when to hit the road. While they were well within their rights to stay and see how everything turned out, he preferred that Mina face this with just him around.

He heard the door open and close several times. Though he knew Wilder and Lydia hadn't left, they didn't return to the basement.

Several minutes had passed. Ever didn't want Mina disciplined like this. He loved her spunky spirit. He stopped the machine and withdrew the dildo. She hadn't enjoyed it, but she hadn't seemed to be in any discomfort either. He found it excessive to keep her on there until Jude and Sara emerged from the playroom. He loosened the restraints and helped her off the bench.

"Are you sore?" He ran his palms over her shoulders and down her arms, trying to see where she was tight.

She shivered. "I'm cold."

Her skin did feel a lot cooler than it had before. The teddy she'd been wearing wouldn't be enough to replace the body heat she'd lost. He shrugged out of his shirt and gave it to her. "Put this on. I'll take you upstairs and help you get dressed."

She regarded his offering warily, but she took the shirt and pulled it over her head. "I can get dressed by myself."

"Mina." He didn't want to leave her side. A sixth sense warned him it could be disastrous. After what he'd made her endure, she had to be in a fragile place emotionally. He hadn't listened to this nagging feeling when he'd gone on that trip six years ago, and she'd ended their relationship. He'd be damned if he'd make the same mistake.

She lowered her gaze, but she seemed defeated instead of submissive. "I'm sorry, Master. I only meant I understand if you need to stay here for your guests."

He slid his arms around her body and held her against him. "Nothing is more important to me than you."

She shivered again, and he had the impression that she was fighting the urge to squirm out of his embrace.

"Honey? Talk to me. Tell me what's wrong. I'm sorry about tonight. I didn't see this coming. I'm very proud of you, though, for the graceful way you submitted." He smoothed her hair away from her face and kissed her temple.

She nodded, but she didn't say anything. He wanted to press her for details, but the playroom door opened, and Jude came out, leading a subdued Sara. Though she let him hold her hand, she kept her gaze fastened on the floor. Her hair was tousled, and her lips were swollen. If they'd gone in there and faked it, Everett wouldn't have called them on not following through with their end of the bet.

Mina might have, though.

Jude regarded him with an expression that was both critical and icy. His gaze flickered down to Mina and back up, dropping a few degrees in transit. "We will never speak of this."

Ever expected Mina to turn around and protest, but she didn't move. He hadn't expected his friend to be so angry. He wanted to say something to set everything right. "Jude, I—"

"Not. A. Word." Jude narrowed his eyes, turned on his heel, and hauled Sara after him.

Ever wanted to speak with Sara, to make sure she was all right. Like Mina, she appeared defeated. In the past, their games had always ended with everyone in high spirits. This time, everything had gone horribly sideways. He let Jude and Sara leave. Right now, Mina was his priority.

He led her around the room, shutting off the lights as they went. Cleanup could wait until the morning.

They made it as far as the living room. Wilder and Lydia awaited them. Lydia had changed into what passed for street clothes for her—a flattering blouse and a skirt. Ever had been hiking with the pair before, and he knew firsthand that Lydia's outdoor look was just as stylish.

Wilder's gaze lingered on Mina. Ever had no idea what thoughts were winging through his brother's mind, and he didn't want to know.

"I guess we'll see you guys later." He motioned toward the door.

Wilder didn't take the bait. "Ever, did Mina know we don't usually cash in our chips for sex acts the last round? That we put those offerings on the menus as jokes?"

While they did sometimes redeem prizes for bondage or housecleaning services, they had never gone beyond flogging or spanking when involving people with whom they weren't romantically connected. The offerings were as much dares as jokes. Perhaps they'd been too arrogant, and now Jude and Sara were chafing at having their collective bluffs called.

Ever shook his head. "I didn't think she would go that far. It was her first time, and she's quite shy. That was my fault. I should have forbade her from playing the last round."

Behind him, Mina seemed to shrink into herself. He couldn't let her feel guilty for playing the game the way the rules had been laid out.

"You have to admit, it needed to be done. Jude and Sara need to work out their issues." Maybe he sounded defensive. So what?

Wild stuck his hand in his pocket and nodded thoughtfully. "I know, but they would have taken it better coming from one of us."

"Sara is very open about her crush on Jude." Lydia stepped forward, abandoning her submissive role, something she frequently did.

Ever disagreed. "Not in front of him, she's not. It's something he doesn't acknowledge."

"I didn't know." Mina pulled her hand from his grip and folded her arms across her body. "I'm sorry. I didn't mean to upset anybody. I thought it was clear they both wanted to be together."

"They don't talk about it." Wilder stepped forward and placed his hands on Mina's shoulders. "I wish I could say it won't be a bumpy ride with those two for a long time, but I'd be lying. Neither of them is going to thank you for this."

Mina nodded and looked away. Ever wanted to take her in his arms and assure her everything was going to be all right, but he needed Wilder to leave first. She'd never liked having a private conversation in front of another person, even Wilder.

Wilder kissed her cheek, whispered something in her ear, and reached for Lydia's hand. Lydia squeezed Mina's hand, but she didn't say anything. The pair moved toward the door.

"Wait," Mina said. "Doesn't Ever owe you a flogging?"

Lydia gave a tolerant smile. "That's okay. Micah already left."

"But Ever and Wild can do it, can't they? It doesn't seem fair that I should ruin the night for everybody. You looked so excited when you asked for your prize." Mina ripped her gaze from Lydia and peered up at Ever with wide, pleading eyes.

He couldn't find the will to refuse her. "All right. Did you want to watch or wait upstairs?"

"It doesn't matter," Wilder interrupted. "We're going home. Maybe next time, if Lydia is a really good girl."

Mina's face fell. Ever crooked his finger under her chin and lifted her face, urging her to look at him. "Did you want to see a flogging?"

She blinked, surprised. "Yes. I want to understand why people like them."

He didn't know why she would be surprised, but like the rest of their issues, that discussion would have to wait for when they were alone. Facing Wilder, he lifted his brows with a silent question. His brother nodded.

"Pet, it looks like you're going to get your way after all. Come on downstairs. I'll get you set up." Wild led Lydia toward the stairs to the dungeon.

Ever swept Mina up in his arms and carried her upstairs. She squeaked and threw her arms around his neck. This was the Mina he'd loved and lost, back at long last. He liked it.

"I won't drop you."

"I know. You just surprised me, that's all."

He captured her lips in a searing kiss. He had every reason to believe things were going to be fine.

In the dungeon, Mina sat on the padded sawhorse with her feet dangling down either side. She had yet to experience this piece of equipment while she was naked, but she still knew its general purpose.

After instructing her to dress in something comfortable, Ever had left her alone in the bedroom. He hadn't told her to meet him in the basement, just that they'd be down there if she wanted to join them, leaving the door open for her to change her mind.

The idea of impact play had held a fascination for Mina ever since John had introduced her to that friend of a friend who, John had said, lived an alternative lifestyle. Mina originally thought that meant the man was gay. It turned out he was, but John had meant the man's leather collar and the fact that he was led around on a leash by his master.

Mina didn't want that kind of life, but meeting the pair had opened her eyes to a world she never imagined—a world that had shed an entirely new light on Everett Burke. She'd wanted to talk to him for years, to track him down and ask why he had never talked to her about the concepts of domination and submission.

Seeing him after her accident had cemented that determination in her head. Divine providence—in the forms of Macy and Isla—had intervened to tell her to take the chance, but after Jude's warning, she wasn't sure whether providence was on her side.

She wore a pair of sweatpants and Ever's shirt. He hadn't asked for it back. Judging by the way Wild had also shed his shirt, neither of them planned to stay fully clothed. Flogging had to be physically demanding work, so it stood to reason they anticipated working up a sweat.

Wilder bound Lydia to the same set of chains hanging from the ceiling that had held Mina captive in front of Ever only the day before. She was completely naked, revealing creamy, dark skin, a finely sculpted figure, and an enviable pair of breasts.

Wilder asked Lydia questions, murmuring in a low tone as he secured the bindings. From having been in that position, she figured he was making sure he wasn't tying her too tight.

The expression on Lydia's face captivated Mina's attention. She appeared excited and serene. Calm energy emanated from her, rendering her positively radiant.

Ever came to stand next to Mina. He touched her hand lightly. "If at any time you need to leave, just do it quietly. I'll understand, but I don't want anything to disturb Lydia's session."

Mina tore her gaze from Ever's future sister-in-law and gave him her full attention. "Have you done this before?"

He took a deep breath as he thought. "Not with Lydia. It's been a while since Wilder and I worked together. He's more into bondage. Lydia's the one who likes the impact play."

"What about you?" She had to know. While she might want to watch someone else go through this experience, she didn't know if she'd ever want to experience it herself.

Ever shrugged. "I don't mind. It doesn't turn me on unless the woman under the lash is mine. This is a favor, a show of friendship and a way to thank Wild and Lydia for their support tonight."

It hadn't escaped her notice that once Wilder had stopped regarding her as the enemy, so had the rest of the crew. She nodded. "How long will you flog her?"

"Wild thinks it'll take ten to fifteen minutes once we get going. We're going to warm her up first." He lifted his hand to caress her cheek.

"Warm her up?"

"Yeah. You can't just start flogging someone. You have to get the blood flowing, get her head in the right space. It can be a very earth-shattering experience if it's done correctly. If not, it's just a beating. There's nothing good about that." He pressed a kiss to her cheek and

173

crossed the room. Wild handed him a pair of floggers. He grasped the long, dark handles and swirled the falls around a few times.

Mina's placement put her well out of the reach of the falls but close enough to see. Ever and Wild put their heads together, exchanging a brief message. She remembered how good the brothers were at reading each other. It seemed time hadn't changed anything for them.

Wild stepped closer to Lydia. The woman was neither blindfolded nor gagged. Wilder started first. She sucked her breath in at the first lick of the flogger. He worked his way around her body, hitting her everywhere. The falls swished through the air, a soft noise Mina didn't expect, and landed on her body with a *thud*.

Mina was under the impression certain places on the body shouldn't be hit. She would have feared for Lydia's safety, but she trusted Ever and Wild too much to do anything but question her source.

The lights blazed brighter, and Mina realized Ever had turned on more of them. It made the red stripes on Lydia's darker skin easier to see. Ever edged closer, adding the sting of his floggers to the effort. After a while, Lydia stopped making those soft sounds.

As if choreographed, the pair danced in a routine that was phenomenal to see. Both men wielded the floggers as extension of themselves. The leather falls flew through the air in a pattern Mina couldn't quite make out. It was elegant and beautiful, and it moved too quickly. The brothers circled her body, subjecting her front and back to the same treatment. Lydia didn't act as if it hurt, but Mina couldn't see how it wouldn't. She truly didn't understand the sense of ecstasy shining from Lydia's face.

Ever's torso was covered in sweat—so was Wild's—and his muscles glistened in the glow of the bucket lights.

After a long time, Lydia's head fell forward. The motion of the falls slowed and stopped. Wilder wrapped his arms around Lydia, supporting her body as Ever released the restraints.

Wordlessly, Ever crossed to Mina, took her hand, and escorted her upstairs to his room. When the door was firmly shut behind them, Mina broke the spell. "Is she going to be okay?"

"Yeah." Ever sat down on an accent chair and removed his shoes. "She's in subspace. Wilder will bring her out slowly and make sure she's warm and comfortable. When she's ready, he'll take her home."

Wild lived a five-minute walk from Ever, though he'd driven tonight, probably becauseLydia hadn't been wearing much and the temperature had dropped down into the fifties.

174

Ever's earlier comment came back and made her think. She sat on the edge of the bed and drew her knees up, hugging them to her chest. "You want to do that to me."

Halfway to his closet with his shoes in hand, Ever paused. "Not unless that's what you want me to do to you." He turned slowly to face her, firmness marking the set of his lips. "But you have to really want it. No pretending because it's what you think I want, and no pressure from what you saw tonight. I did this because you wanted to see it."

There had been other reasons, but from his tone, she deduced this was the only one that mattered. Mina nodded her understanding.

"Get ready for bed, honey. It's been a long day." He headed into the bathroom. After a minute, she heard the shower running.

Much later, a noise woke her. She sat up, listening, but it didn't happen again. Next to her, Ever slept deeply. The day had been long and physically demanding. He'd fallen asleep as soon as he'd hit the mattress. She didn't want to wake him for a false alarm. Besides, she didn't have the impression they were in danger. The sound had likely been a pump kicking on or off. For all she knew, it was the water softener cycling through.

She settled back under the covers and closed her eyes. As time passed, she realized she wasn't going to fall back asleep. Too many thoughts raced through her mind, playing all the bad parts of her life like a cheesy horror movie.

She slid off the side of the bed and grabbed her sweats and his shirt. Then she crept out of the room, closing the door behind her. She slipped the shirt over her head as she tiptoed down the hall, but she paused at the top of the steps to get into her bottoms.

The kitchen wasn't all that messy. She would clean it up, but he'd instructed her to wait until the morning. So she climbed up on the counter and got a cup from the cupboard. When Ever had been formulating his plan for the kitchen, he'd mentioned keeping step stools around. If he had them, they weren't stored in the open, and she wasn't about to go digging in his closets. In all likelihood, this would be her last night in his house.

She ran water from the faucet into the glass. The coolness of the liquid as it slid down her throat served to wake her up completely. She poured the rest into a mug and put it in the microwave. The buttons beeped as she pushed them, and Ever's tired smile greeted her as she turned to find the sugar and tea.

He leaned against the door frame and ran his fingers through his hair, leaving it even more tousled. The look brought back sweet memories, and her heart beat a little faster.

"Do you want to talk about it?" His demeanor might indicate lethargy, but his tone made the question seem more like a command.

She didn't want to talk about it. She wanted to go for a long walk or meditate. She wanted to sit at her desk in California and mourn what could have been. But none of those things would get her what she wanted. Six years ago, she had let cowardice conspire with her doubts and fear to rob her of the only man she'd ever truly loved.

She couldn't let that happen again.

A long, sharp signal indicated that her water was warm. Swallowing her fear, she gave him a tentative nod. "Yeah. Want some tea?"

"Sure. I got some of that apple-cinnamon chamomile you like." He crossed to a cupboard and took down a canister from the top shelf.

His statement bolstered her courage. Ever wasn't much of a tea drinker, and it spoke volumes that he'd gone out of his way to special order her favorite evening tea.

She put another mug in the microwave, and he handed her two tea bags. "Thank you."

He kissed her temple and went to sit at the small table under the window. "I think we should start with the biggest thing and then move on to the smaller issues."

That strategy had never appealed to her before, and it didn't now, but she knew better than to run again. She bought time by making tea.

As soon as she sat down, Ever put a halt to her stalling. His elbows rested on the table, and he curled his fingers around the handle of his mug. "Mina, what scares you the most?"

She thought it was interesting he'd ask her to identify her fear first. It didn't really manifest differently from anxiety. Nobody but Ever had been able to read her like this.

Looking down at the wisps of steam rising from her tea, she rotated her shoulders in a small shrug. "This conversation."

He didn't miss a beat. "What scares you about talking to me?"

"I don't know how to do it."

She made the mistake of lifting her gaze. He caught it, and he held it with the steel in his eyes. "You open your mouth, and words come out."

"It's not as easy as you make it sound."

"It's not as difficult as you think it is." Without surrendering his power over her, he sipped his tea. It had to be too hot, but he didn't seem to notice.

"I don't want to upset you."

He chuckled lightly. "Honey, you can't be afraid of upsetting me. If we're going to make this work, then eventually you're going to upset me, and I'm going to upset you. Then we work it out and move forward. That's what a relationship is."

Hope elevated her spirits and gave her courage. He'd mentioned having a future in an offhand, roundabout way before, but he hadn't spoken so explicitly.

She took a deep breath and let it out. "Jude said you wanted me to fail last night. He said you set me up and I lived down to your expectations."

All traces of sleep left his face. His eyes widened in shock, and then they narrowed. He compressed his lips, fury thinning them. "That's what he said to you when you were on the bench?"

Mina nodded. She was alarmed at his reaction, mostly because she hadn't thought she could upset him so quickly. "I know he was angry, but when he said it, he sounded like he was gloating. Like that's what he expected from me."

Sadness joined anger in the lines around his eyes. "You did a number on me when you left. My friends are loyal. Perhaps too loyal. I'll have a talk with Jude. He can't go around saying things like that to you."

She noticed he didn't deny the truth of what his friend had said. Now that she was in this, she pushed the issue. "Did you?"

"Did I set up a play party just so you'd fail?" He bit his lower lip. "Originally, I think I wanted to make you uncomfortable, to see how you would handle being with my friends. But then when you told me why you left...I should have called it off. I shouldn't have let you decide. You weren't ready for something like that. We aren't ready for something like that."

He closed his eyes and pressed the heel of his hand to his forehead. Mina sat back and tried to control the thunderous galloping of her heart. Jude hadn't been lying. Perhaps he had thrown the words at her with malicious intent. Perhaps Ever's intent had changed. But that didn't make it less true. She didn't know what to say.

"I'm sorry, honey. It was my fault. I'll take care of it. I'll make it right with Jude and Sara." He opened his eyes and placed his hand on the table, palm up, asking for hers. "Mina, I've messed up with you in more ways than that. I'm not a mind reader. I'll always need you to tell me why you're upset. I can't change the past. I can apologize. I can make things right moving forward, but I can't live without you."

Now her heart thundered for a different reason, and her stubborn streak kicked in. She ran her fingertip over the design on the hot mug. "You lived just fine without me for six years."

Ever shook his head. He caught her hand in his. "I survived, but I didn't live. No matter what was going on, I always felt as if half of me was missing. I only feel whole when I'm with you."

She stared down at the way his hand enveloped her smaller one, protected and safe. All this time, she'd been living half a life, too. "Finding out about you the way I did... It scared me. I understand better now, but I'm still learning. Some things I like, but some of the things you want seem like they're designed to overwhelm me. I left you because I was afraid you'd swallow me up and forget I was a person."

Visions of the way her father had taken her mother for granted, yelling whenever anything wasn't exactly how he wanted it, assailed her. But Ever had never raised his voice to her. Perhaps he'd spanked her, but that had only happened after she'd given her permission. At the time, she hadn't really felt she had other options.

"No," he said. "Never. I know what you're thinking, Mina, but I'm not like your father. I was raised to cherish my submissive. That's what I want to do with you—cherish you."

Lifting her gaze, she found his sea-foam-green eyes fixed on her. His expression certainly backed up his declaration, so she took a chance. "No more corporal punishment. I know that's a big thing to you, but I just can't live with it." She could, but she didn't want to, and she didn't feel the need to make that distinction.

Ever's mouth ticked up at the corner in a boyish half smile. "I've already decided to do away with that. Don't worry. I have plenty of other ways to discipline you."

He scooted their mugs out of the way and pulled her across the table. When she was almost completely on top of it, he slung his other arm under her bottom and pulled her the rest of the way into his lap. She luxuriated in the solid warmth of his body cradling hers.

Cupping his hands around her face, he rested his forehead against hers. "I'm sorry I treated you as my submissive without asking you first. I'd never been in love before, and I didn't quite know how to handle letting you in on my dominant nature without scaring you away, but I know that's only an excuse. Life with someone you love isn't always easy, but I can't have you running away from me ever again. I need your word, Mina. I need to hear you say that you're as committed to making this work as I am."

His breath, desperate and harsh, fanned over her lips and chin.

She lifted her hand and feathered her fingertips over his rough cheek. "I love you, Everett Burke. I'm not going anywhere. And I promise to tell you exactly why I'm upset with you from this point forward. Please keep in mind that you might come to regret that."

He didn't chuckle at her warning as she expected. Instead, he claimed her with a deep, probing kiss that promised a lifetime of cherished memories.

"I love you, Mina Sung. I always have, and I always will."

He stood, lifting her easily, and carried her from the room.

"Ever, our tea is going to get cold."

"Don't worry, honey. I'll make sure you're too exhausted to stay awake."

Epilogue

Mina shifted her butt, trying to ease the sharpness from where her hips rested against the heavy butcher-block countertop. This kitchen feature was meant for cutting things, not disciplining submissives who meant well.

Her arms were stretched toward the corners of the rectangular slab, ropes around her wrists holding her in that direction. She was bent over the side, her feet resting on the floor. However, spread so wide, they provided very little support. Additional ropes wound around her thighs and ankles, binding her to the sturdy legs of the movable table she'd brought from California. It had been one of the only furniture items she'd shipped across the country.

She lifted her torso, trying to ease the pain that way, but she found only a few centimeters of movement available.

"Master?"

Ever stood a few feet in front of her at the sink. The last shafts of sunlight streamed through the window, lending an ethereal glow to his light brown hair. The summer sun wouldn't last for much longer. Ever must have thought so as well, because he reached over and flipped on the lights.

"Submissives who refuse to pass the salt don't get to speak. Do you need a gag, honey?"

Oasis had proved to be very thorough indeed. Not only did they require a complete physical of all their employees every year, but the owner of the company stuck her nose in where she saw problems. Being his mother, Macy Burke had violated her son's privacy rights and told Mina that Ever's cholesterol numbers weren't good. Though he was physically fit, his diet needed to improve.

Refusing to pass the salt at dinner would become a small thing once he found out she'd dumped out all his beer. He liked to have one after dinner or when he came home from work. She'd also donated his supply of prepackaged snack cakes. Though she'd replaced them with some healthier options she'd baked herself, she couldn't see him taking that news too well either.

"I need something under my hips, because I think my bones are going to come through my skin."

He left the room and returned a minute later with a thin fleece blanket, which he slid under her hips. "Better?"

180

"Yes, Master. Thank you." She rested her cheek against the smooth grain of the table.

He ran his fingertips down her spine, continuing the caress around to her clit, which he pinched. She jumped and tried to wiggle away, but movement was impossible. He pressed and tapped the little bundle of nerves.

"What else have you done? Confessing will make me go a lot easier on you, because every time I find something new, I will issue a separate punishment."

Attempting a positive spin, she said, "I baked cupcakes."

He paused in his torture. The pantry door was behind her. She heard it open, then close. "You threw out my snack cakes?"

"But I made you something better."

She heard the door to the pantry close, and then his fingers probed her entrance. "I'll give you something better."

His cock breached her opening, pushing inside violently. He fucked her fast and hard. The first flutters of her impending climax had just begun when he pulled out. She cried out in protest even as she felt hot jets of his semen spurting over her lower back and the curve of her ass. This was part of her punishment.

Seconds later he stood in front of her. The fly to his jeans was open, but he'd tucked his cock back into his briefs. "I'm thirty-one. I work out almost every day, and I can fuck you for hours. I'm not in danger of having a heart attack."

She lifted her head and pried as much of her torso up from the table as she could manage. Looking him in the eyes took supreme physical effort. "No matter what you do to me, I'm going to make sure that's always true."

He pressed his lips together in a hard line, but the motion didn't dim the sparkle in his eyes. Though he parked his hands on his hips, she could tell that he'd very much liked her answer. "Anything else you'd like to confess to?"

"You might not be having a beer or two every day. I was thinking maybe once a month."

A muscle in his cheek twitched. He reached for something on the counter behind him. "I think it's time to gag you." He slid the dark green ball between her lips and fastened the straps behind her head.

He grabbed something else from the counter. It was higher than the table, and the angle was bad, so Mina couldn't see what toy he'd chosen to use on her.

Once he was behind her, it didn't take long to realize that he'd grabbed a huge vibrator. The cold lubricating gel made her squirm, but the ropes held her tightly. Then that large, rounded head nudged her entrance. It stretched her wide, a little wider than was comfortable. She screeched a protest behind the gag and tried to jerk away.

Ever chuckled. He put a restraining hand on her lower back and fucked that thing into her small cunt. Though she felt as if she were being split in half, it didn't exactly hurt, so she didn't give the signal to stop. In a strange way, it filled a need that Ever was helping her discover. She liked being forced to submit to him and to the things he wanted to do to her. Once he got over being angry about the changes she was making in his daily life, she planned to ask him for an erotic spanking, a topic she'd discussed at length with Lydia over the past few months.

Biting down hard on the gag, she panted as she coaxed her muscles to relax and accept her Master's will. Beads of sweat broke out along her brow and on her lower back, mixing with the semen he hadn't wiped away.

She cried out when the vibrator bumped her cervix. He paused his actions, giving her time to get used to the feeling of this large-scale invasion.

"You're doing well, slave." The praise went a long way toward easing the stress pulling her shoulder muscles taut.

A ripping sound had her straining to see what he was doing. She wished she were an owl so she could turn her head farther back, because this wasn't working for her. If he'd blindfolded her, then she wouldn't have worried about the sound. Not having the blindfold had become part of the punishment.

A thin, cold strip encircled her upper thigh. She guessed at electrical tape. Ever had picked up several rolls from the hardware store on their last visit. He'd chosen multiple colors after holding them up to her skin to see whether they complemented her tone.

By the time he finished, the handle of the fat phallus was taped securely to her leg. It was going nowhere. The thing whirred to life, and powerful vibrations racked her from the inside out. She groaned and closed her eyes. Depending on his mood, he could leave her like this for up to a full hour. She was going to be walking funny for at least a day. It wouldn't be the first time he'd done this to her. At least she worked from home now, so she wouldn't have to face curious glances and probing questions.

She lost count of how many orgasms that thing forced from her. Tears of agony and bliss wet the table under her cheek. Her juices dripped down her thighs and tickled her calves. At one point, she opened her eyes to find Ever leaning against the counter, eating a bowl of cholesterol-lowering cereal as he watched her submit to his will.

When the vibrations stopped and the bindings loosened, she didn't move. Those orgasms had sapped every bit of energy in her body. She'd lost the ability and the will to control her muscles. Ever lifted her gently and carried her upstairs, cradling her in his arms and pressing occasional kisses to her forehead.

He set her on the bed and disappeared into the bathroom. She heard water running into the bathtub. The sound lulled her to sleep in seconds.

She woke to find his bare chest against her back and his powerful thighs supporting her legs. His arm rested loosely across her stomach. Warm water covered her body, and the scent of lavender filled the air.

"Master?"

"I'm here." He traced a lazy circle on her hip.

"Are you still angry with me?"

"I was irritated, not angry. I would never discipline you in anger." He heaved a sigh. "And no, I'm not carrying a grudge. Next time, though, discuss it with me first. You threw out some damn good beer."

"All right." She wasn't going to apologize, and she was grateful he didn't demand that she do so.

"Straddle me. I've waited almost an hour for you to wake up. It's not nice to keep your horny master waiting."

She shifted forward. Her limbs still felt rubbery. He helped her turn around and position her pussy over his cock. She sank down slowly, savoring the silky feel of him.

"I love you, Ever."

"I love you too, honey. Now ride me a little faster."

"Yes, Master." She braced her hands on his shoulders and increased her pace. At long last, she was right where she belonged.

Michele Zurlo

Michele Zurlo is the author of the Awakenings, Doms of the FBI, and the SAFE Security series and many other stories. She writes contemporary and paranormal, BDSM and mainstream—whatever it takes to give her characters the happy endings they deserve.

Her childhood dream was to be a librarian so she could read all day. Some words of wisdom from an inspiring lady had her tapping out stories on her first laptop, and writing blossomed from a hobby to a career. Find out more at www.michelezurloauthor.com or @MZurloAuthor.

Lost Goddess Publishing

The Doms of the FBI Series

Re/Bound (Doms of the FBI 1)
Re/Paired (Doms of the FBI 2)
Re/Claimed (Doms of the FBI 3)
Re/Defined (Doms of the FBI 4)
Re/Leased (Doms of the FBI 5)
Re/Viewed (Doms of the FBI 6)
Re/Captured (Doms of the FBI 7)

The SAFE Security Series

Treasure Me (SAFE Security 1)
Switching It Up (SAFE Security 2)
Unlocking Temptation (A SAFE Security Short)

The SAFE Security Trilogy: Mercenary Hearts

Forging Love (A SAFE Security Novella: Mercenary Hearts prequel)
Coming Fall 2019:
Drawing On Love (Mercenary Hearts 1)
Broken Love (Mercenary Hearts 2)
Shards of Love (Mercenary Hearts 3)

Awakenings

Letting Go
Owning Up
Serving Sophia

Safeword: Oasis Series by Michele Zurlo

Wanting Wilder
Mina's Heart

Paranormal by Michele Zurlo

Dragon Kisses 1-3
Blade's Ghost

MM Romance by Nicoline Tiernan

Nexus #1: Tristan's Lover by Nicoline Tiernan
Nexus #2: The Man of His Dreams by Nicoline Tiernan

Anthologies

BDSM Anthology/Club Alegria #1-3 by Michele Zurlo and Nicoline
Tiernan
New Adult Anthology/Lovin' U #1-4 by Nicoline Tiernan
Menage Anthology/Club Alegria #4-7 by Michele Zurlo and
Nicoline Tiernan
Discovering Desires Anthology by Michele Zurlo

Check out Re/Bound (Doms of the FBI 1)

Blurb: Picking herself up after the devastating loss of her master is more difficult than Darcy anticipated. Just when she needs someone the most, a handsome Dom steps in. Theo is thoughtful, dominant, and demanding—everything she needs. He pushes her boundaries, tests her limits, and takes her to new heights. With him, she remembers what it is to feel joy and love and a firm hand on her ass.

Agent Malcolm Legato is after a corrupt businessman, and Darcy is his ticket into the upper echelon of Snyder Corp. As he cultivates her as an asset, he falls hard for this feisty submissive, and he knows he'll break her heart the moment she finds out he's been lying to her all along.

When it all falls apart, will Darcy be able to find the strength to forgive Malcolm so they can build a life together and the courage to bring justice to the man she loved and lost?

With twists of rope and plot, this action-packed story will make you laugh, cry, and squirm in all the right ways. With Re/Bound, Michele Zurlo delivers a smart, bold, and sexy tale.

Warnings: Bondage, D/s, S/M, salsa dancing

Praise for Re/Bound:

"It's not hard to find yourself lost in this book and unable to stop reading...RE /BOUND is a must read." *The Romance Reviews*

"A bold, smart, and sexy story that is the perfect combination of romance and dominance. The author does a superb job of explaining the psychological elements behind the relationship, needs, behaviors, and connection that is between Malcolm and Darcy. The blistering sex is filled with smoking hot delights, kinky pleasures, and tender seduction." *The Romance Studio*

A *Night Owl Reviews* Top Pick! "This was a very absorbing and entertaining read with an action-packed ending that will leave you breathless. The connection that Darcy and Malcolm share is stunningly beautiful. Highly recommended."

Excerpt:

She paused at a door three-quarters of the way down the hall. Her gaze fell to the floor. After the awkwardness had passed, the rest of the night had gone well. He had kept the conversation on innocuous topics and had learned a lot about her relationship with Victor Snyder. The prick had her thoroughly and completely snowed. She considered him a friend and a benefactor.

He hooked his finger under her chin and encouraged her to meet his gaze. When she complied, he rewarded her with a smile. Without a doubt, she was one responsive submissive. Yataines had trained her well.

He cupped the side of her face and traced his thumb over her eyebrow. Adjusting the position of his hand, he repeated the caress along her lower lip. She trembled a bit, but she clearly awaited his command. His earlier intention had been an impulsive act of affection. It had taken all his willpower to keep his cock from saluting her submissiveness.

"I had a nice time tonight, Darcy. Thank you for making this trip worthwhile."

Her eyes widened a bit, and he knew she wanted to ask if he'd decided against seeing her again now that he'd found out about some of her baggage.

He replayed his caress of her lip. Suddenly he needed to taste her lips more than anything in the world. "Can I kiss you?"

She began to nod, but she caught herself in time. She swallowed and licked her lips. "Yes, I'd like that."

Malcolm had never once taken the trust of a submissive lightly. Part of him wanted to play the gentleman and leave her alone. A larger part of him needed to know the flavor and texture of her kiss. He recognized the blurring of the line between his cover identity and his real self, and he couldn't keep from crossing it.

He feathered his lips over hers, a reverent caress that teased a small sigh from her. That tiny sound proved to be his undoing. He traced the seam of her lips with his tongue, and she opened for him. He cradled her head with one hand to hold her close, and he snaked the other around her waist to press her body closer.

She moaned and leaned into him as he directed with the pressure of his hand on her back. He tasted her lips and teeth. He sampled the roof of her mouth and tangled his tongue with hers. A piece of his heart he'd never before used came to life. It beat a furious staccato rhythm he felt echoed in her chest. Blood rushed to his cock. He thrust a knee between her legs and ground against her.

She mewled, and her fingers dug into his shoulders. Inflamed with her flavor, he moved his lips to sample her neck. She moaned and threw her head back.

The sharp crack of it hitting the door brought Malcolm back to his senses. He had shoved her against the door, and he had ravaged her with everything in his arsenal. He released her abruptly, keeping one hand close in case she needed more than the door to hold her up.

She gazed up at him, her eyes heavy-lidded with desire and blurred by shock. She took a deep, ragged breath and pushed away from the door.

Malcolm ran a shaky hand through his hair. "I'm sorry. You consented to a kiss, not a public mauling."

A little laugh escaped before she could bite her lip to keep it inside. "Now I'm wondering what will happen if I consent to a public mauling."

The visions she evoked meant he would need an icy shower before going to sleep. Wisely he changed the topic. "I'd like to see you again. Can we have breakfast together? I could swing by around eight, and we could walk down together."

Malcolm didn't know whether he asked her for the mission or because the pounding heart in his chest wanted to shrivel up and die at the thought of not seeing her.

She nodded. "I'd like that."